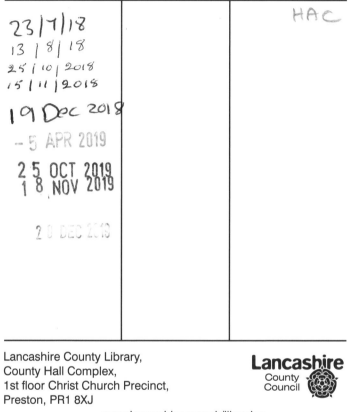
Lancashire County Library,
County Hall Complex,
1st floor Christ Church Precinct,
Preston, PR1 8XJ

Lancashire
County
Council

www.lancashire.gov.uk/libraries

LL1(A)

TILL THE END OF TIME

1939. Cathy lives happily with her family in Australia, oblivious of the onset of WWII in Europe. In England, young Tom, devastated when his mother leaves the family home in Leeds, is determined to enlist as soon as he is of age. He joins the Royal Navy and is sent to the Far East, arriving in Sydney. Tom meets dance teacher, Cathy at a ballroom and it soon becomes obvious they are destined to be together. But what are their chances of keeping their romance alive when it is inevitable that, once the war is over, Tom must sail back to England?

TILL THE END OF TIME

TILL THE
END OF TIME

by

Shirley Heaton

Magna Large Print Books
Long Preston, North Yorkshire,
BD23 4ND, England.

British Library Cataloguing in Publication Data.

A catalogue record of this book is
available from the British Library

ISBN 978-0-7505-4398-9

First published in Great Britain 2015 by Aphrodite Publications

Published in Large Print 2017 by arrangement with
Shirley Heaton

Magna Large Print is an imprint of Library Magna Books Ltd.

Printed and bound in Great Britain by
T.J. (International) Ltd., Cornwall, PL28 8RW

155349904

To my dear friend, Marie for her kindness, understanding and support

Chapter 1

1939

Tom heard the door close and the tapping of footsteps across the back yard. The gate clattered shut. Startled, he sat upright in bed and, drowsy-eyed, he peered at the clock. But his brow furrowed when he focused on the time. It was only twenty-five past six; it was too early for Dad to be leaving for work. Who could it be out there? Surely not a burglar – what did they have to steal? *Nowt* was his answer. Concentrating hard, he listened more intently. Those were not a man's footsteps. They were a woman's and he couldn't imagine a woman being a burglar.

He stuck his arms in the air and stretched his skinny body before slipping his long legs out of bed, hitching up his pyjama bottoms and plodding over the cold lino to the window. The numbness spread rapidly from his toes to the soles of his feet, and he realised that if he didn't wear his slippers he would get the dreaded chilblains. Typical English weather! But he had no time to waste. There was something wrong. He could sense it.

When he lifted the curtain and peered through the nets, his heart gave a heavy thump and his eyes, still dazed with sleep, opened wide with shock. Mam was hurrying across the cobbles and along the back street towards the main road at the end. She was wearing her best coat and floral headscarf. He frowned. She couldn't be going shopping. In any case it was too early for that.

The cold was beginning to penetrate even more as he tiptoed to the bedroom door and gently turned the knob, hoping not to wake his brother Billy who was still fast asleep in the double bed they shared. He bounced down the stairs two at a time and dashed through the living room into the kitchen. There on the table was a note. It read:

Harold. Leaving with Sid. Take care of the kids. Alice.

He did a double take, his eyes now huge and tinged with horror. It couldn't be true. Why was she leaving? They hadn't done anything wrong! And who the heck was Sid?

Dragging his Dad's army greatcoat from the back of the door he slipped it around his shoulders, but when he tried to open the door he realised Mam had locked it behind her. His mind, now racing in a maelstrom of panic and fear, he shot to the corner of the kitchen, opened the cupboard doors to the sink and leant over for the spare key hanging up on the back wall. He grabbed it and dived towards the door, his hand shaking as he slotted the large mortise key into the lock.

He threw open the door and stepped outside, fixing his gaze on the main road at the end of the street. Mam was standing at the tram stop. And when Tom spotted the small suitcase on the ground beside her his stomach gave a violent jerk. His face was bone-white now and he stood there like a robot, staring and unable to move. Within seconds the number six-thirty tram turned up and his Mam stepped on to the platform. In numb disbelief he watched her as the tram set off again. The destination at the back read *Manchester*.

Pulling himself up sharp he shouted, 'Mam, no!' Staring wildly, he ran barefoot through the back yard and on to the cobbles. The greatcoat fell from his shoulders. 'Come back, Mam,' he bellowed.

For a few fleeting seconds his Mam glimpsed over her shoulder, her face sketched in guilt, but then she quickly looked away. The conductor pushed her inside and that was it. She was gone.

'What's all the noise about our Tom?' Harold Crossley was standing behind him, shaking his head and scowling as he stared after the tram. But it rattled along the main road gathering speed and finally disappeared around the corner. 'What the dickens is going on?'

Tom, a wiry lad four or five inches taller than his father, slipped an arm around Dad's shoulders and led him back into the kitchen. Plainly still in an emotional state, he struggled for composure and then he pointed to the note on the table. 'You'd better read that, Dad.'

Harold picked up the scrap of paper and read. Although his face was drenched in apathy, it registered no apparent shock. He shook his head. 'The penny's dropped now. I might have known.' With a sudden glimmer of understanding, he took a deep breath. 'Your mam's spent a lot of time doing Sid Barraclough's cleaning since his wife died. But how long does it take to clean a cottage that size?' Hurt and humiliated, his mouth tightened and, fighting hard now to control his anger, he mumbled under his breath, 'You bitch, Alice. I've been a bloody stupid fool.' He sat down, took a Woodbine from the packet on the table and lit it, holding it between his thumb and forefinger and inhaling deeply.

Tom rubbed his arms to get the circulation going again. 'You mean they've had it off and now she's gone away with him?' He tightened his arms around his body and hugged himself.

Harold nodded stiffly. 'That's right, lad.'

'But what about us?'

'What about us?' Harold repeated. 'You see what she's put.' He stabbed his finger on the note. 'That's it now. She won't be coming back. You know what she's like – wouldn't dream of backing down once she's made her mind up.' He stood up decisively. 'It'll have to be down to our Dot now to see to things for us.'

'But Dad, you can't expect our Dot to do everything. She has to go to work every day, and she's tired when she comes home at night.' Concerned to protect his sister, Tom shook his head.

'Aren't we all? Someone has it to do. God knows, I've enough on going out to work at the foundry without having to wash and iron.' He stretched across and ruffled Tom's hair. 'Don't worry, lad. We'll all muck in and do what we can for her.'

Shoulders slumped, Tom dragged his feet slowly back upstairs, his stomach shaking like jelly as though it didn't belong to him. He stared at little Billy lying there and his problems seemed to multiply. He felt a sudden panic but, as Dad said, they must get on with things and try to cope

14

as best they could.

Standing there shivering, he mulled things over in his mind. Come to think of it, Mam had been a bit strange recently. One minute she had no time for any of them, rushing about like a scalded lop, and the next minute she was making treacle toffee to surprise them when they came home from school. Looking back Tom could only guess it was her guilty conscience playing up. But she didn't have a guilty conscience now, did she? And as for the relationship between her and Dad, half the time they were totally at each other's throats. So maybe the place would be quiet without Mam.

He padded through the bedroom, unable to feel his feet. He stared down at his toes. They were going blue. He buried them in the rag rug next to the bed and closed his eyes, hoping for some warmth to seep through. How he wished it was a bit warmer in the bedroom when he got up of a morning. It was fine at night with the oven plate wrapped in a blanket to warm the bed and keep it nice and snug, even though he always slipped it over to Billy's side.

His thoughts turned to the lads at school. He shook his head. He'd no desire to be mollycoddled like that set of Moorhead sissies, bragging about the gas fires in their bedrooms. Two of them even had proper central heating, radiators and that. But what do you expect when their dads had pots of money and they lived in great big houses, not like this tiny little back-to-back where you couldn't hide a farthing without someone spotting it. That lot didn't have to share a bedroom either, or go down the back yard to the privy. They had proper bathrooms. Show-offs! Cocky buggers!

He dragged his clothes from the chair beside the bed and slipped them on. But as he turned to leave the bedroom he caught his knee on the iron frame of the bed. 'Bloody 'ell,' he cursed as the bed shook. He rubbed at the stabbing pain and stared again at the sleeping Billy, hoping his brother would sleep another half hour before getting up.

But six-year-old Billy had obviously been disturbed and it was only minutes later when he wandered into the kitchen. The note had been left on the kitchen table and when Tom tried to snatch it up Billy grabbed it and ran off laughing as though it were a game. But when he discovered his mam had left he began to bawl.

'I want me mam. Where's she gone?' Noisily adamant, he banged his fist on the tabletop. And then he pressed the heels of his hands to his eyes and tried to wipe away the tears. Tom knew Billy desperately needed her. But she wasn't about to come back, not for anyone.

That was the last they heard of Mam. Not that it bothered Tom. He was determined they would not be visiting, even if they knew her address. It was a long way from Leeds to Manchester. And after the way she'd treated them, did he care if he never saw her again? If Dad could remain calm and show no emotion, so could he. At fifteen you didn't let anyone think you were soft. Not like those namby-pambies at school.

But his reaction was nothing but bravado. Deep down Tom was gutted when Mam left. Holding back hot tears of frustration and anger, his lips felt dry and tight and the nerves jangled inside him.

He turned away, trying to knuckle away the tears as he walked over to the sink to fill the kettle. Dad would need a brew now that he was up out of bed, and especially after what had happened.

Tom tried to lock his sadness away and, once things settled down, all he could think about was getting right away from the place. It was a pity he couldn't leave school until the summer. How he wished he had chosen to go to a secondary school instead of the grammar school. But Dad had said he should give it a chance even if they had to scrimp and scrape to keep him there. To start with the uniforms cost a packet but, give him his due, Dad tried his best even though the clothes were not always new. The ones Tom was wearing in his final school year were second-hand. Dad had bought them from Keith Wilkinson's mam. The only trouble was the royal blue jumper was pilled and faded now, the blazer a skimpy fit. But he would be leaving soon so what did it matter?

His thoughts went back to his dilemma and he concluded he had no chance of moving anywhere with little money and nowhere to go. Had he chosen to go to the secondary school, he would have been working full time by now and he could have been earning a weekly wage. His part-time job sweeping the floors in the evenings at Barber's joinery shop paid a shilling a week. He worked hard, and that was a princely sum compared with some part-time jobs. But how was he supposed to save? To start with, Dad took nine pence – and you couldn't blame him after the way he'd supported Tom through grammar school – but that only left Tom with three pence to last him the week.

It was then his mind latched on to a secret plan. Dad always switched the wireless on to the Home Service of a morning. More often than not it was still on when he left for work and Tom listened to the news whilst he was getting ready for school. For weeks they had been talking about another war looming. Dad had fought in the First World War – not that he ever said a great deal about it. Tom reckoned it was too horrific for him to recollect, let alone discuss with anyone. So surely Dad would not complain if Tom enlisted as soon as he was old enough. But he wouldn't mention his plans to Dad, not just yet, not until it was time to look into it. So roll on the next two years. At seventeen Tom would be old enough to enlist.

At the other side of the world in Australia's Sydney suburb, St Peter's, Frank Ellis sat down in his armchair, a sigh of satisfaction escaping his lips. He'd been on his feet working behind the scenes in the city's Paddy's Market since the early hours of the morning and it was a relief to rest his legs. *Peace and quiet* were the words floating in his head and he picked up the daily newspaper, staring avidly and in somewhat of a daze before starting to read the front page. It was his first opportunity to relax and, although his wife, Marjorie, was aware he disliked being disturbed when he returned from work – just twenty minutes, that's all he asked – she seemed anxious to broach a subject which concerned her.

She stood looking down at him, coughed nervously and folded her arms. *What now*, he thought.

'I take it you've heard the news,' she challenged. 'Menzies is calling for military service volunteers to serve at home and abroad. And apparently abroad means the Middle East. What do you think about that?' Her voice faltered and her mouth trembled. But, seemingly in an effort to control her emotions, she took a deep breath.

Frank digested her words in silence. And then he looked up from his newspaper.

'To tell you the truth, I don't know what to think. But I suppose he has to pick up volunteers one way or another. At least they're not being press-ganged or conscripted like in some countries.' He smiled. He always knew how to ease the situation even though it was a serious matter. 'They were all buzzing with it down at the market. One or two of the younger lads were getting excited and talking about enlisting.' He shook his head. 'But I'm telling you now, it'll not happen.'

She seemed to disregard his final words. She had her own opinion and he supposed she was entitled to have her say. 'Enlisting? Well I am surprised.' Marjorie shook her head. 'I think the Prime Minister's jumped the gun. The war is in Europe, not here in Australia.' She fingered the tablecloth nervously before straightening it at the edges. 'And who's going to come over here and attack us? Surely Hitler's not interested in Australia.'

Frank sighed and folded his newspaper. Did he ever get a minute's peace? His day had been hectic and it was heavy work down at the market, especially when it was crates of watermelons or coconuts they were handling. And now all he wanted was a quiet moment or two to read his newspaper, find out what was going on in the world, instead of Marjorie's ear-bashing as soon as his bum hit the armchair. But he kept calm and suppressed the surge of irritation. It was no use letting on he was getting steamed up.

'You'd be surprised, Marj. What you don't seem to understand is that we're Allies with most of Europe, and the Commonwealth countries. We owe it to them to join in. We're so isolated over here, if we were attacked, we couldn't possibly defend ourselves without their help. We haven't enough men, or women for that matter. And the Japs are causing a bit of a stir with the Chinese. You never know what might happen.'

'Well, I suppose you're right there but I wouldn't be happy if our two decided to join up. They both have good jobs and I'm sure they wouldn't want to lose them.'

Now Frank understood why she was whinging. It wouldn't be about Freddie or Danny losing their jobs. It would be Marjorie worrying about losing her sons. Frank smiled. Neither of them was old enough yet. And he had to re-assure her. He didn't want her upset thinking the boys would be off to war any day now.

'I agree with you there Marj. But they can't sign anything without my permission; they're not old enough. So don't fret. And I'm ninety-nine per cent sure most of the young lads at the market won't get away with it. Some of them are only sixteen.'

'Exactly. If the lads are up front with it, their parents will certainly not sign. But some of them can be a bit devious like my brother Stan, running off without even telling us. And he never came back you know.' She sniffed and began to fidget. 'You should dob the lads in Frank if they try it on.'

'I won't need to dob them in. Their parents will soon find out and see to that.'

Marjorie huffed as she finished laying the table before sitting down and picking up her crochet work. She smoothed out the front to the dress she was making for her daughter, Cathy. Crochet dresses were all the rage for the young girls and Marjorie always made sure Cathy didn't miss out.

But she had to get the matter of enlistment off her chest. She couldn't let it drop. 'If Freddie or Danny even mention it to you Frank, put them straight won't you?' Her brow creased heavily as she turned her attention back to the crochet work.

'I don't think I'll need to. They know what's what.'

Looking a little mollified, Marjorie looked up as the door flew open.

'Who knows what's what?' It was Cathy returning from school, her bottle green jumper slung over her arm and a dish in her hand.

'Nothing you need to bother your head about, lady.' Marjorie smiled and put down the crochet work before moving to the worktop in the kitchen.

Cathy followed her and plonked the dish down. 'There you go; veggie pie for tea.'

'Good on you. I'd forgotten it was cookery today.' Marjorie lifted the tea towel covering the dish. 'Lovely tucker! How about bangers and some nice, tasty gravy to go with the veggie pie?' She opened the pantry and lifted the dish of

21

sausages from a cool slab. 'Dad brought them home from the market. Look how meaty they are.'

'They do look good, Mum.' Cathy smiled and leant on Dad's armchair. 'You've beaten me home today, Dad.' She kissed him on the forehead and his face relaxed into a smile. As long as they didn't take his little girl away, that's all he cared about, especially if Menzies introduced conscription. She was still an innocent fourteen-year-old. But there was no knowing when the war would start and when it would end, hopefully before she was eighteen and eligible for call-up. Granted, Frank didn't want to lose the two lads either, but he was sure if they were called up they could fend for themselves.

He pulled Cathy towards him and rubbed his stubbly cheek on hers. 'Last delivery at the market two thirty today. Only took half an hour to unload. I was home about half three. Thought I'd get back and help Mum around the house.' A wide grin spread across his lively face. He winked.

Cathy's huge brown eyes opened wide and she flicked her rich brown hair over her shoulders, suppressing a giggle. She loved their banter.

Marjorie turned and pointed a finger at her husband. She smiled. 'Fat chance of that Frank!' She shook her head. 'You wouldn't know the head of a broom from the handle. Besides, you're too busy reading your newspaper.'

Frank's eyes twinkled as he opened up his newspaper once more and began to stare at the print. But he was neither focusing nor concentrating. His mind was filled with thoughts of his family. Granted he could be a bit of a nark at times, especially when he was tired, but he couldn't have married anyone more adorable than Marjorie if he'd been given the whole of Australia to choose from. After years of being passed around from pillar to post and being sent to an orphanage as a young lad when his Ma died and his Pa had abandoned him, he'd met Marjorie and – snap – that was it! They had married within the year. Living with her was like being in heaven. He really should tolerate her yacking on when she was concerned about the family. He looked up and watched her as she smiled towards Cathy. What more could he want? He loved her with a grand passion. She had given him two handsome sons and a beautiful daughter. He couldn't have been happier.

Cathy slipped her arm around Mum's shoulder, popping a kiss on her cheek and giving her a squeeze. 'That's a joke, isn't it Mum? Imagine Dad preparing the tucker. He wouldn't know where to start. And what sort of concoction would he serve up? He can't even boil an egg!'

Marjorie's face became a serious mask, but it failed to cover the laughter in her eyes. 'Give him his due, Cathy. He might manage beans on toast.' She nodded her head, rolled her eyes and lifted her eyebrows.

'Or egg on toast, or cheese on toast...' Cathy continued the joke and laughed at Mum whom she knew was proud of the way she looked after all their needs. Mum would have had a fit if Dad had tried to involve himself in what she regarded as her job.

'I'll have you know I can cook a nice fillet of barramundi, and I'm a dab hand at roast chook, or tiger prawns cooked with a touch of garlic. What about all the fruit I bring home from the market? I can serve up stewed apples and custard, plum crumble...' He stopped and racked his brain to think of more dishes at which his wife excelled.

Marjorie waved her hand in the air as though to clip him around the ear, but her hand hovered above his head and he took hold, kissing the back of it. She shook her head and smiled. 'What am I going to do with you, Frank Ellis?'

Frank laughed and turned to the sports results on the back page of the newspaper, anxious to know how the Wallabies had done against the Barbarians.

When Cathy turned towards him to make some other amusing comment, she noticed the front page of the newspaper was facing her. She stared at the picture and headline. 'HITLER RE-CEIVES AN ULTIMATUM.' Underneath it read: *'Hitler's territorial ambitions quashed. Chamberlain guarantees Poland's independence and vows to come to her aid if attacked by Hitler.'*

What was all that about? She had heard the boys at school talking about someone called Hitler threatening to invade Europe. But it was of no interest to her. Wars were for boys. And wasn't Chamberlain the prime minister of England? That was thousands of miles away. So why were people over here so concerned? This Hitler guy wasn't invading Australia, so why should it worry them?

Harold Crossley found it difficult to cope after Alice walked out on them. Instead of getting on with his life, he would sit in the chair moping and feeling sorry for himself. At first, Tom sensed how Dad must be feeling and, in his mind, he made allowances. 'We'll get over it, Dad. Don't worry.' But when Dad gave up his job on the pretext he had to look after the family, Tom changed his tune. Dad was not the one looking after them. It was Dorothy. Up before six she would see to the washing and hang it out in the back yard before Dad even dragged his bones out of bed. And then she would get Billy ready for school, rubbing his hands, neck and face vigorously with a soaped-up flannel, making sure his shoes were polished and checking that he was wearing a clean shirt.

Fortunately Tom had been able to look after himself since Mam had left, and for that matter well before then. She had been out of the game for ages, preoccupied with other things, and now he knew what those other things were. And, despite Dad's casual comment about them all mucking in, they were empty words. There had been no input whatsoever from him.

It was Dorothy Tom felt sorry for now, not Dad. After she had sorted Billy out ready for school, it was time for her to leave for work, and Tom's turn to look after Billy. More often than not Dorothy left it until the last minute. She was forced to run across the cobbles and out into the main road to catch the number sixteen tram which took her to the city centre. She never missed it. She had worked in the large Woolworths store since she left school, first of all on the haberdashery counter and later on sweets and confectionary. She was a good worker and the boss had mentioned making her a supervisor once she was eighteen. And with that in mind, the last thing she needed was to be late for work.

A few minutes after Dorothy had left, Tom did his stint. He would set off for St. Winifred's Infants School with Billy, before continuing on to Harefield Grammar. Sometimes he was a few minutes late for school and, unfortunately, the teachers made no allowances for the fact that his Mam had left them. Once or twice, especially if old Bates, the deputy head, (who felt he was entitled to mete out punishment willy-nilly) was checking in 'lates', Tom was given the cane. His backside would be stinging all morning and he would sit there seething. The bloody idiot was a sadist. He seemed to revel in giving 'six of the best' to anyone he felt warranted the cane, and his callousness was no less than chilling. And at times like that some of the Moorhead lads guffawed and could be sarcastic, even cruel. But Tom let it wash over him. He preferred being tough. They were wrapped up in cotton wool by their mams. The last thing he wanted was their kind of life with someone wiping his arse for him!

But they sure knew about it if they got on the wrong side of Tom. He would only take so much. He had a reputation for being good with his fists, and secretly the others thought he was a bit of a low-life – well Tom knew that was the excuse they bandied about. Boxing was for working class lads not for them. But Tom used his boxing only in a sporting way, not to get into a fight, but merely as a deterrent. He had never had to use the skill, except in the ring. And that was the way he'd been taught by Charlie Weston, the instructor at the club. 'Boxing is a sport, lads,' he would say, 'never to be used in temper. You must learn to control that, and get rid of your anger in some other way.' And that's how it was with Tom.

He was eight years old when Dad had enrolled him at the Tennyson Boxing Club for Boys. Tom was not an aggressive child and, at first, he showed a complete lack of interest, but it was something Dad had pushed him into. And Tom had to admit that despite his earlier reluctance, in the end, the training had served its purpose. But he only used it as a challenge if any of the other kids tried to set about him. He only had to put up his fists and their muffled laughs would cease. They knew not to push their luck. And what he enjoyed most of all was watching the faces of those cocky posh kids when he did so. He could have made mincemeat out of them. They were scared shitless and they soon backed off without 'mummy' there to stick up for them.

Tom counted the days until he was old enough to enlist and get away. He still had his School Certificate to sit and after that, in theory, his schoolwork was finished. Not that the teachers looked at it in that way. There was a series of end of term events before he would be allowed to leave. Some of them were sporting events and Tom didn't mind those, especially the athletics. He could beat the lot of them with his eyes closed. So why did they look down on him? Why did they regard him as a misfit? He was brighter than most academically, and he could wipe the floor with them at most sports. In a way he was superior to them. And that's the way he secretly thought of himself. One of these days he would show them.

When the war broke out in Europe in 1939 Tom listened avidly to the wireless. There was plenty of action and he was itching to get involved. It had all started with the Jerry attacking Poland, and after that there was all hell let loose. The Soviets attacked Finland and our lot kicked them out of the League of Nations. Meanwhile Churchill was voted into power, replacing Chamberlain.

The Battle of Dunkirk – that was something else. One of the neighbours, Mr. Gosforth who lived through the passage at the front of the row, had been there. When he returned the excitement mounted. Everyone in the street was talking about it. Tom was well impressed especially when he heard about those tiny fishing boats mucking in with the destroyers and picking up over three hundred thousand troops from France between them, bringing them back home to safety. Churchill was right when he said it was a miracle. And then in 1941 the Jerry moved on and invaded Denmark and Norway to get hold of Sweden's iron ore. And so it went on.

Tom began to speculate. Where would he be sent when he joined up? The Americans had created a secure zone in the Atlantic to protect British convoys. That could be exciting, leaving for the Atlantic. But failing that, hopefully he would be sent to where there was some action! Meanwhile he had a job of work to do. The Head-master wanted him to stay on at school and sit his Higher School Certificate. But that was not for him. He decided to get a job where he could earn as much money as possible. He felt the need to pay Dad back, mainly for the support and the clothing through the Grammar School years.

After seeing an advert in the *Chronicle* for building-site workers, Tom applied. Dad was not best pleased when Tom announced he intended taking up a bricklaying job, but he was adamant. What he failed to mention to Dad was that he intended to enlist for the forces the minute he was old enough. And when the time came, he mistakenly thought Dad would be proud.

'I don't know what we're going to do without your wages, our Tom. Happen I'll get our Dot to do a bit of overtime at Woollies. They do a bit of shelf stacking after closing time.' He shook his head. He thought more about Tom's wages than the fact that his son was about to face the dangers of war. 'It's our Billy who's the problem. But he'll soon be plenty old enough to look after himself.' He dwelt on his words. 'It won't be long I suppose before he's fixed up with a job.' His eyes lit up. 'I could get him a paper round. That'd help.'

'You must be joking, Dad. At his age? They wouldn't allow it.' Tom had it on the tip of his tongue to ask Dad why he didn't get up off his arse and apply for a job himself. But it was a waste of time. It was for sure he'd argue against it and put on the pathetic act. Tom could even forecast the exact words he would use. 'Nay lad, I can't work the state my back's in, and it's getting worse.' A bit of exercise would have done him the world of good. It wasn't surprising his back was stiff when he never moved out of the chair. But that was no longer Tom's problem.

Tom was over the moon when he was given his

first choice, the Royal Navy. No more waiting now. Today was the day of action. He stood at the door, suitcase in hand ready to leave. His plan had finally come to fruition. It was late nineteen forty one and he was a strapping seventeen year old with regular features and light brown wavy hair.

He set out for the tram, dwelling on the situation he was leaving. Billy was just eight now and he took some watching. But Dorothy had no qualms. She was eighteen and had taken over that responsibility since Mam left.

Tom pulled his thoughts together. His enthusiasm mounted as he thought of doing his bit for his country. But now he was leaving home, he knew the parting would be a strain.

'I'd like to go to the station with you, Tom. Give you a proper send-off,' Dorothy explained.

'Can I go as well,' Billy begged. But Dad cried off, saying his back was too bad to be gadding about. That was his excuse but Tom knew differently.

The tram took them into the centre and they crossed over to City Square. It had started to drizzle and Dorothy slipped a plastic rain-mate over her headscarf and pulled it tight under her chin. She linked her arm through Tom's and gripped Billy's hand as they walked across to the station. Tom tried to appear light-hearted, laughing and joking, and making a valiant attempt to contain his emotions. But it was so hard to steel himself especially when he took in the state of them both, standing on the platform with tears in their eyes as they waved him off at Leeds City Station.

'I'll miss you our Tom.' Dorothy dabbed at the tears rolling down her cheeks. 'Take care won't you, love. Come back soon – safe and sound.'

'Don't you fret, our kid, I'll be as right as a bobbin. If anyone tries it on with me, I'll give 'em some stick.' He shook his fist and laughed, but it was a false laugh.

'Don't go, Tommy!' Billy wailed as he tried to break free from Dorothy's grip. But she strengthened her grip.

Tom stared hard as he waved, all the while trying to control his emotions and remain strong. But his heart was heavy and it tumbled in his chest. All he wanted now was for the train to leave the station so that he could quit this bravado and mope in peace.

Chapter 2

1941

Tom placed his bag on the luggage rack up above, sat down and stared ahead. He leaned back and let his mind wander. His stomach did a nosedive. Poor Dorothy! He was leaving her behind to face all the responsibility. But would it have made any difference had he stayed back? Probably not. In any case, if Dorothy had her way, she would be out of it in no time, and no doubt take their Billy with her. It made him smile when he brought George Swanwick to mind. The lad had been pushing his

31

luck and hanging around for over a year now. Tom was sure that once Dorothy came of age, she would agree to marry him. He was dead keen and Dorothy was sweet on George. You could say they were courting – in a loose sort of way.

Alone, in a deep pool of silence, Tom realised it was the first time he had travelled on his own, and he was filled with a mixture of apprehension and excitement. The train was destined for London where he would change and continue on to Portsmouth. He pulled himself together. At last his dreams had come true. Brimming with hopes and ambition, he was off to join the Royal Navy and experience some action. But, once underway, he knew he would have to keep his wits about him. He would need to change at Kings Cross and, never having been to London before, he hoped he could find his way around without getting lost.

As the train slowly trickled out of the station, a young man appeared in the corridor, opened the carriage door and stepped inside, placing his holdall on the luggage rack above before sitting down opposite Tom. The two of them studied one another intently. Tom guessed they were of a similar age.

The young man smiled. 'You're not travelling to Portsmouth by any chance are you?'

Tom was startled at his comment. This was too good to be true. Bright with surprise, he was quick to reply. 'Yes. I'm joining the Royal Navy.' His voice held a note of pride.

'Me too. That's exactly where I'm heading. I thought you looked the type.' He held out his hand. 'Mike Lightowler.'

Tom liked the comment about looking 'the type'. He smiled to himself, assuming the guy meant the tough, athletic type. Mike certainly looked it. Tom took his hand and shook it. 'Tom Crossley. Where are you from, Mike?'

'Shipley, near Bradford. And you?'

'Hunslet in Leeds.'

'Pleased to meet you Tom.' He sighed. 'I've just left Mum and Dad at the station. Mum was crying her eyes out – you know what they're like.'

Tom was knocked off balance by this unexpected comment. Since Mam had left, he had tried to maintain scant regard for her, and he was reluctant to think about her. She had never contacted them since she left two years ago. And now Tom was off to fight the enemy and she wasn't even aware he had left. For one irrational moment he felt a tiny ember of anger still burning in his heart.

He took a deep breath and stopped himself from showing even the slightest degree of emotion, knowing himself well enough to realise it would take very little to fan that tiny ember into full flame. He closed his mind to Mam, kept his cool and nodded. 'I know what you mean.'

'I'm training to be a chef.' Mike shuffled to the end of the seat in the corner next to the window, settling down and making himself comfortable. 'How about you?'

'I'll be in communications. The Morse Code's like a second language to me. I learnt it when I was a kid.'

'That should stand you in good stead then,' Mike offered.

'It's a start,' Tom agreed. 'What made you choose catering?'

'I've always been interested. Mum's a really good cook and Dad's a baker, so you could say it runs in the family.'

Tom relaxed. Relief seeped through him and all negative thoughts were quickly brushed from his mind. 'I'm glad we've met up, Mike. To tell you the truth I was dreading getting lost. This is my first ever train journey.' He grinned.

'Don't mention it, pal. I was thinking the same myself. Skipton's as far as I've been on a train. We'll sort it out between us.' They both laughed and Tom was grateful he now had an ally in Mike. He seemed a decent enough sort, and best of all, he was someone to share the responsibility of finding the connection once they reached Kings Cross. Two minds were better than one and, together, they'd cope.

It turned out to be much easier than they had expected.

'We needn't have worried,' Tom said pointing to the endless stream of young men heading for the Portsmouth train. And that was when the camaraderie began.

When they reached the camp at Portsmouth, Tom realised his apprehension had been unnecessary. He shrugged it off when the banter between the lads started. He was so carried away that he had no time to think about what he had let himself in for.

Tom and Mike were billeted in the same Nissen hut, a prefabricated building made from cold, corrugated steel. The ends had wooden frames covered in weatherboard and, once inside, a draught wrapped itself around them. Tom shivered and rubbed his arms.

'I'll tell you what, Mike, I don't know how we're supposed to keep ourselves warm in this place. It's bloody freezing.'

Mike laughed. 'I'll say but they'll want to toughen us up. That's their little game! But I must admit the slightest wind nearly blasts us back outside into the cold.'

'We'll make the best of it.' Tom stared at the ugly metal stove at the far end of the hut and shook his head. 'Pity we don't have a bed nearer the stove. That would have been a bonus, although I keep reminding myself this is wartime – we're not on holiday in some swanky hotel.' A wide grin spread across his face as he walked the length of the hut to the stove, rubbing his hands together and anticipating the warmth.

But then his face took on a look of despondency and he gazed distantly to the far end of the billet. He supposed the conditions were little worse than those at home. His bedroom with the cold lino and the windows iced over with the frost had hardly been a comfort. His stomach rippled when he thought about home and he began to worry that Billy would be lonely sleeping in the big bed all by himself. But commonsense told him to stop and think, and he cast the thoughts of home from his mind. He could not go on tormenting himself about what was happening there. Everything was being taken care of. At least Dorothy knew what was what.

He began unpacking his bag and searching for

the photos of Billy and Dorothy. He stared at them and reminded himself he must stop fretting. He looked around to find somewhere to put them, somewhere he could always see their cheery faces. He glanced across the billet to check out what the others were doing and it seemed common practice to stick any photos on the wall behind the bed. Tom decided to do likewise and, as he did so, Mike narrowed his eyes and peered across at the wall.

'Who's the girlfriend?' He walked across to look a little closer.

Tom's face cracked into a smile. 'She's not my girlfriend, she's my sister.'

'She's some looker, I'll say that for her!' Mike whooped. Some of the others wandered over and one or two of them nodded in agreement.

Tom said nothing and kept on unpacking. But he grinned and his heart gave a bounce of joy. There was nothing like a few compliments for him to feel proud of his sister. One of these days she would make a good wife for some lucky guy. Maybe the lucky guy would be George Swanwick.

After sorting through their kit bags and un-packing, they assembled in the common room. There was an undercurrent of rumbling when the training officer entered.

'Quiet you lot. I'm not here to waste time,' he barked. Stern-faced, he cleared his throat and waited until the mumbling stopped. Briskly he continued. 'During the next few weeks you will be transformed from civilians into sailors. And now is the time to make a start. So let's get on with it.' He pulled himself upright. 'You will be supplied with the full able seaman's uniform and told how to look after your kit. You'll learn the basic skills you will need to rely on throughout your career, including physical and military training, familiarisation with life on board and working with equipment. You will also be taught the history and traditions of the Royal Navy.' He nodded stiffly and searched the faces of the recruits to make sure they were listening. 'In two days' time you will be transferred to training ship HMS *Omnipotence* where a rigorous programme will commence.'

They returned to the billet where they were allocated a full kit including hat, tunic shirt and jumper with the traditional large light blue-jean collar edged with three rows of tapes, and bell-bottom trousers.

The officer in charge of supplies pointed to a pair of the bell-bottoms he held in the air for all to see. 'You must ensure the seven horizontal creases are kept sharply pressed and in immaculate condition at all times,' he remonstrated. 'Failure to do so will incur a severe penalty.' Rumour had it that the creases signified the seven oceans of the world but no-one knew for sure. One of the tips for keeping the bell-bottoms well creased was to place them neatly folded under your mattress at night.

The recruits were given a little time to practise the skills of folding and pressing, but for some it proved difficult, especially Mike. He picked up the tunic and made a valiant attempt for the umpteenth time to press it. 'This is driving me crackers,' he wailed. Tom guessed his friend didn't have a clue. The more he tried the more he pressed several creases in entirely the wrong places.

Frustrated he slammed the iron down on the board. 'It's a waste of time trying. Mum's always done it for me. But I suppose I'll have to learn.' He lowered his voice. 'Otherwise I'll be in big trouble.'

'I'll say you will,' Tom assured him. 'It seems to me you've been mollycoddled, pal!' He grinned. 'There's nothing to it once you get some practice in. Here let me show you.' Tom took the shirt and smoothed it out on the board with his hands, pressing first the sleeves and the back, and then turning it over to the front. 'Here. You do the front like I've done the back.' He handed the iron over to Mike. 'I've been doing this at home since Mam left us. Dorothy didn't like it at first. She was worried I'd scorch things. I did to start with but, trial and error, Mike, that's the way.'

'There'll be plenty of that.' Mike picked up the iron and tentatively pressed the front of the shirt. After replacing the iron on the board, he lifted the shirt in the air. His brows lifted as though in surprise. 'How about that?' He smiled broadly.

'Not bad, Mike. You'll get used to it.'

Within the week they left the draughty Nissen hut and were moved to the training ship. Tom looked along the huge deck. 'This is more like it. I wonder how long it'll be before we set sail.'

'I expect it'll be a while. It won't be until after the training,' Mike replied.

That very day physical training began. 'The PT instructor's strict,' Mike whispered, 'and the training's rigorous.'

'It suits me,' Tom said knowing it was something at which he excelled. He was used to physical activity and he enjoyed pushing himself to the limit.

And the time spent on parade each day practising marching drills and manoeuvres became monotonous but the men soon carried out the exercises flawlessly and in accordance with the warrant officer's instructions. 'The focus must be on teamwork,' he stressed. 'We encourage recruits to work as a single unit, something you will eventually be proud of.'

Once the training was complete Tom was ready to get down to some real work, he was ready to fight for his country. He felt a stirring of pride in his chest. Able Seaman Thomas Crossley. The name had a certain ring to it and, as he stood in line during the parade in Portsmouth, it gave him a great deal of pleasure to be a part of it.

Cathy closed the door to Mr. Dallarup's office and tried to keep a straight face, but a smile worked its way from the corners of her mouth and her eyes shone with excitement. She couldn't believe it. She'd only been working there for two years and here he was offering her the job of junior secretary. Of course she knew she could do the job. She was confident about that. She'd been covering for Agnes Bishop for over six months now. Poor old Agnes! She'd had to take leave to look after her elderly mother who was now bed-ridden. Her aunt had offered to look after her sister but Mrs. Bishop insisted it had to be Agnes. Mr. Dallarup held the job open until things could be sorted. But it seemed once old Mrs. Bishop had made it clear that she wanted nobody but her daughter to look after her, it meant Agnes was forced to resign. It was then Mr. Dallarup had no alternative but to appoint someone else. And that someone was Cathy.

'You look like the cat that got the cream. What did he want you for?' A voice broke into her thoughts.

Cathy slipped her hand over her mouth. 'You'll never believe it, Rita.' She could hardly contain herself. 'You knew Agnes's mother was crook with arthritis, didn't you? Poor Agnes has been forced to leave.' She frowned and shook her head but then her eyes were filled with delight. 'Mr. Dallarup has only given me her job. What do you think?'

Rita smiled and slid an arm around Cathy's shoulder. 'I'd heard her mum was bedridden and Agnes was off work, but I didn't know she'd actually resigned. In any case, you deserve the job, Cathy. You've been doing it long enough – and there's no-one else in the office capable.' Rita was Cathy's best friend. Not only had they spent their school days together, they now worked together too, Cathy as a shorthand typist and Rita a comptometer operator. You could say they were almost inseparable.

Cathy shook her head. 'You're biased, Rita,' she replied, her eyes alight with pride. But that's how they were with each other. And despite their closeness it was a compliment. Surely Rita wouldn't have said it if she hadn't really meant it.

Cathy rubbed her hands together, an expression of joy on her face. But then she paused and added, 'Oh, my goodness, it's just occurred to me. What about Gloria?' She pulled a face and

40

sighed. 'She's not going to be happy about it. She's been here longer than me.'

'I suppose it might have crossed Mr. Dallarup's mind to consider Gloria but, anyone with any sense can see it wouldn't be smart to appoint her. She's bone idle, Cathy. She spends too much time in the washroom, gazing at herself in the mirror, powdering her nose and combing her hair. She'd never get the work done. The boss must have known that. And she's nowhere near as bright as you.'

'Thanks for that. I'm over the moon.' She slipped an arm through Rita's. 'Wait until I tell Mum and Dad.' She paused. 'And it means a rise in salary too – a good one at that.'

'Lucky you.' Rita squeezed her arm, her voice holding no resentment or envy. 'All I can say is that it's your treat tonight after we finish at the ballroom studio. Smoothies all round at Johnny's Milk Bar.'

Cathy tipped her nose in the air. 'I'll go better than that. How about if we go to Collinson's Restaurant after work and order afternoon tea?' Collinson's was the most prestigious of Sydney's restaurants, more in the style of one of the top English establishments rather than a more in-formal Australian one. It would take all of Cathy's pocket money and more, but it was worth it.

'Now you're talking. But are we suitably dressed?' Rita looked down at her modest short-sleeved blouse and skirt, mockingly pursing her lips and fluttering her eyelids.

'If we can afford to pay the price, we're suitably dressed.' Cathy laughed, checking her own sleeveless dress, one her mother had made for her. 'But don't expect to make a habit of it.'

'That's disappointing,' Rita said in jest. 'I was hoping it might be a regular occurrence.'

'Only when you're promoted,' Cathy replied, pointing a finger towards her friend and laughing. 'Just remember it has to be your turn next.'

They sat near the window and looked out into the busy highway as they tucked into cream cakes. It was still quite hot outside even though it was well after five o'clock. 'These are delicious,' Rita mumbled, rolling her eyes in ecstasy.

'Aren't they just?' Cathy relished the taste and licked the cream from her lips as she poured tea into Rita's cup. 'I think I can squeeze out a drop more.'

The string quartet started to play Mozart, and Cathy took in the four oldies, one on double bass, one on cello, one on viola and one on violin. 'It's such a relaxed atmosphere in here with the music playing in the background.' She looked around her and then lowered her voice. 'Although I must say it's not exactly my type of music.' She grinned.

'Nor mine. But we didn't come in here for the music, we came for the cakes.'

'Exactly.' Cathy finished her cake and whispered, 'I feel real posh! I wonder what the poor people are doing.' She reiterated one of Dad's standard jokes, the one he always came out with when he was enjoying himself.

'Don't start getting snooty just because you've been promoted to junior secretary. And don't forget I'm the number one comptometer operator.' She pulled a face. 'But I take your point. I

42

do feel upper crust sitting here sipping tea from a china cup. Pity you couldn't afford the treat on a regular basis.'

Cathy tapped her on the back of the hand. 'You're pushing your luck, Rita O'Shaunessy. As I said, it's your turn next.' She giggled as she looked at her watch and collected her handbag from the seat beside her. 'We should be getting off now. You know how prickly Miss Jagger can be if we're late.'

'I'll say. It wouldn't be sensible to get on the wrong side of her. After the final ballroom exam Thursday, assuming I pass, I'd like to stay on and teach dancing in the evenings.' She looked to Cathy for confirmation. 'She did mention it some time ago – teaching dancing – didn't she? And the extra money would be useful.'

'She seemed keen for us to help. Surely we'll pass after all the years we've put in.'

'I do hope so, but I don't like to take things for granted.'

'Nor me, but I'm sure we'll be fine.'

It was the following Thursday when the two left Dallarups and made their way to the park where they sat in the sunshine and ate sandwiches before heading towards Segar's Dance Studio.

'By the way, what did your mum and dad have to say about your promotion?'

'Mum was quite blasé actually. She said she knew I could do it, and Dad was as proud as punch. He gave me an extra two shillings pocket money he was so pleased.' Hesitating for a moment, she slipped the brown paper wrapper back in her lunch box, and then she continued.

'Talking about Mum, she wants me to go straight home after the exams. Gran's coming to tea and she'd like to see me before Dad takes her home.' Cathy pulled a face. 'I know it's a bit of a pain but I did promise.'

'That's a pity. I thought we might celebrate the end of the exams and go to Johnny's.'

'Sorry, Rita. But I can't go back on my word. And Gran will want to know all about my promotion too. Mum's been bragging to her as usual.' Cathy exaggeratedly shook her head. 'You know what they're like.'

Rita tutted. 'Absolutely! I know what you mean. Dad's a bit like that. It's so embarrassing.'

'I'll say. But let's get in there and get it over with.' As Cathy held the door open for Rita to enter, she spotted Miss Jagger talking to a man she assumed was the examiner. 'Haven't seen him before,' she whispered.

Rita turned her head to study him. 'Me neither.'

Cathy pushed open the door to the cloakroom and slipped off her jacket. Her stomach gave a tiny flutter. It wasn't that she was nervous about the dance exam itself, but about the expectations of her family, especially Mum. From being eight years old Cathy had always passed her exams with distinction. It was the pressure of staying at the top that gave her the willies. It's easy to go up when you're down, but there's nowhere to go when you're already at the top. And this was the final exam – and a stiff one at that.

But it all went smoothly. Mr. Tonks, the examiner seemed to be impressed. And once the exam was over Cathy left Rita in the city and took the bus. As far as she was concerned she need not have worried. She was confident she had sailed through without putting a step wrong. Fingers crossed she'd done enough to gain that distinction.

There was a succulent aroma of cooking as Cathy walked into the kitchen and through into the living room. And Gran was more than complimentary about the job.

'You obviously take after our side of the family.' She smiled sweetly and Dad, who was sitting behind her, shook his head in dismay. Cathy looked at him and smirked behind her hand knowing that Gran's normal reaction was to take the credit, especially since Dad had had quite a poor upbringing. But he had come good with the job in the market. He was a supervisor now. He did help the men out when there was a large delivery, but he had climbed the ladder pretty quickly and was earning good money.

'But Frank's done well, Ma,' Marjorie was quick to point out.

'At the market, yes.' She shrugged and looked away. A backhanded compliment if ever there was one.

But no one took any notice of Gran. And that put a stop to the conversation about promotions and inherited intelligence. Gran had become quite rigid in her old age and she always tried to take the credit for any of the family's accomplishments. Like when the boys passed their exams and went to Gledhill High.

After a few minutes silence, which was rare when Gran was at the house, she looked Cathy up and

45

down. 'Is that your dance class dress, Cathy? I hope you don't wear it for work. Isn't it a bit short, dear?' She frowned and pursed her lips.

Marjorie was quick to defend her daughter. She took a steadying breath. 'Shorter dresses and skirts are the vogue now, Ma. That's the recommended length in view of the shortage of fabrics.' Before she could react Marjorie flashed a smile at her mother to keep the conversation light. 'I thought you always kept up with the news. Everyone's been talking about the new fashion. It seems to be popular now it's been accepted.'

'Wouldn't do for me. That's all I can say.'

'No-one's expecting you to wear anything that length, and you don't need new clothes in any case. It's wartime, Ma. You've surely heard the new slogan, *Make do and Mend*. Skirts just below the knee, straight lines, no puffed sleeves and all that. We've all got to pull in.'

'Well I don't hold with it, war or no war.' She folded her arms and shook her head.

'I don't agree with you there. We all have to do our bit. I bought a new treadle sewing machine last week. I've been saving up for it for ages. It's a beaut! I made Cathy's dress, the one she's wearing and I'm about to make one for myself in a similar style.' She went across to the sideboard, opened a drawer and rustled through some papers before pulling out a packet. 'Here take a look at this. It's a lovely pattern and they've been reduced to five pence a pattern at Stitchcraft.'

Gran narrowed her eyes and sniffed. 'I'm surprised at you Marj. Fair enough the short length might be fine for kids but you're going on forty.

You'll look like mutton dressed as lamb in something as short as that.'

Cathy was puzzled. Was Gran referring to her when she mentioned 'fine for kids'? How dare she refer to her as a kid? And she wants to make her mind up. First of all she disapproves of Cathy's knee length dress and now she seems to be changing her mind. Was she backing down?

'But Mum doesn't look forty does she Gran?' Cathy burst in. Why did old people have to be so straight-laced?

At this Gran perked up. 'Well I think it runs in the family this business of looking young for our age.' Gran patted her hair at the sides with the palms of her hands.

There she goes again. That was what annoyed Cathy. Everything complimentary was put down to Mum's side of the family – not that Mum agreed with Gran. But Dad received no credit whatsoever. His side of the family were non-existent as far as Gran was concerned. But did he care? Not two hoots!

Cathy took the time to study Gran and tucked away the urge to comment. She was only in her early sixties and yet she wore a black dress, black stockings and black shoes with a fur wrap slung around her shoulders. And it must have been twenty four degrees outside. But as far as Gran was concerned it was autumn coming on winter and one wore a fur wrap, cold or not. And as far as wartime rations were concerned, there was no convincing her that everyone had to make the effort.

'Well I suppose if you've bought a treadle then

you'll have to make your own clothes.'

'That's right. And I don't know whether you know this, Ma but you need twelve coupons for a dress and six for a hat. With Cathy and the boys growing so quickly, I can't keep up with it, I don't have the coupons to spare to keep on buying bigger sizes.'

Cathy waited for a response from Gran. Maybe she would offer Mum some of her coupons if she had no intentions of buying herself new clothes. But no, she was not about to give way.

When Dad set off to take Gran back home Mum sighed with relief.

'I don't know sweetheart, your Gran's always such a Job's Comforter. Why can't she appreciate we're trying our best.'

'I know she's my Gran and she's your Mum but I'd take what she has to say with a pinch of salt if I were you. Sometimes I think she does it on purpose just to rattle you. Quite honestly I think she's a teeny bit jealous.'

Marjorie started to laugh. 'You've got Gran off to a tee. You're good at weighing people up, Cathy even at your age.' She turned on the tap and filled the kettle. 'Well let's forget about what she said and have a cup of tea.' She set the kettle down on the stove and turned to Cathy. 'Now tell me, Cathy. How did the dancing go? We didn't get down to discussing that with Gran being here. How do you think you've done?'

Here she goes again. Cathy smiled. 'Not bad, Mum, but we'll have to wait and see won't we.'

But their light-hearted conversation was interrupted when Cathy's brothers, Freddie and

Danny returned with Dad. Frank, now stony-faced, followed them through into the kitchen.

'Don't look so glum, Frank. What on earth is the matter?' Marjorie gave a nervous frown.

'It's not good news, Marj.' Frank kept his eyes fixed on her. 'That letter Freddie received in the post was only his call up papers.' He shook his head and turned to Freddie. 'I don't know! Why didn't you mention it this morning, son?'

'I didn't want to upset Mum so early in the day. You know she gets up to see us off. The post was here for half six. I had an idea what it was when I saw the colour of the envelope but I didn't open the letter until I was on the tram on my way to work.' He threw the envelope on the kitchen worktop. 'Here, take a look.'

Marjorie ignored the envelope and began to snivel. 'I knew it.' She dabbed at her eyes. 'I don't know why our lads have to be involved. Come here Freddie,' she said, tears now rolling down her cheeks. She held out her arms. 'What am I going to do?'

'Stop worrying, Mum. I'll be back before you know it,' Freddie replied as she pulled him towards her.

Frank intervened. 'I keep on telling you, Marj, we have to do our bit. We'd have no chance if we were attacked. We need the Brits and the rest of the Empire behind us. I look at it this way, most of us down at the market look at it as a priority. We need to have a united approach and try to be of some value.'

'That's fine, Frank but no-one else seems to be pulling their weight,' she said sulkily.

'We have to give them chance for the penny to drop but once they realise how crucial it is, they'll follow suit, they'll make the effort.'

Cathy knew how upset Mum was at the thought of losing her first born, eighteen-year-old Freddie, to fight with the allies. She would be listening intently to the wireless day in day out, worrying and fearing for Freddie's safety as he moved into the battle zone. She'd be dreading anything happening to him. But that wasn't all. She would be fretting about Danny too. He would be seventeen soon and he'd be the next to go.

All was quiet for some time. The news had subdued events for that day. There would be no more speculation about Cathy's exam results. But that was somewhat of a relief to her. Mum always put her on a pedestal. She had high expectations and, although Cathy felt the exams had gone well, in her head she always quoted one of Mum's favourite sayings, *Don't count your chickens until they're hatched!*

'Crossley,' Chief Petty Officer Roberts called out before handing Tom a travel pass. Tom stared hard as he fingered it and, on reading the contents, a look of disappointment clouded his face. After their trips out to sea, mainly guarding the waters around England and Scotland, he had hoped they would be travelling abroad, but it appeared that wasn't to be. He waited until the officer had done his rounds before calling over to Mike who was sitting on the edge of his bunk. 'Where to?'

Mike looked up, sullen-faced, and lifted his pass in the air. 'Greenock.'

Tom's face eased into a tentative half-smile. 'Snap!' He was delighted that at least they would be travelling together even though it didn't sound to be anywhere exotic, or a place where they would be in the thick of the action. After sparking off a friendship on the train down to London, the two had become best buddies.

'Hope we're on the same ship.' Mike's face eased into a smile and his heavy boots clattered as he crossed over to where Tom was standing. He gazed over Tom's shoulder. 'Your destination's identical to mine, but that doesn't mean we'll be on the same ship.'

Tom pointed to the ticket. 'We'll soon find out. Tomorrow morning, seven-thirty train up to London, and then on from there.' He sat down on his bunk, now unfolding the sheet of paper accompanying the pass. 'Hang on, it says exactly which ship. I'll be joining HMS *Swallow*. How about you? Go on. Get it opened. Have a look,' he urged, pointing to the folded sheet.

Without hesitation, Mike opened the order document and turned to Tom, his mouth drooping at the corners.

Tom slapped him on the back. 'Come on. Don't keep me in suspense!'

Mike threw his hands in the air and bellowed. 'Me too!'

Tom gave him a gentle punch on the shoulder.

'Stop having me on,' he said between gritted teeth. And then he let out a roar. 'That's great! Wherever we're going on the *Swallow* we'll give 'em what for when we get there.'

'This is going to be our first real voyage. We've

51

completed the training and had plenty of experience guarding the coastline. That's something under our belts.' Tom lay back on his bunk, clasping his hands together and slipping them behind his head.

'I'll say. Let's hope we'll be sent abroad.' Mike folded up the order, slipped it into the envelope and turned to go back to his bunk.

'Somewhere with plenty of action.' Tom shouted after him.

Mike turned. 'Great minds think alike,' he clichéd.

They left as planned the following morning, still with no notion as to where they might be heading and, when they reached Greenock, they were immediately issued with thermal underwear and large, fur-trimmed hooded jackets.

Tom held the jacket out in front of him. 'By the look of this lot we won't be heading for the Mediterranean.' He felt a tinge of disappointment but he laughed. 'More likely the Scottish highlands.'

Mike picked up the woollen long johns and waved them in the air. 'You're right there, pal! I know what you mean. It's for sure we won't be heading for the tropics in these granddad pants,' he joked. 'It's more likely to be the Arctic.'

After a great deal of speculation, they listened to the captain's announcement.

Tom laughed and shook his head. 'Right again Lightowler. No sooner a word than a deed.' Mike was spot on. The Arctic it was to be.

For several months they were attached to one of the Arctic convoys and the warm clothing helped to keep out the severe cold when the sailors were on deck. But their duties were to guard the waters. Times were uneventful and Tom was getting itchy feet. He wanted to be involved; he wanted to see some action.

It was four months later when their taste of the icy Arctic climes came to an end and they sailed back to Scotland. After a low-key march through Greenock to join HMS *Resolute*, despite the cold wind and the heavy rain, crowds of well-wishers braved the inclement weather and gathered there to see them off.

Once on board the *Resolute*, they were issued with tropical kit and this gave them a clue as to their future destination.

'Wow. This looks promising. New ship, new experience.' Tom held the kit out in front of him. 'Looks as though we'll be taking a holiday in the sun.'

But Captain O'Neill soon made it quite clear it would be nothing of the sort.

'Listen carefully, men, and make sure you take in every word I say very seriously.' He glanced around the room. 'This is no joy ride. The orders I have received are based partially on factual information from the War Office, and partially on their speculation.' He clasped his hands together as the men stared expectantly, some smiling, some wearing a frown. 'There have been rumblings about possible uprisings in the Far East. After the United States' oil embargo on Japan, it appears the Japanese are planning to seize European colonies in Asia with the intention of exploiting the resources of Southeast Asia. The Allies are set in readiness to counter attack.' He paused before continuing. 'We are to join the Eastern Fleet to provide air-sea rescue facilities for those airmen brought down by the enemy during their attacks from the air. The ship is provided with hospital facilities, essential for the injured airmen. Although we shall not be directly involved in battle, it does not mean we are immune from attack.' He took a deep breath. 'Every man is expected to be vigilant and, once we reach the Indian Ocean, always remember one careless move can bring the whole ship down. Think about your fellow men, your friends,' he nodded, 'and your families.'

These new instructions gave Tom the buzz he was looking for and he felt immensely proud to be part of the operation. He turned to Mike.

'This is it then. It looks like we're off to where it's all happening.'

Mum was nowhere to be seen when Cathy entered the house. Dad was sitting in his chair his newspaper on his knee staring into space. It was unusual for him not to be reading. Cathy went over and kissed him on the cheek.

'You're in a world of your own, Dad. Where's Mum?'

'She's lying down, treasure. She's in a right old state and I'm not surprised. She was devastated when she found out Danny had only gone and signed on. He's left without even a goodbye.'

Cathy couldn't believe what she'd heard. The boys usually told her of their plans and if she'd made a promise she always kept it. But this time Danny had been secretive. He obviously couldn't trust her not to tell when it was something as important as running off to war. She knew he'd been envious of his brother for some time. But Cathy had the feeling he hadn't thought it through properly, he'd glamorised the role of serviceman.

'How did you find out?'

'One of the men at work told me. His lad has gone off with Danny.'

'I'm surprised, Dad. Danny could have made it official. We could at least have seen him off.'

'I doubt that would have happened not without your mother making a scene. Neither of the lads is of age as yet. Harry Chambers is not much more than sixteen.'

'Harry Chambers? He's a couple of months older than me but there's eleven months between me and Danny. At least he'll be seventeen next week.' She sat on the chair arm. 'They must both have said they were seventeen. What's going to happen?'

'Dick Chambers has had a word with the police. I don't know about Danny seeing he's nearly seventeen but they'll be sure to bring Harry back if they can get their hands on him. Dick is furious. He's been down to the barracks but it seems the unit moved to Townsville this morning.'

'Are you going to dob Danny in to the police?'

'Your mother wants me to do just that. But what's the point? It'll only cause a scene. Danny will be seventeen by the time it's all sorted and if they send him back here he'll only resent us. I've told your mother what I think but she's adamant.'

'I think you're right, Dad.' She slipped an arm

around his shoulder. 'We'll have to trust that he doesn't get into any trouble and that he stays safe.'

'I wish your mother could be as optimistic and put it all into perspective, Cathy. She'll be in bed mulling it over in her mind. I'll get the blame for not doing anything about it but it won't be the first time she's had a go at me.' He smiled. 'And I know what you mean. Danny's always been one to get himself involved. Where there's trouble, there's Danny.' He gave a heavy sigh. 'Come on, treasure. Let's get some tucker sorted.'

Cathy smiled to herself. What Dad meant was for her to sort out the meal. But he worked hard down at the market and he deserved to be waited on from time to time.

Although she put on a show of bravado for Dad's sake when she went into the kitchen her stomach began to churn. She loved both her brothers so much even though they teased her constantly. And she hoped with all her heart that they would stay safe.

Chapter 3

1941–1942

It was early December when HMS *Resolute* left Portsmouth for their destination in the Far East. The crew were optimistic that, provided they encountered no hostilities during the passage, they would be allowed to celebrate Christmas on board.

The ship headed for the English Channel where, after the German occupation of France and the Channel Islands, great care had to be taken to stay within the allied-held area, which was no more than a thirty square kilometre block.

'There's no way we can afford to put a foot wrong,' the captain explained. 'The enemy are going to be on the lookout for potential targets.'

It was a stormy night and Tom stood watch on deck in the torrential rain, the strong blustery winds cutting all the way through to his bones. He pulled his rain gear tightly around him and cupped his numb hands together to shield the match he was furtively trying to light. But the match was damp and his attempt was unsuccessful. The heavy rain continued to hammer down on to his frozen hands and he had to beat them together to revive the circulation.

When he heard a voice behind him, he glanced over his shoulder. 'Want a light?' Mike whispered.

Startled, Tom nodded. 'Yeah, thanks,' he replied, gratefully accepting the light from his friend and, as he drew on the cigarette he took the greatest care for fear the glow would be seen by the enemy.

'You were in a world of your own there, pal.' Mike stood next to him and leant on the rail. 'Something on your mind?'

'Only that I was wondering what'll be in store for us when we get there.' But as he drew on the cigarette he felt a hand on his shoulder.

'Clink for you, laddie if I catch you with a fag

57

in yer hand again.' Robbo snatched the cigarette from Tom's hand, dropped it on to the deck and ground it viciously under his foot.

Tom cleared his throat and stared back at the sergeant.

'Got a problem with that?' Robbo asked.

Undaunted by the sergeant's scowl, Tom smiled. 'No Serg. Sorry about that.'

'You will be if it happens again!' The sergeant strode away. The others knew Robbo had no problems with Tom. In fact they were aware he liked the lad but was determined to keep an eye on him. They'd caught Robbo's words, 'At times he has too much fire for his own good.'

'You were lucky there, Tom,' Mike whispered, stepping out from the shadows. 'Me too!'

'I know. We'd better watch it in future.' Tom stared out to sea. 'Have you any idea of the time, Mike?'

'It was going on for eight when I came up here.'

'That's a relief. About another half hour and I'm off duty.'

The crossing turned out to be uneventful and, eventually, the ship headed south into the Atlantic Ocean. But when they reached the Bay of Biscay the swells rose to eighteen feet and some of the men moaned in agony as the ship pitched and rolled.

Mike was one of those men. Tom had managed to escape seasickness, but Mike had complained he felt nauseous. He groaned continuously, fighting hard to control the sickness. Tom looked across at his friend who was lying on his bunk. Staring down at his ashen face, Tom reflected on the time he told Mike about Mam leaving. Mike had understood immediately how Tom must have felt.

Tom pulled his thoughts together. 'Is there anything I can do to help, Mike?' He stared down at his friend whose face now seemed to be completely drained of blood.

All that Mike could mutter was, 'I'm going to die.' He clutched his abdomen and anxiety filled his eyes. 'My gut...' But his words were cut short when the voice of Lieutenant Driver came over the intercom.

'All hands on deck. The captain has an urgent message.'

The Lieutenant's announcement caused uproar down below. Most of the men down there were off duty, some in bed fast asleep. Tom felt his senses being bombarded with the noise of the men shouting and complaining to each other, some of them writhing about and wailing.

'Bloody 'ell, it must be serious if we've to shift our arses up top when we're off duty,' someone called out.

'Off your backsides you lot,' Robbo bellowed from up above.

Tom hurriedly slipped on his tunic and bell-bottoms. When he was ready to leave Mike behind he said, 'I won't be long, pal. I'll tell Robbo you're a bit green around the gills.' He grinned, hoping his jokey comment would help to cheer up his friend. Mike did try to laugh but his eyes betrayed the pain he was suffering.

Once assembled, Captain O'Neill appeared. Before making an announcement, he paused, staring into space for a long moment as though composing his thoughts.

'I have received very bad news from the war office concerning a devastating blow for our allies, the Americans. On Sunday the seventh of December the Japanese carried out a surprise attack on Pearl Harbor, one of the US naval bases in Hawaii.' His face was a mask of gravity, his words clipped and his delivery slow and precise.

'The main aim of the Japanese was to sink the American fleet's aircraft carriers, but fortunately they were out at sea and the Japanese failed. However, during this sneak attack many of the United States Navy battleships, cruisers and destroyers were lost, as well as a great number of aircraft. Two thousand four hundred personnel were killed and twelve hundred and eighty wounded, such was the severity of the bombings.' There were groans and gasps of surprise from the men.

The captain lifted his hands to silence them. 'As a consequence the United States, Britain, our other European allies and China have declared war on Japan.' There were more gasps from the men, but the captain held up his hands once more. 'Quiet, there's more. The attack was apparently meant to deter the United States from intervening in Southeast Asia and the day after Pearl Harbor the Japanese army invaded Malaya.'

He took a deep breath. 'The potential task we were sent to carry out over there has now become reality. Rumour has it that the Japanese will attack Singapore. We are to join the convoy standing off in the Andaman Sea ready to make our way south towards Malaya and Singapore.'

The captain retired to the bridge, leaving the men in huddles. They turned to each other and a buzz of conversation began again, some of the men raising their voices and speculating, others coming out with gloomy mutterings. But Tom was more intent on getting back to Mike to see how he was coping. And he decided not to elaborate on Captain O'Neill's announcement. It was more important that he get help and make sure Mike was made more comfortable.

'What was all that about?' Mike asked.

'The latest instructions, Mike. But let's try to get you more comfortable. It's a good job this is a hospital ship. I'll get one of the medics to take a look at you.'

'I'm not the only one suffering, Tom,' Mike mumbled. 'They've probably got their hands full already. I'll be OK.'

'Don't try kidding me on with that line. I'll be back in a couple of minutes.'

The doctor prescribed medication to help calm the seasickness and it was a matter of hours before Mike started to feel the benefit. 'I must try to pull myself round now I'm feeling a bit better,' he said, a glazed expression on his face. 'Sorry about this.' He closed his eyes. 'I wouldn't wish it on anyone.'

'Stop worrying, Mike. These things happen and it takes time to clear. As soon as the pills kick in properly I'm sure you'll feel much better.' He sat down next to Mike. 'Besides, you're doing great. I'm only relieved it's not me.'

Despite the medication it was more than a week before Mike had his sea legs back and, once things appeared to be under control, Tom told

61

him the full story about Pearl Harbor and the consequences.

Mike shrugged. 'Takes some believing, all those poor buggers killed. We need to watch our backs, that's all I can say.'

Later that day Captain O'Neill addressed them again. 'It has become crucial we make haste to the Andaman Sea and with that in mind I'm afraid I'm going to have to curtail all Christmas celebrations, or at least postpone them. I appreciate you were all looking forward to some respite, but we have no time for partying. Our priority is to get there as quickly as possible.' He smiled for the first time in a while. 'But don't worry there'll be other opportunities to celebrate once our task in the east is complete.'

After hugging the Portuguese coastline their journey took them through the Straits of Gibraltar and into the Mediterranean Sea. Although the captain was especially vigilant, it was quite peaceful as they sailed along the North African coast towards Egypt and Port Said, considered to be the most important city north east of the Suez. There had already been attacks in that area. But, despite their fears, they managed to re-fuel and continue their passage without event through the well-guarded Suez Canal.

Eventually they left the canal behind and entered the Red Sea. And, after a journey free of conflict, they headed through the Indian Ocean and onwards to Colombo in Ceylon, their eventual destination being the Andaman Sea and the coast of Malaya.

Christmas over, it was January 1942. It was

then the men heard that The United Nations had been formed and the Atlantic Charter had been signed.

A month after Cathy's final ballroom examination a letter arrived. Marjorie Ellis fingered the envelope and checked the name across the top. It was addressed to Cathy and sure enough it was from the dance awarding body. Marjorie, now anxious to know the results, stared at the envelope, hoping her daughter had once again excelled. She couldn't wait to find out.

Should she open it? Marjorie stared at the envelope and reasoned that since Cathy was still a minor she, as her mother, had every right to open any correspondence addressed to her daughter. After all it could have been something serious that Marjorie needed to know about. What the hell? Why not? She took a knife from the kitchen drawer and slit the envelope across the top. Slowly unfolding the sheet inside, she stared avidly. The result read: *Distinction.*

Marjorie was delighted. She smiled to herself. Sure enough Cathy had been awarded the top grade once more, and this was her final ballroom examination. She shook her head. Why did she need to bother checking the result? She should have known. And she couldn't wait until Frank came home to tell him the good news.

But Frank refused to listen. 'Don't tell me how she's done. I'd like to leave that for Cathy to tell me.' He shook his head. 'You shouldn't have opened it Marj. It takes away the element of surprise for Cathy.'

'She won't be surprised.' Marjorie couldn't help giving him the hint. 'She knew she'd done well, she told me so.' But, after the way Frank had reacted, Marjorie was now beginning to wonder if she had done the right thing opening the envelope although, as usual, she convinced herself she had every right to check her daughter's mail.

When Cathy returned from the office that evening, Marjorie took the envelope from the mantelpiece. 'Your results are here,' she said beaming as she waved it in the air. She started to hand it over. 'I knew you could do it. Here you are. Check it out for yourself.'

Cathy stared at the envelope and turned it over, looking pointedly at the slit. 'But it's been opened already.' Her forehead crumpled into a frown. 'Why, Mum?' she shook her head. 'Don't you think now that I'm old enough I should be allowed to open my own mail? You had no right to do that.'

'I haven't told you the grade, Cathy. I've left that for you to do. Come on. Your Dad's dying to know how you've gone on. Don't keep him in suspense.' After Cathy's reaction Marjorie began to feel ashamed she'd opened the envelope, no matter what her reasoning. And the guilt stayed with her.

Cathy looked to Mum again and blinked her eyes in annoyance before pulling out the sheet from inside the envelope. 'You've spoilt it for me. And for Dad too I reckon.' She opened the sheet. 'It's no good telling you, Mum, you already know but Dad I've made distinction grade. That's a relief.'

'Well done, Cathy. You deserve it after all the

hard work you've put in.'

Cathy continued to give Mum a look of disapproval, but she couldn't keep it up for long. Dad was giving her a hug and she knew Mum wanted to do likewise, but by now she realised Mum felt sheepish.

Later that evening when Cathy met up with Rita they conferred. Rita had been graded Merit and not distinction. When she challenged Miss Jagger about the grade, she was told she had been a borderline candidate but that the examiner had decided she was not quite a distinction grade.

It was obvious Rita was disappointed but she tried to cover it. 'It doesn't matter to me. I'm still teaching the boys and earning my one and six a night. I'll get over it. It's all done and dusted now.'

'But we were as good as one another,' Cathy insisted. 'We always have been. I can't understand it.'

'Don't forget you're taller than I am. I probably didn't have as good a stance as you, although I always try to hold myself upright, pull in my stomach and hold my shoulders back.' Rita smiled. 'Come on let's get on with the dancing. I can't be bothered thinking about it anymore.' The two of them turned, left the studio and headed for the main ballroom.

Tom's mind was constantly flooded with thoughts of Billy and Dorothy. At times his conscience played havoc. But what could he have done had he stayed back home? His country needed him and, had he not volunteered, he felt sure he would have been called up for service anyway. And what

65

was the point in getting maudlin and dwelling too much in the past? It was time to think about the future and concentrate his efforts on the war and the tasks before him.

Mike interrupted his thoughts.

'I hope we get some mail through from England. We haven't heard a dickey-bird since we left Portsmouth.' He placed his clothes neatly at the bottom of his bunk and lay on top of the mattress, his hands clasped behind his head. 'I thought Mum and Dad would have written by now.'

'Yes, I was expecting to hear from Dorothy. I can't help wondering what's happening back in Yorkshire. All I hope is that Billy's not causing her too much trouble.' Tom folded his bell-bottoms and pressed down the creases as he had been taught. 'Our Dot's good at letter writing, much better than I am. I was sure she'd have let me know by now how things were going.' He slipped the bell-bottoms under his mattress and spread himself out on top of his bunk.

'It depends where we stop now as to what comes through. There was nothing in Port Said so, fingers crossed, it won't be long before the next port of call.'

'Wherever that might be...' Tom started, but before he could continue, he heard the voice of the captain over the PA system. They were to assemble up above.

'As we approach the Andaman Sea we will soon be joining the convoy standing off ready to pick up the wounded. The Japanese have taken and occupied Singapore and I have been advised they are pushing north and heading for Burma. It is possible enemy submarines are waiting in the area, and we may be attacked. We must be more than ever vigilant. I intend doubling the number of men on watch. You will do four hours on duty and four hours off. Mr. Roberts has the rota. Watch duties will commence immediately.'

Tom and Mike looked at one another. Reality was here, staring them in the face. The captain had said Japanese submarines. 'We wanted action.' Tom slapped Mike on the back. 'We're in the thick of it now! Not that it's the sort of action I'd envisaged.'

'Me neither.' Mike shook his head. 'It'll be hardgoing trying to spot the periscopes from up above, especially in the dark, and that's when the subs tend to strike.'

'It's got to be done, Mike. I don't relish the thought of one of their subs sneaking up on us.'

'Nor me, but I'm sure we can beat 'em!' Mike smiled wickedly. 'Robbo reckons they shouldn't give us much trouble. He says most are only the size of two pen'orth o' copper.'

Tom grinned. Mike could be outspoken at times, even though he was quoting Robbo. But Tom liked him for that. And the feeling was mutual even though they came from differing backgrounds. Although Tom had a bright mind and a light heart, something essential in those gloomy times, he hadn't been brought up with a doting mother in a middle class district. He was from the backstreets where life had its hardships and you fought for survival. The war hadn't come as a brutal shock to Tom and he admired his friend for surviving as well as he had.

Tom found the four-hour stints on watch in the Andaman Sea more intense than he had ever experienced. The search for signs of sub conning-towers in the vast ocean was so exhausting that it made every muscle in his body ache with sheer fatigue. He rubbed his eyes. In the dark of night it seemed that periscopes bobbing along above the water might have caused the tiniest ripple. Sometimes he thought he was seeing things and, by the end of the stint, he was so tense, he felt ready to drop. His first priority was to get his head down, and yet when it was time for him to take a rest, his mind was still active and he found it difficult to get even an hour's sleep.

And he was not the only one affected in this way. His shipmates were hollow-eyed and flagging too. With only a short break to refresh themselves the sailors were often still weary when they resumed watch. But it was vital the enemy be prevented from firing torpedoes at the convoy of Allied troops.

The Japanese were ferocious in their attack and when the dogfights began the small rescue boats were constantly on the alert, ready to retrieve the casualties from the frenzied waters of the Andaman Sea. Men were dropping from the skies like the tiny, fluffy dandelion clocks Tom used to catch in his hands when he was a little boy. But this was not some childhood game, these were airmen clinging on to their parachutes and falling into the churning mass. Tom glanced up. These men were precious and, each and every one, whether British, American or Japanese, needed to be rescued, dead or alive.

The boats sped back and forth returning to the mother ship and off-loading the casualties. And when Tom was up above he caught sight of two Japanese airmen who were still alive and being ferried back to the ship. He seethed inside. As they neared the ship pandemonium broke loose as the other duty men pointed and shouted towards the oncoming rescue boat. But the officer in charge issued an order. 'Quiet you lot. Bring those men in and take care not to lose them.'

The seamen quickly got the message and, with deliberate movements, they lifted the captives to safety. But it was obvious that the courageous Japanese prisoners were ashamed after being captured and taken on board a British ship. They were reluctant to step on board and spoke to one another in frenzied tones in a language none of the crew could understand. And when they struggled to throw themselves over the ship's rail and back into the murky depths, it was apparent their joint decision had been to commit hara-kiri. But the captain had earlier insisted that all casualties be rescued unharmed whatever their nationality. This also meant that they must not harm themselves.

But Mike could not hold back his irritation. 'Why the captain didn't let the buggers throw themselves back in there I'll never understand.' He paced up and down becoming more and more heated. 'They're the enemy.'

One of the others on duty, a broad-shouldered, heavy-muscled man, struck a defiant gesture, fixing his gaze on the Japanese prisoners, staring them boldly in the face and giving an arrogant shrug. 'Sneaky, yellow bastards!' he muttered under his breath.

There was a chorus of laughter from the other men. But Tom rationalised, sharpening his perception of the situation. Although he understood why the others were resentful and scoffing at these characters, many with poor eyesight and buckteeth, he had a touching faith in human nature and he was not in favour of that sort of comment. His jaw clenched. 'Point taken. They are the enemy. But Robbo says it's the policy to capture and not to harm the men. It's to do with some sort of agreement under the Geneva Convention. Don't ask me what it's all about.'

'You're too soft for your own good, Yorkie,' the big man retorted.

Tom laughed. 'I suppose I am, and having said that, I doubt if they'd give us the same leniency if we were captured by them. Would they stand by the agreement?'

'I'd hope to hell they would, but I doubt it.' Mike spit out the words with undisguised annoyance before the two of them went back down below.

'It looks wonderful, Cathy. Fits like a glove!' Marjorie Ellis clapped her hands as her daughter slipped on the pink crepe de chine dress, closed the side zip and tossed back her shiny hair. Cathy carefully smoothed the dress down at the sides.

'Are you sure, Mum? It's not baggy around the waist is it?' She tugged the fabric gently.

'Baggy? Not at all.' Marjorie took her daughter by the shoulders and turned her around. 'Film star good looks and a lovely figure. That's my girl. You've a real talent too. You handle that sewing machine like you've been doing it all your life. You'll make someone a good wife one of these days.' She paused. 'And save him money too.' She beamed proudly.

'You would say that, Mum. I'm your daughter.' Cathy's lovely brown eyes sparkled as she popped a kiss on Mum's cheek. 'But I keep on telling you I've no interest in marrying, not yet. Besides there's no point talking about getting married when I haven't met Mr. Right,' she insisted.

'You'd do well to be sensible and consider Mrs. Grant's boy, Geoffrey. He's been sweet on you since you joined the youth club. He has a good job at the Commonwealth Bank, and Irene tells me it's the biggest bank in Australia, branches all over the place. You could do worse. She reckons their Geoffrey could end up being a manager at one of the branches when he passes his final exams. How about that?' She smiled brightly and waited for Cathy's response.

Cathy smiled to herself. 'For goodness sake, Mum. Geoffrey Grant! He's just not my type. And he must be going on thirty now.' She shook her head.

Marjorie took in a deep breath and huffed. 'You'll learn one of these days, lady.'

'But Mum, once the war is over I want some fun. Surely there's more to life than marrying and settling down.'

'Well your Dad and I didn't miss out. And how do you mean you want some fun? You've had lots of fun. We were never against you going to Segars. You enjoy that don't you? And you've done well there with your medals,' she bragged. 'You're out nearly every night of the week.'

'I know, Mum, and I do enjoy teaching at the dance studio, but...'

'There you go. They're paying you one and six a night,' Marjorie stressed, 'and free entry the other nights. What more do you want?'

'I want to try somewhere else. Rita tells me the *Trocadero* Ballroom in Sydney is popular. We've decided to try it.' She swallowed hard, knowing Mum might not approve.

'The *Trocadero!*' Marjorie was aghast. 'Your father and I don't want you getting mixed up with that sort,' she blustered. 'You don't know what those foreigners are up to half the time. Here today gone tomorrow,' she clichéd.

'You're exaggerating, Mum. For a start, what about our own lads? And the so-called foreigners are Americans and Brits. Don't tell me you don't trust the Brits. After all we can't criticise our own roots.' She smiled sweetly now.

'I don't know about that, Cathy. Your Grand-dad was Scottish. Look how he treated his family. He left your Dad and Auntie Mary in an orphanage in Sydney when their mother died.' Marjorie sniffed and, in a dramatic gesture, turned her head away.

'But what alternative did he have, Mum? He was a ship's captain. He couldn't abandon his ship. He needed to get back to England.' She knew they were empty words and she didn't believe in them herself. But she had to try and put a point across and defend her reasoning.

'Oh, yes. But he could abandon his children, is that what you mean? And why didn't he come back for them?' Marjorie was adamant. 'Your poor Dad and Auntie Mary never saw him again.'

'Don't go on, Mum. Besides, we could teach some of the boys at the *Trocadero* the basic steps. Most of them haven't a clue how to dance. They've never had the chance to learn. They've been fighting for their country – and some of them are younger than me. Don't you think they deserve a break? It'll be fun teaching them.' She looked directly into her mother's eyes. 'Anyway, we've made up our minds about the *Trocadero*, and that's the end of it.'

She turned away. She was old enough and sensible enough to look after herself, thank you very much. Mum would make any excuse to discourage her from going to the ballroom. And why did mums have to start planning for their daughters to marry once they reached eighteen? It was as though it was a slight on them personally if plans for a wedding weren't in place by the time their girls were twenty-one. It wasn't a competition! And all this talk about being left on the shelf. For goodness sake! Going on for eighteen, she wasn't ready for big decisions. She wasn't an 'old maid' yet. What did Mum expect?

She sighed. Mum had obviously been talking to Irene Grant and between them they'd hatched a plan to have a go at matchmaking. Fair enough Mum wanted security for Cathy, and Mrs. Grant wanted to choose her future daughter-in-law for herself. But Cathy was adamant. She was definitely not going to be the chosen one. She stifled a smirk. Wait until she told Rita. She'd crease herself at the thought of Mum suggesting she marry

Geoffrey Grant.

'Well, your Dad's not going to like it.' Marjorie interrupted Cathy's thoughts. 'I know what he thinks of the *Trocadero*.'

'Hard cheese, Mum.' The words slipped out and Cathy lifted her hand to her mouth, knowing she'd gone too far.

Marjorie took a deep breath. 'Don't adopt that attitude with me, Catherine Ellis. And you know I detest those stupid sayings. I don't know where you get them from, really I don't.'

'Sorry, Mum. I didn't mean to answer back. I only said it in fun.' Cathy slipped her arm around Mum's shoulders and gave her a squeeze. After all hadn't Mum been generous enough to hand over her own clothing coupons so that Cathy could buy the fabric. 'Please, please, don't get annoyed, Mum.' She smacked a kiss on Mum's cheek.

And before Cathy dropped herself into more hot water, she turned and went into her bedroom to change. She'd better play it cool otherwise Mum would make an issue of it. And she didn't want that. If she kept things on an even keel, Dad would give in. They were allies, especially if Mum got on her high horse. Or if any of her brothers started picking on her. Not that they had the chance these days. Cathy was full of smart answers. The boys were easily irritated and they quickly backed off, especially if they thought she was about to get the better of them.

That evening she put on the new dress and left quietly before Mum could continue to put on the pressure, and before Dad came home from his job at the market. He started in the early hours and was usually home by mid-afternoon, but there must have been a large delivery to unload. If, when she saw him later, he created about the *Trocadero*, she could always sweet-talk him. It would probably be the following night before he had the chance to tackle her about it, but by that time he'd probably have forgotten, or calmed down. Unless of course Mum wound him up again.

Rita was waiting down at Circular Quay when Cathy stepped off the bus and ran towards her, making sure she didn't catch the heels of her black patent court shoes on the cobbles.

'I nearly didn't make it,' she called out.

'How do you mean?' Rita asked.

'Mum was annoyed when I mentioned going to the *Trocadero* next week. She more or less said the guys who go there are up to no-good.' She giggled.

'Well, we won't know until we get there, will we? So come on and let's see what it's like.'

'Not tonight, Rita. We promised to meet Nancy and Gwen at the new floating dance floor off Luna Park.'

'Yes, I know that, but when you mentioned the *Troc* I thought you'd changed your mind and arranged to meet them there.'

'No. It was just that Mum was in a good mood when I finished sewing and I thought I'd broach the subject to see what her reaction would be. But it was just as I thought. And then what do you think? She had the nerve to suggest Geoffrey Grant would be a good catch for me!' She collapsed in helpless laughter.

'I don't believe it. Geoffrey Grant? He must be

all of thirty.' Rita joined in the laughter. 'Although I must say he's quite handsome if you like that sort of thing.' By this time the other two girls had arrived on the scene. And the laughter was infectious.

'It's as well Mum's not a fly on the wall,' Cathy blurted out. 'She'd have a fit!'

'I know what you mean. Mine too if she knew what we were up to!' Rita slipped her arm through Cathy's and they set off towards Luna Park.

A loud cheer rang out as HMS *Resolute* sailed into Darwin and anchored. Respite at last after their intensive surveillance in the Andaman Sea. Tom's excitement rose and he held his breath when a large mailbag was brought on board. Would his luck be in? Hopefully news from home at last. He picked up the envelope and stared hard at the handwriting. The letter was from Dorothy. His hands were shaking as he ripped it open. But his heart sank when he read the contents.

Dear Tom,

I'm sorry to have to tell you like this but Dad passed away earlier this week. He came down with the flu and then pneumonia set in. There was nothing we could do. It was sad to see the state he was in, and I don't think he made any effort to pull himself round. I honestly think he wanted to go. Thankfully he didn't suffer for long.

Don't worry though because I'm coping fine and getting over it, Billy too. I've made all the necessary arrangements for the funeral. Unfortunately I don't know where you'll be when you receive my letter but I know it would be difficult for you to travel back home in any case. We'll both be thinking about you, Tom.

Tom looked at the postmark on the envelope. The letter had been posted five weeks earlier. The funeral had been and gone and besides it would have been impossible for him to have returned to England.

You won't believe this but Mam had the cheek to show her face on Wednesday morning. She was after scrounging some of the furniture, and she asked about Dad's bankbook. But I gave her short shrift and refused to let her see it – not that there'll be much left after the funeral expenses have been paid. Mam wanted Billy to go back with her but he insisted he preferred to stay with me and George, and we're glad to have him. In the end she got the hump and left for Manchester with a flea in her ear.

On a lighter note George and I got engaged last month. You know we've been going out together for ages. We've talked things through and decided to get married as soon as we feel a reasonable period of mourning has passed. We'll all live together in the house at Back Rushton Street. I think the landlord will let us stay, especially when he realises George and I are to marry.

We're all missing you, Tom and hope to hear from you when you get a chance to put pen to paper.
Lots of love
Dorothy

Tom stared at Dorothy's neat handwriting and read the letter again. Tears were stinging the backs of his eyes and began to steal down his cheeks, not so much for the loss of his Dad whom he'd loved dearly, but more for the plight of Dorothy and Billy. But then he rationalised and felt sure they would cope as long as the landlord allowed them to stay on in the house. And of course Dorothy would soon have George to care for her, Billy too.

He was still clutching the letter and staring into space when he heard the roar of the men down below. He leaned forward and placed his forearms on the bulwark, quickly pulling his thoughts together, aware of the sound of someone clambering up to the top deck. He brushed the damp from his cheeks and turned. It was Mike who was gripping the rungs as though there was a fire down below, a huge grin on his face. He dashed across to the rail where Tom was standing. 'Did you hear that?'

Tom did his best to control his emotion. 'Yes. What were the lads cheering about?'

'It's good news, Tom.' Mike joined him, rubbing his hands together. His eyes lit up. 'We're bound for Sydney. According to Robbo we're being replaced – but only temporarily. How about that? The pilots, Brits and Yanks, have left the ship to join their own units but we're taking the two Japs to Sydney. And that's a good enough excuse for me – just to get away from it all for as long as they'll allow.'

'I can't believe it!' Tom turned to Mike. 'I'm desperate for a break.' He thought about his family again and realised this might take his mind off things.

Mike took a long, hard look at his friend. 'Are you OK, Tom? You're looking a bit pale. Is there something up?'

Tom held up Dorothy's letter. 'It's Dad. He's passed away. And the funeral's been and gone. It's all over with.'

Mike placed his hand on Tom's shoulder. 'I'm so sorry about your dad. I'd no idea you'd received a letter. I wondered where you were.'

Tom nodded and explained about Dorothy and George. 'At least once they're married they'll take Billy in hand. He'll be well looked after.'

'I'm sure you're right.'

Tom didn't want to inflict Mike with his problems. He certainly didn't want to subdue him when he was so psyched up about sailing down to Sydney and going ashore there. He gave a heavy sigh and quickly changed the subject.

'It's good news about sailing to Sydney.'

'You can say that again. We're due for a spot of off-duty if we're lucky.' Mike rolled his eyes and grinned. 'We might have a chance to sample the talent.'

Tom smiled back at Mike and tried to enter into the spirit of things.

'Exactly, given half the chance.'

And although it would take time to overcome his sadness, Tom felt a rush of excitement at the thought of a new experience.

Chapter 4

1942

It was a hot evening but there was a light wind coming from the ocean. The two sailors, bell-bottoms flapping in the breeze, stood on the quay gazing over the water at the floating dance floor. The music drifted across and the name on the sign stood out, *Neptune's Palace*. A small ferry stood by to take the dancers the short distance to the place where the dance floor was anchored in the harbour.

Tom tried to curb his excitement as he pointed to the illuminated sign. 'We've nothing like this at home. It looks great.' His eyes sparkled. 'Fancy your chances, Mike?'

Mike, his gaze fixed on a pretty girl in the queue, was startled into replying. He turned to face Tom. 'I fancy her if that's what you mean.' He nodded towards the girl whose silky blonde curls shimmered in the breeze as she chattered animatedly to her friend. 'Some of these Aussie girls are fab lookers.'

Tom followed his gaze. 'Wow. I see what you mean. She's a real cracker!' He turned back to Mike pointing to *Neptune's Palace*. 'What do you think about going over there? Are you game?'

Mike nodded his head and grinned. 'Nothing's going to stop me.' He pulled a face. 'The problem is I have two left feet when it comes to dancing.'

Tom laughed. 'Same here, but the music's great. And a bit of female company wouldn't go amiss.'

Mike grinned. 'It would not.' He replied with emphasis on each word. He nodded. 'Come on. Let's make the best of tonight. It might be the last chance we get.'

Tom's smile faded. 'You're right there. We might never be here in Sydney again. What with the war still raging it's anyone's guess what'll happen next. We could be back in the thick of it any day now.'

'Then what are we waiting for? Let's do it.'

Decision made. They joined the happy throng queuing for the ferry. Mike, seemingly mesmerised, still had his eye on the blonde girl but then his smile turned into a frown. One of the American soldiers slipped an arm around her shoulders.

'How about if we tag along with you little lady,' he drawled, addressing the blonde girl.

Mike raised his eyebrows and nudged Tom. 'Typical,' he murmured as he watched the guy.

'Over-familiar, that's their trouble,' Tom added. But in his heart he knew his resentment was nothing more than his own lack of confidence. When it came to approaching the opposite sex, the confidence to do so was something he lacked, mainly through his inexperience. He took a deep breath. But now was the time to make a start, provided the opportunity arose.

Once at *Neptune's Palace* they headed for the bar.

'How about a pint of beer and a rum chaser, Mike? I think we've earned it don't you?'

'You can say that again!' He grinned sheepishly. 'I need a bit of courage before I give it a go on the dance floor.'

They stood at the bar surveying the dancers and it wasn't long before Tom spotted a willowy, dark-haired girl arriving. Her friend was an equally attractive redhead.

He nudged his pal. 'How about cutting in on those two?' he suggested, pointing furtively.

'It's not taken you long to pick the good-lookers,' Mike replied, smiling broadly. 'But let's wait for a slow dance. I can just about get round the floor if it's a waltz but I've no chance with a quickstep and I'm even worse tackling a foxtrot.'

'Same here!' Tom continued to stare at the two girls. 'I fancy the dark-haired one in the pink dress.'

'That's fine. The redhead in the green is more my choice. We'll keep an eye on them. They've only just arrived and won't be in a hurry to leave.'

Tom continued to stare vacantly at the girl and his thoughts turned to home. He'd never been shown any affection, except from his sister, Dorothy. He absently shook his head. And that one thought led him to reflect on his life in Leeds before he enlisted. Apart from the news about Dad, he'd received no more mail from home, but neither had anyone else. He knew Dorothy would have written again, that was her way, but somehow or other the mail was slow to reach the ships.

Mike's words interrupted Tom's thoughts and he emerged from the past.

'Penny for 'em!' He nudged Tom.

Momentarily Tom's mind blanked. He shook himself and, not wanting Mike to know he was thinking about home, he rolled his eyes and fixed them on the girl in the pink dress. 'I think I've died and gone to heaven.' He grinned. The dress she was wearing showed the lovely curves of her figure.

'What?'

'Hmm...' When the girl turned Tom couldn't concentrate on what Mike was saying. He took in her delicate features, directing his gaze to her huge brown eyes, still yet beautiful as she watched him. He held them and when he plucked up the courage to wink her eyes warmed and faint dimples flirted in her cheeks. She shyly turned away and his breathing quickened. 'I think she likes me.' There was something about her he could not resist.

Mike stared after Tom as he stepped forward. 'What makes you think that?'

'Something in the way she looked back at me.'

'So what? It doesn't mean she wants to dance with you.' He grinned. 'But I must say, I fancy the redhead. Come on it's a slow one. Let's cut in now.'

Cathy gazed back at the sailor. He was tall and upright with classic good looks and light brown wavy hair. She liked what she saw. He looked smart in his uniform and so handsome too. And those clear, riveting glacial blue eyes. She could no more break away from his gaze than she could stop her heart from beating faster. Her stomach fluttered. And then the firm, sensual lines of his mouth slowly relaxed into a devastating smile and lit up his wonderful eyes. He winked.

Feeling the hot flush on her cheeks, she turned

away, embarrassed. But that wasn't like her. She'd met lots of guys, especially at Segar's when she was teaching them to dance. She was never embarrassed. She turned back to look again. There was something about him she couldn't resist but she didn't know what it was. All she knew was that she was drawn to him.

The minute the band struck up a waltz, he approached her.

'Would you like to dance?' he asked. She smiled and accepted.

The minute they stepped onto the floor she knew why he'd chosen the waltz. He thought he had the steps off pat but Cathy knew he needed dance lessons. Despite trying to guide him around the floor, they kept on stumbling and, when she looked down at his feet she realised he was getting the waltz mixed up with the quickstep.

Lifting her head to face him and correct his steps as diplomatically as she could, she was momentarily speechless when she saw his sexy mouth, neatly curved and not too wide. She shocked herself when the thought came into her head that she could easily stretch over and kiss those inviting lips.

But what was she thinking? It was not her way to allow such thoughts invade her consciousness. Disciplining herself she cast the idea from her mind, now regarding him as coolly and as steadily as she could, even though her heart was in her throat.

'It's a waltz,' she whispered.

He bent his head towards her until they were cheek-to-cheek and whispered back. 'I know, but

I had to get you to talk to me somehow.'

His words broke the ice. He was chatty, he made her laugh and the bonus was that he was English. They had no language problems and that had to be a good start.

They found a table and sat out the next dance. 'Would you like a drink?' Tom asked her.

'A lime and lemon, please,' she replied and when Tom went to the bar she waved to her friend. 'Over here,' she mouthed.

Rita and Mike joined them but Cathy became so wrapped up in Tom they sat deep in conversation for most of the evening. Occasionally they danced and although Tom was no Fred Astaire Cathy enjoyed her time with him. And he seemed to appreciate her efforts when she tried to put him right about his dance steps without being too pushy or making it obvious she was teaching. When the music finally died down after the last waltz, Tom squeezed her hands and pulled her towards him.

'I've enjoyed your company, Cathy. I'd like to walk you home if that's all right?'

Cathy's heart did a tiny somersault. Although she would like that, she didn't want him to think she was a pushover. She let go of his hands. 'I'm with Rita,' she told him, steering clear of a direct answer and pointing across to her friend who was busy having a good old chinwag with Mike. 'We always go home together.'

'Then let's make it a foursome,' Tom suggested.

He was certainly taking the initiative and she smiled, admitting to herself he seemed the honourable sort. She took his hand in hers. 'I'll make this the exception.'

'How do you mean?'

'You don't think Rita and I are in the habit of letting any Tom, Dick or Harry...' She lifted her hand to her mouth. 'Whoops, Tom. That's not what I meant. It came out before I'd thought it through.' She laughed. 'Not that I'm intimating you're just any Tom...' Stop talking, she ordered herself. You're getting yourself into a mess!

Tom pushed his mouth down at the corners but his action did nothing to dilute the laughter in his eyes. 'What exactly do you mean then?'

'You know what I mean. You're teasing me now.' When she turned to face him, he took her hands in his, gently pulling her towards him and locking his quiet eyes on hers. And now her heart gave a hard knock against her ribs.

He pulled her even closer. 'You are gorgeous, Cathy,' he maintained. 'I can't believe my luck that I've met someone as lovely as you.'

Cathy was impressed at his compliment and she tucked away the urge to snuggle into his arms. It was too soon for such familiarity. What would he think of her? She edged slightly away and tried to cover her embarrassment, laughing and adding, 'I bet you say that to all the girls.'

His gaze dropped to her mouth and then once more he pulled her close and nuzzled his face in her hair. 'You've got me wrong, sweetheart,' he whispered. 'I meant every word I said.'

Cathy gently eased herself from his arms, pointing and changing the subject. 'We're getting left behind. Rita and Mike are miles ahead.' She grabbed his hand and started to tug.

With a deliberate movement Tom started to run,

pulling her after him. 'Let's go then.' His eyes lit up and he flashed a dazzling smile in her direction.

Her stomach wallowed in pleasure, and she let him pull her along, her high-heeled shoes clicking in rapid flurries on the pavement as she put on speed. Then she began to giggle and she tripped on a loose paving stone. When Tom turned to save her, she fell into his arms.

'Wow! You're fit for nothing but the egg and spoon race,' he joked, looking at her feet and pointing, 'especially in those shoes.'

She caught her breath and giggled again. 'I didn't expect to be running in them.'

Tom wagged a finger. 'You were the one who said we were getting left behind.'

She lifted her head and gave him the slightest peck on the cheek. 'I know. But we're going to have to love you and leave you now, Tom. I don't want Mum or Dad at the door looking out for me and seeing me with you.' She slipped her hand over her mouth. 'I've done it again, opening my big mouth.' She smiled. 'I didn't mean it like that, but you know what parents are like! At least you're English.'

'Thanks for the back-handed compliment.' Tom grinned. 'Are you sure you'll be fine from here?'

'Don't worry. Rita and I always walk home together.' She gazed across at Rita who was in the throes of a passionate embrace with Mike. 'Come on, Rita,' she called out. 'I've got to be in before midnight, or else I'll be in Dad's bad books.'

Rita withdrew from Mike's clutches. 'Coming!'

'Does Rita live nearby?' Tom asked.

'In the next street.'

'That's handy.'

He kept hold of her hands and Cathy could tell he was reluctant to let go. 'When can I see you again?' He gave a look of eager expectancy.

'How about meeting at the *Trocadero* on Tuesday?'

'The *Trocadero?*'

'Yes. It's not far away. You can see it from Segar's.'

'Sounds good.' He stretched across and kissed her on the lips. 'I'll see you then.'

For the next few days all Cathy could think about was seeing Tom again. And when she called at Rita's house the following Tuesday she was bubbling with excitement as they set out for the *Trocadero*. 'I hope the manager's impressed when we turn up for our interview,' she breathed. 'But most of all I can't wait to see Tom again.'

'Don't bank on seeing him, Cathy. I have an open mind when it comes to them turning up. Remember those two we arranged to meet again at Segar's?'

'I do, Rita. All I can say is that it didn't bother me when they didn't come back.' She frowned. 'But with Tom it's different.'

They entered the *Trocadero* and asked for the manager.

The pompous Mr. Williamson came along to interview them and he was certainly impressed.

'I can see you've both had good experience at ballroom, and at teaching. And you're well qualified. Technically you're spot on.' He rubbed his hands together. 'I like what I see. How about if I give you a week's trial teaching the boys?' His voice took on a more serious tone. 'But no jitter-bugging. Some of the Yanks are into that but not you two. It's strictly ballroom for you girls,' he insisted.

'That's great, Mr. Williamson.' Cathy spoke for the two of them. 'When do we start?'

'There's no time like the present,' he offered. 'If the boys get some success, they'll come back again.'

Cathy and Rita looked at one another and laughed. 'Come on Rita. Let's join the other girls and give it a whirl.' Cathy tapped Rita on the shoulder. 'He would say tonight wouldn't he when we've arranged to meet up with Tom and Mike?' she whispered. 'I need to look out for Tom and make sure he gets a bit of tuition.'

'They certainly need it, both of them.' Rita nodded her head and smiled.

It was late when Tom and Mike were relieved from on-board duties and well after nine o'clock when they arrived at the *Trocadero*. They paid the one and six entrance fee at the door and wandered through into the ballroom. In unison they stared up at the crystal chandelier in the centre of the ceiling as it twirled around and around, flashing its light on the dancers' faces. Tom, anxious to see Cathy, glanced around the dance floor hoping to spot her. He noticed a group of Americans at one corner of the room doing some sort of jive and he shook his head.

Mike followed his gaze. 'Show-offs,' he retorted.

Tom laughed at Mike's comment but the minute he entered the room his sole intention was to find Cathy and his gaze turned once more to the main area of the ballroom. He searched avidly and when he finally spotted her she was involved in what appeared to be an intense discussion with her partner, an American marine. A surge of disappointment flowed through him and he felt a tiny pang of jealousy.

He tapped Mike on the shoulder. 'I think we've left it too late,' he mumbled. 'She seems to be involved with the guy she's talking to.'

'Don't give up hope so easily, Tom. She's probably chatting to him, nothing more.'

'It looks like more than a chat to me,' Tom replied bitterly.

'But we can't expect them to sit around waiting until we finally turn up. And you can see they've plenty of choice.' Mike smiled 'But lighten up. I'm sure they'll come over when they see us.'

'I suppose you're right. It's just that I've been all keyed up looking forward to tonight and I've probably taken things too much for granted.' He tried to relax and when he looked again Cathy turned towards him and waved.

His heart tumbled in his chest and he stood there as though transfixed. He took in the look on her face, and the back of his neck began to prickle. A shimmer of need wavered inside him. But he pulled himself up sharp. He would have to watch out. He'd earlier thought things through and told himself he couldn't afford to take anything so seriously when he was in a country thousands of miles from England. Once the ship left Australia they'd probably never set sight on the place again. It would be so easy to become besotted and too involved. That would never do. Anyone with any sense could see it wasn't smart, especially when they'd be leaving for the Pacific pretty soon. He couldn't afford to daydream and mope around when he had a huge responsibility towards his shipmates. He needed to keep his mind firmly on the job.

He felt an elbow dig on his upper arm. 'Pull yourself together, old pal. They're coming towards us,' Mike offered.

Tom pulled himself up. At least she recognised him and she'd now left the other guy standing. He gave her a beaming smile. 'Sorry we're late.'

'Don't worry about it. You're here now, that's the main thing.'

'We had extra drills before we were allowed to leave. But now that we're here let's dance.' He held out his hands.

'Just the one for now, Tom.' Cathy cast a glance towards the entrance. 'The manager, Mr. Williamson, has returned. Rita and I are teaching the boys – a special arrangement with the boss. Having said that we finish at ten. We can dance together then.'

'Teaching here? You didn't mention it. I thought it was only Segar's.' Although he was late in arriving at the *Trocadero*, he expected to have Cathy all to himself.

'We didn't know when we arrived tonight. We had asked Mr. Williamson last week and he said he'd think about it. We didn't expect to start immediately.'

Tom smiled and took her hands in his. 'So you're not annoyed we're late. At least we've made it. And it's just me being impatient. I couldn't wait to get here and see you again.' He looked at his watch. 'That's fine, Cathy. It's nearly ten now.' As he took her in his arms, relief flowed through him when he realised she must have been teaching the serviceman she was dancing with when he arrived, nothing more.

Cathy spotted him standing there as though in a trance. Her heart gave a little skip. At last he was here and he was even more handsome than she remembered. But Mr. Williamson had insisted they teach until ten which meant she couldn't afford to concentrate all her efforts on Tom. The minute the manager slipped out of the ballroom, Cathy made a beeline towards Tom.

She guessed he was disappointed at first but when she clarified the situation and told him about their agreement with Mr. Williamson he seemed to relax and didn't mind waiting until they finished.

Once the tuition was over she danced with Tom for the rest of the evening. And when the last waltz came to an end at eleven o'clock he asked if he could take her home again, insisting he walk her all the way to the door. But Cathy was nervous. She didn't want anyone to come outside and see them, not that she was ashamed of Tom but she knew what Mum was like, especially after the conversation they'd had about Geoffrey Grant.

When they reached the front path Tom turned to her. 'When can I see you again?' He slid his hands on her shoulders. 'I hope you do want to see me.'

Cathy didn't answer straight away. She slipped her arms around his neck and looked into his pleading eyes. After a few seconds she smiled and withdrew her arms, reaching up to rub the back of her hand on his cheek. 'Don't worry, Tom. Of course I'd like to see you again.'

Tom's face relaxed. 'Then how about Tuesday?'

'I teach my dance class on Tuesdays now, like I did tonight. Are you free Wednesday?'

'As far as I know,' he replied, trying not to look too smug. He kissed on her cheek and set off towards the gate.

'Hang on,' Cathy called after him. 'We haven't decided where we're meeting.'

Tom gave a sheepish grin. 'That's a point. Stupid me. It would be useful.'

'How about the *Trocadero* again, seven thirty, Wednesday?'

'Great! I'll see you...' Before he had the chance to finish what he was saying the door opened. Cathy's father was standing there peering out into the darkness.

'Oh it's you, Cathy,' he said. 'It's getting late. Who's that with you?' He came out on to the top step to look more closely. 'Don't rush off young man. Come inside.'

Tom turned to face Cathy's father who was smiling broadly now, his hand on Cathy's shoulder.

'Come in and meet Mother.' He beckoned to Tom and went inside. 'There's a young man to see you, Marjorie.'

Cathy took in his words and cringed, dreading what Mum would come out with. This was exactly what she didn't want! Dad was a good old stick, but it was Mum she worried about. Tom followed her inside and stood on the doormat.

'Don't stand on ceremony young man. Come in.' Marjorie Ellis looked him up and down and then focused her eyes on Cathy. 'And who's this handsome young man you've brought in to see us?'

Tom caught the words and blushed. Mum had embarrassed him. Cathy flinched, sighed deeply and pulled a face at her. Typical. She always had to have her say. What a showing up!

'This is Tom. He's from England and he's in the Royal Navy.'

'We can see that by the uniform. Come and sit down.' Dad folded his arms. 'How long are you over here?'

'I'm not sure, Mr. Ellis. Hopefully a few more weeks.' He paused. 'But I must get back to the ship now. Thank you for asking me in.'

'It's a pleasure young man. Maybe we'll see you again sometime.'

Cathy took in Tom's words. He'd said he would be in Sydney a few more weeks. Then that would be the end. Her stomach began to churn and her heart seemed to flip over in her chest. Once the war was over he would leave for England and she probably wouldn't see him again. But she tried not to let it worry her. She must take things a day at a time. At least they'd made arrangements to meet up again.

On the following Wednesday Cathy's excitement turned to dismay.

'Your Aunt Maud seems to be recovering nicely

from her operation, Cathy,' her mother announced. 'We'll go along and see her tonight.'

'But, Mum, I've made arrangements to go out with Rita.' She didn't mention she'd be seeing Tom.

'I think you owe it to Aunt Maud to visit. After all you've always been her favourite.'

Cathy knew that was true and it wasn't that she didn't want to see Aunt Maud but did it have to be tonight? 'Couldn't we go tomorrow, Mum?'

'I've made arrangements to go tonight. Surely you can see Rita another night.'

In normal circumstances that would have been fine but what about Tom? If she didn't see him tonight they'd lose touch and she wouldn't be able to make any more arrangements.

'But Mum I said I'd see Tom. Where is the hospital and what time are you thinking of leaving?'

'Visiting is seven until eight but we need to set off early. It's a bus into the city and then another one out to Bexley. What time did you arrange to meet?'

'Eight o'clock.'

'You could be there for eight fifteen. That's all it takes to get back to the centre.'

Reluctantly Cathy seemed to have no alternative than to promise her mother she would travel to the other side of the city.

The traffic was heavy when they left the hospital. It seemed ages standing there waiting for the tram and it was late when Cathy arrived at the *Trocadero*. Rita was already in there.

'Sorry I'm late Rita.' Cathy looked around. 'Aren't the boys here yet? I hope Tom remembered where we arranged to meet.' Cathy stared anxiously. 'They can't have left. The HMS *Resolute* was still anchored in the harbour when I passed.'

'I noticed too. But maybe they've extra drills like before. And of course they'll remember. It's not as though they haven't been to the *Troc* before. Give them time. They're bound to turn up. They were late the last time we made arrangements. It's not all that easy for them to get away, Cathy.

'I suppose not,' Cathy agreed. But when the clock struck eight thirty she turned to Rita. 'It doesn't look like they're coming. And Tom seemed so keen too. But I don't hang about for any man, and half an hour's beyond all reason.'

'I agree it is, Cath.'

Cathy didn't answer directly. She wasn't disappointed; she was devastated. She liked Tom more than she cared to admit. And what upset her more than anything was that she wouldn't see him again. They hadn't even exchanged addresses. But she'd get over it, she was sure. She lifted her chin. 'There's plenty more fish in the sea,' she replied beginning to think Mum had been right when she'd said *they'll love you and leave you*. And now the evening was spoilt. Normally Cathy would be up on the floor for every dance. But not tonight.

'There's no point moping,' Rita insisted.

'Who's moping?' Cathy's reply was sharp and she regretted her tone the minute she uttered the words. She slipped her arm around Rita's shoulder. 'Sorry. I'm taking it out on you but I'm so disappointed.'

'Me too but I'm not prepared to let it get me down.'

'Agreed. Come on. Let's go over and show those two how to do the foxtrot. They haven't a clue,' she added, lifting her voice and smiling.

She kept a look out for Tom but he didn't turn up. She tried to tell herself their time together had been nothing but a casual fling, but deep down she knew that for her it was more than that. She'd been looking forward to seeing him again, but it was apparent he'd stood her up.

Rita linked her arm through Cathy's as they set out to walk home from the *Trocadero*. 'I'm still surprised they didn't turn up.'

'It doesn't surprise me,' Cathy had to admit. By now, she was not only disappointed but a tiny spear of anger kept shooting through her. How dare Tom say how lucky he was to have met her and then stand her up like this?

'I suppose not,' Rita acknowledged. 'But they didn't seem flighty types.'

'I agree.' Cathy tried to reason things out in her mind, now wondering if she had judged the situation without thinking it through. 'Perhaps we're jumping to conclusions. We really don't know what's happened, do we?'

But as Cathy looked towards the water she stared open-mouthed and her face turned ashen. The first thing she noticed was that Tom's ship had left the harbour. She opened her mouth to speak but the words stuck in her throat. Amazed, she turned to Rita and swallowed, giving herself time to calm down. Her eyes were enormous with apprehension and a ripple of emotion passed through her. 'I don't believe it!' She shook her head and pointed across the harbour to the

97

place where the ship had been docked. 'They've left, I'd say in some sort of rush if they hadn't time to let us know.'

Rita's gaze followed hers. 'Well that explains it.'

'It does. And all the time we thought we were being stood up.' She tore her gaze away from the space where the ship had been docked. 'I feel bad I said those things about Tom. It didn't cross my mind the ship might leave. Will we ever see them again?' That was the question bombarding Cathy's mind.

HMS *Resolute* set sail on Wednesday evening, eight o'clock sharp. The captain had received orders for his ship to patrol the Arafura Sea north of Darwin, once more to aid in the rescue of pilots, mainly American, who may be stranded in the sea during a series of dogfights with the Japanese.

As they sailed out of the harbour and through the narrow channel between the North and South Heads, Tom began to reflect on his time in Sydney. After the earlier ordeal in the Indian Ocean, the short stay in Sydney had been a welcome relief. And meeting up with Cathy, that was something else.

The clock in the communications room where he was working at the switchboard said eight-thirty. His stomach stirred vigorously. What would Cathy be doing now? She'd no doubt be in the *Trocadero* having given up on him. She'd probably be dancing with some other lucky serviceman. And by this time she would be wondering why he hadn't turned up, the obvious answer being that he'd stood her up. Tom was overwhelmed with frustration at the thought. But there was no way he could have sent a message to let her know they would be sailing north.

He only hoped that at some time in the future the *Resolute* would sail south again and dock in Sydney's harbour. He felt a pinprick of anxiety and his heart began to beat more urgently now. Whatever happened he must see her again. But then what? When the war ended the ship would return to England and that would be the end. They'd be thousands of miles apart.

Chapter 5

1942

Time seemed to pass slowly. For weeks Cathy's mind was full of Tom and the time they'd spent together. But during her darker moments when pessimism took over she began to dwell on what might be. What if something disastrous had happened? Tom could be injured or even worse. Dare she hope she would see him again?

Realising her negative thoughts were futile, common sense took over. It was time she stopped moping. There was a war on. Tom had been fortunate enough to visit Sydney and, best of all, she had been lucky to meet him. For all she knew he could be back in a month or so. And before she'd even met Tom she'd looked forward to the time when the dance exams were over and she could earn a few extra shillings a week by teaching. Knowing that would be her salvation and with a positive attitude she was determined to get on with her life.

Pulling her thoughts together she looked at her watch. It was seven o'clock and when she followed Rita out of the studio and into the main ballroom the place was empty. But in fifteen minutes the doors would be open. She managed to compose herself, concentrated her gaze towards the entrance and waited for the first of the servicemen to arrive.

The minute the doors were flung open the men flooded in, some searching the ballroom for partners, some hanging around down the sides, too shy to come forward. The glamorous Miss Jagger crossed the ballroom and tapped the shoulders of two British sailors who were standing there. She beckoned them to follow her and led them across to Cathy and Rita.

'There you go. I'll leave you to do your own introductions.'

At first Cathy felt a little nervous, but she knew she must try to put the boys at ease. 'I'm Cathy, my friend is Rita, and you're...'

'I'm Andrew.' He was tall, strongly built and good-looking by any standards with deep-set hazel eyes and auburn hair.

'I'm Jack.' The quieter of the two was slightly shorter with fair hair and vivid blue eyes.

'Pleased to meet you,' Rita chipped in. 'Where are you from? I can tell you're English.'

'You're not far off,' Andrew replied, grinning. 'We're Brits and I'm from Scotland.'

'Sorry.' Rita put her hand to her mouth. 'I'm pretty poor at accents, although English and Scottish seem very little different.'

Looking a little embarrassed, Jack came forward. 'But I'm English. I'm from Lancashire.'

'You're right on one count, Rita.' Cathy smiled at her friend, and they laughed off Rita's mistake. 'Andrew, I suggest seeing you're taller than Jack you partner me.' She took his hand and led him to one corner of the ballroom. 'We're going to start with the waltz. It's a slow dance so hopefully it'll be easier to pick up than the quickstep. Before we start let me tell you it's supposed to be a smooth dance with just a little bit of rise and fall. Your head should always be upright and looking over my right shoulder.' She took Andrew's hands and she could feel he was shaking. She laughed. 'Don't worry. I'm not going to bite you!'

He grinned. 'Thank goodness for that,' he joked.

'Place your right hand round my waist and take hold of my left.' The music began. 'Follow me and make your steps quite long ones.'

That was a start for Cathy. She found the experience enjoyable but, as the music faded away after the last waltz, she looked down at her feet. They were aching and she guessed they would be covered in bruises the next day, not so much with the dancing itself but with so many feet stepping on hers. But most of the servicemen were appreciative and wanted to come again. To Cathy that was the only reward she needed.

The evening over, she went into the studio and changed into her outdoor shoes, placing her dancing shoes in a brown paper bag and tucking it under her arm. When they left the building Andrew was waiting outside.

'I'd like to see you again, Cathy. Is there any chance?' He took her hand in his and stared into her eyes. 'It's been a great evening. I've really enjoyed your company and I think I've improved.'

'I'm sure you've improved. There's no doubt about it.' Cathy removed her gaze and focused on her friend, Rita. This was all quite sudden and she was not sure she wanted to see Andrew again, other than on a dance instruction basis. Her mind was still very much taken up with Tom and no one could be a substitute for him. 'I don't know, Andrew. We're taken up here at Segar's two nights a week, and we've another two nights at the *Trocadero*. It's not easy to make arrangements to meet anywhere else.'

'That's a pity. We're having a bit of a celebration on board Wednesday – nothing swish, just a meal and dancing on the open deck afterwards. The captain thinks we're due a break, a bit of a treat. We've been up in the war zone for months. We're allowed one guest each. I'd love you to come. How about it?'

'Wednesday is a Segar's night. I don't know what Miss Jagger's response will be.' Cathy looked to Rita for some sign of agreement. 'What do you think?'

'It is a bit tricky.' Rita paused. 'Although I don't think she'll mind.' Rita turned to Jack and smiled. 'Let's be straight with her, Cathy, and ask outright.'

'I suppose that's best,' Cathy replied, still not sure that she wanted to go, although it did sound as though it could be a fun evening. 'All we can do is ask Miss Jagger.' She turned to Andrew. 'We'll check it out but don't hold your breath.' She smiled. 'Where do we meet if we manage to sort it?'

'Our ship, HMS *Victor*, is docked at Port Hacking. How about meeting at Circular Quay, six thirty? If you're not there by seven, we'll assume you can't make it. There'll be transport available to take us across the harbour. Is that OK? What do you think?' He pulled Cathy closer. 'Please try,' he begged.

'I'll do my best.' Cathy moved slightly away from Andrew. She didn't want to give the wrong impression and lead him on. 'Let's hope we see you then.'

'We'll be there,' he called out, his face wreathed in excitement as he waved his goodbye.

Cathy frowned as they set off towards the bus stop. 'I don't know if we've done the right thing there, Rita. I like Andrew but I don't want a serious commitment.' She linked her arm through Rita's. 'I don't know what Mum and Dad will say.'

'But it'll be a change for us to get away from Segars and do something different.' She took a deep breath. 'I don't think I'll mention it to Mum and Dad. What they don't know they can't fret about.'

'How do you mean?'

'Dad might not be too keen. He might put his foot down and tell me I can't go.'

Cathy was quiet for a few moments. She was used to being straight with Mum and Dad, but as Rita had pointed out, did she have to mention it?

103

It wasn't lying if she kept quiet about it.

The two sailors were waiting when Cathy and Rita arrived at Circular Quay and, once they took the ferry and reached Port Hacking, Andrew took them on board the ship where the deck was milling with sailors and their visitors. Through a gap in the crowd Cathy spotted the huge buffet set out towards the bow of the ship. She hadn't expected such a lavish arrangement.

Andrew took her hand. 'Come on Cathy. Let me introduce you to some of my friends,' he said proudly as they began to circulate. But when she was asked to dance by several of his shipmates, he didn't appear too happy. Cathy hoped it wasn't a streak of jealousy. After all this was a social event, purely and simply. Fair enough Andrew had invited her but it didn't mean she belonged exclusively to him. She belonged to no one. And it would be rude. She continued undeterred.

And eventually Andrew seemed to relax and, at the end of the evening, he kissed her gently. 'I'll see you again, I hope.'

'We're always at Segar's or the *Trocadero*.' Cathy was reluctant to arrange a date with him. She preferred to keep things loose. But he seemed happy enough with that.

It was late but still very warm outside when Andrew stood at the quayside waving to Cathy who was leaning on the ferry rail and returning his wave. 'Wasn't that great,' she said turning to Rita.

'Much better than I expected and I'll tell you what,' Rita replied. 'We were popular with the sailors, especially showing them the dance steps.

But I don't think Jack was impressed.'

'Nor Andrew, but we're only friends, nothing more.' Cathy turned and sat down on a wooden seat at the stern of the ferry. 'I'm still missing Tom,' she confessed. 'I know it's stupid of me but after meeting him, I'm reluctant to become involved with anyone else.'

'But you might never see Tom again. What's the point, Cathy?' Rita turned away from the rail and sat down next to her friend.

'You're right, I suppose, but that's just the way I feel.'

Rita changed the subject abruptly. 'I reckon we'll have plenty of clients once we're back at Segars.'

'Clients?' Cathy shook her head. 'Don't say that, Rita. When you call them clients it sounds like something else.' They both started to giggle but, startled by a bright spotlight dancing across the harbour, they stopped abruptly.

Cathy jumped up from the bench. 'It looks like they're searching the harbour for something.'

'I can't think why, unless someone's fallen in.' Rita took a deep breath. 'I hope not.'

They stared ahead searching the water for anything suspicious and it was then the ferry seemed to pick up speed. They reached Circular Quay within minutes but when Cathy looked at her watch she gasped out loud. 'I didn't realise it was so late. Mum'll kill me when I get back.'

'Why what time is it?'

'I haven't looked at my watch all night but it's already one o'clock.'

Rita popped her hand over her mouth and pulled a face. 'Looks like I'll need an excuse.'

'What are we going to do? There aren't any more trams. Eleven thirty is the last one.'

Rita gave her a blank look. 'We can't walk back!'

Cathy took out her purse and emptied the coins into her hand. 'I've just about enough money for a taxi back.'

'We'll go halves,' Rita offered after counting her money out loud.

They stepped off the ferry and struggled in their high-heeled shoes across the cobbles. Within a couple of minutes a taxi came towards them. Cathy waved it down and the car came to a standstill. 'Where to?' the driver asked.

'St. Peter's,' Cathy told him as she slipped into the back seat and Rita followed closing the door behind her.

The driver turned his head before leaving. 'You're sure you can pay,' he enquired.

But before either Cathy or Rita had the chance to reply a heavy boom echoed from the harbour. The driver jumped physically.

'Bloody 'ell. What was that?' He shot from his cab and dashed across to the edge of the water, searching the harbour for any sign of explosion. 'It looks like something's blown up in the harbour, Garden Island I think,' he called out. 'I hope no-one's been hurt.' Shaking his head, he climbed back into his cab and set off towards the suburbs.

Cathy pulled herself up in the seat and whispered, 'If something's blown up in the harbour, we've had a lucky escape.' And then her thoughts turned to Mum and Dad. She had tried not to think about them during the evening, but now she was worried. She'd have some explaining to do at this late hour. And the only way was to come clean.

When she tiptoed into the house and quietly pushed open the door into the living room Dad was sitting upright in his chair waiting for her.

'Sorry I'm late Dad,' she said, lowering her voice in case her mother heard. 'I didn't realise what time it was.'

He stared back, straight-faced. Cathy knew he was annoyed. 'I'd like you back in the house by half eleven in the future young lady. Mum's gone to bed. She was tired out.' He took a steadying breath and then continued. 'I'll cover for you this once, but not again. You know what Mum's like.'

Cathy crossed over and kissed him on the forehead. 'Thanks, Dad. I'm sorry I've kept you hanging around waiting for me when you have to be up and out of bed so soon in the morning. It won't happen again, promise. I'll go straight to bed now. See you tomorrow.' Relieved that he had not asked where she had been until the early hours of the morning, she headed for her bedroom.

Marjorie Ellis shook her head. 'And where did you get to last night, madam? Stayed late at Segar's no doubt.'

Cathy's stomach gave a series of gentle flips. Mum had no idea about last night's little jaunt. She hadn't mentioned anything and was obviously unaware of the time Cathy arrived home. She'd made an assumption she'd been to Segar's as usual and Cathy was not about to dispute it. Her intentions last night to own up about her visit to the ship had faded and besides, she'd lost her nerve.

'I don't know, Cathy. You're never so late getting out of bed and rushing about like this in the morning. You'd better get your skates on. Toast and vegemite. Is that all right for you?' Mum seemed miles away. She was listening to the wireless in the background, and seemed to be concentrating on the news.

'That's fine, Mum.' Cathy tried to shake off the tiredness. The last thing she wanted was to rush about. But she had no time to sit at the table. Grabbing a slice of toast from the plate she took a bite, still dreading Mum asking any more questions about last night. But fortunately for Cathy, Mum seemed to be more interested in listening to the news. She turned up the sound. Cathy too had been listening but with blank incomprehension and then an item stopped her in her tracks.

'In the early hours of this morning a Japanese submarine entered the harbour and blew up HMAS *Kattabul.'*

Mum gasped. 'But that's one of our ferries.'

'HMAS *Kattabul had been converted into accommodation for our forces. It was moored at Garden Island.'*

The words fell into place. And now, filled with a strange feeling of unease, Cathy listened avidly. It was then the terrible realisation dawned. The loud noise last night over Garden Island – that was it, that was the explosion!

But Mum interrupted, urging her on. 'Hurry up and get ready, Cathy. You'll be late for work if you don't put a spurt on.'

Cathy missed a chunk of the newsreader's

words but she continued to stare into space, her mind still filled with the incident the previous night. Before she left she listened more carefully and took in more of the news item. *'It is thought the torpedo was intended for* US...*'* She checked her thoughts and the voice trailed off as she picked up her things and rushed out of the door. Last night she had behaved irresponsibly and foolishly. But she'd promised her father it wouldn't happen again. She must set off for work and, hopefully, arrive in time to tell Rita about the outcome of the incident in the harbour.

It was five minutes to nine when she reached the office and, breathless, she dashed into the cloakroom, hoping Rita had not yet moved out into the office. Rita was at the door ready to go to her desk when Cathy caught up with her.

'I've been dying to tell you. You won't believe what happened last night after we left the ship.' Her face was flushed.

'How do you mean?'

'Remember that spotlight searching the harbour?'

'Yes.'

'And then the boom in the harbour?'

'Yes. What about it?'

'I can't believe how lucky we were to get to Circular Quay before it happened,' she announced.

'Lucky? Why's that?'

'I heard it on the news this morning. One of the watchmen spotted something large caught in the anti-submarine net in the harbour. Guess what! It was a Japanese submarine. It's a wonder we weren't still there at the party. They raised the alarm at half past ten. And what do you think? The two Japanese submarine officers must have known they'd been spotted. They deliberately blew up their submarine and killed themselves.'

Rita was open-mouthed. 'Killed themselves? I don't believe it. Are you sure?'

'Positive, and not only that, you know that loud rumbling when we were getting into the taxi.'

'You mean when the driver got out and said he thought something had blown up?'

'Exactly. Well it had. Apparently the Japs fired a torpedo at one of the Yank's ships, USS *Chicago*, but it missed. The torpedo hit one of our ferries, HMAS *Kattabul*.'

'Stop it, Cathy. You're really scaring me now. We missed out on that by the skin of our teeth.' Rita sighed deeply. 'Thank goodness we left when we did.'

'Mum would go spare if she knew. I was going to tell them both if they asked where I'd been, but neither of them mentioned it. Dad was still up but Mum had gone to bed. I think it might be best to say nothing. She'd be watching me like a hawk if she knew.' Cathy took a deep breath. 'The worst thing is that some of the sailors were killed. They don't know yet exactly how many sailors or what nationality they were. Obviously some will have been our boys. I hope Andrew and Jack weren't affected.'

'Me too. But I wouldn't think so. You said the name of the ship was *Kattabul*. That wasn't the name of their ship was it?'

'No but we don't know how close the *Victor* was to *Kattabul*.' Heaving a sigh Cathy turned to move out of the cloakroom into the office. She continued to whisper. 'They've been pulling sailors out of the sinking vessel all night. If we hadn't left when we did, we might not have been here now. They've stopped all ferries from entering the harbour until further notice, unless it's a matter of urgency. And they've stopped all lights on ships – only those that are necessary.'

'All I can say is that it puts a stop to our little jaunts. Even if we're invited we can't go there again Cathy. Mum and Dad hit the roof when I was so late back. At least I got away with not having to tell them where I'd been. It's disappointing but we have to be sensible.'

'I'll say.' Cathy sighed deeply and shook her head. And then she turned to Rita again. 'Oh and I forgot. Bondi and Rose Bay waterfronts have been bombed as well.'

'Those belong to the rich-listers.' Rita pulled a face. 'But you don't expect that, do you? None of us is safe. I hope I'm still allowed to continue at Segars. Dad's likely to ground me if he thinks there's some sort of warfare in the harbour.'

'I know what you mean. I'll get exactly the same reaction from Dad, Mum too.' Cathy frowned. 'But surely our lot will have stopped them by now.'

'Let's hope so. Fingers crossed nothing else happens. I think I'd go crazy if Mum and Dad stopped me from going out at night.

'I'm not even prepared to think about it.' Cathy pushed open the door to her office and left Rita to continue upstairs to sales.

It was not until a week later Andrew appeared at

111

Segar's. Cathy approached him. 'I'm so relieved to see you, Andrew. I was worried after the news about the Jap submarines. Thank goodness you've survived.'

'Glad to know you care.' Andrew slipped an arm around her shoulders. 'We were actually quite a distance away. But we did see the flash when the *Kattabul* was struck by the torpedo. It was devastating.'

'I think that's the last time I'll be allowed to come to the ship. We had a lucky escape last week. If we'd been half an hour later we wouldn't have been able to leave. The harbour closed soon after we left. Mum and Dad had no idea where I was. They would have sent out a search party for me.' Cathy started to guide him around the ballroom.

'Don't worry about it, Cathy. The harbour's been cleared now. There were six midget subs. The first one was spotted and the two Japs blew up their own sub and killed themselves once they knew they were trapped. And then another two were attacked with depth charges and committed hara-kiri rather than be captured by the enemy.'

'Hara-kiri? You mean suicide? How can they do that?'

'Don't ask me but I've heard that's what they're trained to do. I'm just as flabbergasted as you. I think there's some sort of shame in being caught by the enemy.'

'According to Dad, the submarine attacking Bondi and Rose Bay was a mother sub and it got away.'

'That's right. But going back to the midget subs, the coastguards found the bodies of the four Japanese crewmen. They'll be cremated in Sydney and have full military honours.'

'So I heard and Dad says a lot of Australians are up in arms about it, but he reckons if we show respect it could help to improve conditions for allied forces in Japanese war camps.'

'I agree. But let's not talk about that. I've been looking forward all week to seeing you again.' His eyes lit up and he flashed a smile before nuzzling his face in her hair. 'And there's something I need to tell you.'

'Oh, yes and what's that?' Cathy challenged, hoping it was some sort of joke or tall story he was about to tell her and nothing too personal. Andrew seemed to be making more of the relationship than she wanted.

His mouth sagged at the corners and the laughter was gone from his eyes. 'We set sail again on Thursday. We're going north. The Japs are attacking Malaya and we've been called up there. They don't tell us any more than that, but I guess we'll be standing off shore somewhere waiting for things to happen.'

'You must be disappointed about that. But maybe you'll be back some day in the future.' Cathy tried to remain light-hearted.

'I do hope so. If I get the chance I'll write. Will you write back to me?' he begged. 'It gets so lonely when you're at sea. We all look forward to reaching port and checking for mail.'

'Of course I will, although I've plenty on, what with my full-time job and the studio most nights. But I'll do my best.'

Andrew was reluctant to leave. Cathy felt sorry

for him on that score but he was becoming far too serious for her liking.

And she had to admit to herself Tom was forever at the forefront of her mind. How she wished she could have seen him for a final time and given him her address. At least they could have written to each other. But it was no use looking in retrospect. She must remain optimistic and hope to see him again in the future.

Chapter 6

1943

Tom tried to cast all thoughts of Cathy from his mind but the more he tried, the more the vision of her danced before him. But his idle daydreaming was cut short when an urgent message came through for the captain. Within minutes they were told of the revised orders from the War Office. They were to continue north to the Andaman Sea and on to Burma where it seemed they were more urgently needed. The Japanese had landed there and captured British soldiers.

Another call came through almost immediately and it was remiss of Tom not to switch off his own receiver when he connected the captain to his superior. Reprimanding himself for allowing his mind to drift he was left in a quandary. Should he switch out now that the conversation was in full flow? The problem was they would probably hear the click and know he'd been listening. He decided to stay connected, hoping no-one would enter and make a noise.

That was when he heard the complete plan from the War Office. A select group of forces known as the newly established SAS had been sent into the Burma jungle to provide a decoy and help as many soldiers as possible to escape to the coast. The captain was not given explicit details of this decoy plan, but he was instructed that his ship must stand by off the coast of Burma where his men should keep a look out in readiness to pick up the soldiers as soon as they appeared.

On the first evening Tom was on watch duty at its stern keeping a look out for any escapees as the ship ploughed through the waves. They eventually dropped anchor and, as far as they were aware, the Japanese had not penetrated that area of the coast. But still the ship remained in darkness allowing the crew a clearer view of the sandy beach in the bright moonlight where, hopefully, the soldiers would appear. Tom gazed over to the starboard side of the ship facing the beach. There was no sign of life.

Suddenly he heard a noise coming from the port side facing the open sea. He couldn't weigh up what it could be. But, trying not to make a sound, he crossed over and his eyes caught a movement at the rail. Could it be one of the British soldiers, an escapee who'd swum out to the ship? They were anchored not too far away from the beach and he realised that would have been possible. But he knew that, whoever it was, he must remain silent. He couldn't afford to call out and warn his colleagues for fear of startling whoever was now climbing on board.

It was then he heard a clattering noise. A hook appeared at the rail with a rope attached. The minute a head appeared, Tom realised the intruder wasn't a British soldier. It was a Japanese sailor.

He must stop the intruder from climbing aboard! Lunging forward towards him, Tom drummed hard on his knuckles, releasing the sailor's hands from the rail. There was a loud splash. He leant over the rail and watched the Japanese sailor plunging heavily into the ocean. But what amazed him was the sight of a Japanese submarine, which had surfaced alongside the *Resolute*. His instant reaction was to warn his colleagues. He turned back from the rail but he was brought down from behind. It was then an inky blackness engulfed him.

Marjorie picked up a tea towel and dried the cups and saucers. 'What's happened to that young man, Tom, you brought back here?' she asked Cathy. 'You've not mentioned him for a few weeks.' She placed the crockery on the worktop next to the draining board. 'Dad thought he was a decent sort – for a Pom that is.'

Cathy looked up from the magazine she was reading and frowned. Mum was quoting Dad, but she hadn't said she agreed with the compliment. That was typical. Compliments didn't come easy from Mum.

'Dad's right. He is a decent sort, Mum. But the ship left a month ago. There must have been some crisis. He didn't get the chance to say goodbye.'

Marjorie shook her head and pulled a face. 'Just like the rest! Here today, gone tomorrow,' she clichéd.

'It wasn't like that,' Cathy protested, a flicker of regret in her gaze. 'Why on earth would he leave without letting me know?'

'Well I keep on telling you, you'd be better off with someone more reliable.'

Cathy blinked her eyes and sighed. There was no prize for guessing who! She re-focused on the magazine, but she didn't take in the words dancing before her eyes. Her mind latched on to Tom's departure and then to Mum's comment. Don't say Mum and Irene Grant were still at it, trying to throw her and Geoffrey together.

'Dad's about to light the barbie, Cathy. He's managed to get his hands on a nice bit of steak from Barry, you know, that nice butcher at the market. And he's brought a few links of those tasty sausages.' She rubbed her hands together. 'It's a long time since we did anything like this, what with the war and everything.'

'But I'm not really hungry, Mum. Rita and I had arranged to meet this afternoon. We thought we'd go down to Cronulla. The lifeguards are holding a swimming contest, you know, just a bit of fun. It'll be a laugh.'

'Really, Catherine, it is Sunday,' she stressed. 'I think you owe it to Dad to stay back here. He's getting the barbie going now. We always have Sunday lunch together.'

Cathy sighed, knowing it was always her full name, Catherine, when Mum was reprimanding her. And what of it? She saw Dad every day, so

117

why was the weekend any different? Mum was trying it on again.

'But we usually have Sunday lunch at lunchtime, not in the middle of the afternoon. That's why I arranged to meet Rita.' A fierce determination swept through her. 'The weekend is the only time I get to do something different.'

'Well, that's the way we're doing it today.' Mum sniffed and nodded her head. 'And you can't say the weekend's the only time. What about during the week? You're at Segars most nights.' She folded her arms. 'And don't look at me like that. You look as miserable as a bandicoot!'

Not that again! But she probably did look miserable. What could she say? Mum was right, she supposed. And if she insisted on going out, she would be throwing kindness in Dad's face seeing he was making a special effort. Not only that, she would never hear the end of it from Mum. Decision made. She would have to pop round to Rita's and tell her she couldn't make it to Cronulla, not for the start of the contest at any rate. But maybe they could go down there mid-afternoon if the barbecue was over and done with by then.

With that in mind, she decided not to change out of her navy tailored shorts and pale blue seersucker blouse. She'd be ready to slip away once they'd finished eating.

Rita was naturally disappointed but there was nothing they could do.

'Let's hope you can get away soon. I'll be around. I've nowhere to go.'

When Cathy turned the corner into Brackhill Road she noticed a car parked outside the front gate. She frowned. That was unusual. Someone must be visiting, but who could it be? They didn't have many friends or relatives who owned cars. She walked down the side path and into the back yard.

The minute she stepped foot on to the patio she knew what had been going on behind her back. It came to her very clearly. A deep sigh trickled through her. The truth was out and Mum's secret plan had come to fruition. There standing beside Mum were Irene, Walter and Geoffrey Grant.

Cathy's face lost its glow. Feeling a bitter stab of annoyance she gazed gloomily at the scene before her. So that was it. The car belonged to Geoffrey.

When she entered the yard Dad sidled up to her. 'I know it's not your choice, but don't chuck a wobbly, treasure. Put up with it for your Mum's sake,' he whispered before turning back to the barbecue and heaving a sigh. It was obvious Dad wasn't enamoured either.

Geoffrey beamed and then they exchanged glances, his roving eyes looking her up and down. 'Lovely to see you, Cathy. You look gorgeous.' He hovered over her, giving her a light kiss on the cheek. 'How's the job going?' His question was patronising and he was obviously trying to use his charm but, to Cathy, his words were empty, his tone condescending.

He stroked her cheek with his hand and her body became rigid with tension. She backed off, putting a little distance between them. He was quite a handsome man with strong, regular features, but there was something about him that irritated her. She slapped a false smile on her face and roused herself to answer his question. 'I'm really enjoying it, thank you. And you? Are you still at the bank?'

'I've been appointed manager at the Sylvania branch. I've lots of prestigious clients there. I spend most of my time giving advice.' The smug look on his face told her he was interested only in bragging about his own status. What was happening in her life was of no real significance to him.

But two could play at that game. 'Congratulations, Geoffrey.' She flashed him a beaming smile. 'I had a promotion myself a while back. I'm Mr. Dallarup's secretary now.' She may as well get that one in. No doubt Mum had already been boasting about it, especially if Mrs. Grant had been giving her an update on Geoffrey. She studied Geoffrey's face for some sort of reaction.

'Really!' he replied crisply, his mouth twitching with a flicker of humour. 'Well done you!' But it was clear from his manner and the obsequious response he had a total disregard for anyone except himself. He believed himself to be superior.

Unwilling to meet his gaze for fear she would say something she would later regret, she made no effort to hide the coldness in her tone. 'But I suppose that's nothing in comparison with your promotion.' Her words held a hint of sarcasm but she fluttered her eyelids and smiled sweetly once more.

'Indeed.' Geoffrey's lips curled into a smug smile.

Mum gave her a withering look and Cathy made an effort to lighten her tone. She turned to Dad in the hope of changing the subject. 'How long's the food going to be? I'm starving.' She wasn't of course. She wasn't even hungry, but she had to say something, otherwise if she dwelt on the words of this supercilious buffoon and gave her reaction, he would wish he'd never come along.

'Nearly ready, treasure,' came the reply.

But Geoffrey ignored the comments. He wasn't about to change the subject. 'Of course a man's future career is much more important than a woman's,' he stipulated, a peevish look on his face. 'Once a woman marries, it's her duty to look after her husband. It's for sure no wife of mine would be allowed to go out to work.'

So a woman was nothing but a chattel to play nursemaid and be a slave to her man. Cathy was not prepared for such a biased statement and, swept with indignation, she raged inwardly. But what was the use letting him see she was in total disagreement when she knew his opinion would never affect her. She shuddered to think of what life would be like for the woman who agreed to spend her future together with him. Purgatory – that was the first word that came to mind. Would anyone ever break down those Victorian barriers?

After his comment about wifely duties, Cathy clamped up. She had nothing to talk about, simply because they had nothing in common. The awkward silences were filled with quiet, inconsequential conversation until Geoffrey found his feet once more. And then his voice droned on and on.

Cathy closed her mind to what he was saying, thinking instead about Tom. Tenderness flowed over her as she thought of him. He was kind and caring, not an obnoxious twerp like this one. But

121

her reverie was broken when Geoffrey took her gently by the shoulders and smiled. 'You know, Cathy, it's time we saw more of each other don't you think?'

She lifted her head in a contemptuous gesture, a tight smile on her lips. But she spoke courteously. 'I haven't a great deal of time these days, Geoffrey. I seem to be taken up most nights with my teaching.'

The supercilious smile left his lips and he sniffed. 'Teaching? What's all that about?'

If he came out with another condescending remark, to be sure she would grab her bag and leave or, better still she could grab him by the throat and throttle him. But before she could give that idea serious thought Mum came to the rescue.

'Cathy teaches ballroom at Segars. It's the top dancing school in the state you know. And she's passed all her exams with distinction.' Brimming with pride, Marjorie looked to Irene who smiled back acknowledging Cathy's success.

Geoffrey arched his dark eyebrows. 'Dancing, I see. That could come in handy. I get plenty of invites to the balls at City Hall. I meet lots of dignitaries, VIP's, royalty and the like.' He slipped an arm around Cathy's shoulder and whispered in her hair. 'My dancing's a bit rusty. Perhaps you could teach me a thing or two, Cathy.'

Cathy refrained from answering, quickly disengaging herself from his grip and turning her gaze on Mum. She glared. How dare Mum set up this get-together without even mentioning it? It was obvious Geoffrey thought it was cut and dried. And then a single thought crossed her mind. She hoped he didn't think that she had been part of the little game to invite him along to the barbecue. That was the last thing she wanted. Seething, she gave Mum a 'wait until we're alone' look. But Mum gazed adoringly at her daughter and smiled pleasantly. 'Come along now. Let's eat before it gets cold.'

How Cathy managed to get through the barbecue without slapping Geoffrey's face she would never know. She watched as he bent his head to place a forkful of steak in his mouth and she noticed his hair was thinning at the crown. Not only did he have the opinions of an old man, he was beginning to look like one too.

Tom slowly gained consciousness, blinked his eyes and peered, trying to recollect where he was and what was happening. He had a sudden fleeting memory of the Japanese sailor disappearing into the brine. He shook his head to clarify his thoughts and tried to move his hands and feet but he soon realised he'd been tied up in some strange chamber within what he believed to be the submarine. His stomach gave a violent flip. He'd been taken captive by the Japanese.

The boom-boom of a kettledrum meted a regular beat inside his head. It kept on resounding and wouldn't stop. All around him he could hear shouting, wailing and gentle sobbing. He lifted his shackled hands in front of him and touched a sore spot close to his temple. When he removed his hand his sticky fingers were covered in blood. His eyes were still bleary and he tried to focus on those around him, vaguely recognising some of his fellow crewmembers crammed in beside him, many wounded, some still unconscious. He searched the chamber for the captain of the *Resolute*, but there was no sign of him. Had the Japanese sailors disposed of him?

As his vision began to return he took in the position of the small chamber. It led to the main body of the submarine where everything seemed to be happening. And although the doors to the front and the rear of the small chamber were still open, Tom felt claustrophobic. But he knew, despite the injury to his head, he must steel himself to stay as calm and alert as possible, he must ignore the noisy cries of his shipmates, most of whom seemed to be in a far worse state than he was.

Within seconds the penetrating sound of crashing levers and screaming hooters added to the background noise invading his consciousness. Chaos erupted. The throbbing in his head refused to go away. He lifted his shackled hands, held his head and closed his eyes.

It seemed the submarine was watertight and ready to submerge. He reckoned the sound of the hooters must be the 'all clear' signal. The crash dive began with the sound of water gushing into the ballast tanks. Thrown into a kind of stunned despair, he knew that any hope of escape had now disappeared. They were in the hands of their captors and, although he'd been determined to steel himself, now he couldn't stop his own desperate cry.

But as the thought crossed his mind that they were undeniably trapped, his mind was filled with even more torment when the submarine started its descent. He heard a plaintive cry through the loudspeaker and, although the words were in a foreign tongue, they were garbled. Something was wrong. The man calling out sounded desperate. And then came a sudden click, the voice was cut and the intercom went dead.

All eyes turned to the indicator panel where Tom could just about make out that all the lights were green. But despite this, an almost tangible anxiety swept through the submarine as the voices of the Japanese sailors soared to a high-pitch, their shrieking and wailing becoming more and more frantic. Tom looked around and some of the men in the compartment beside him complained of a 'fluttering' sensation of the ears.

Within seconds a wall of water hit the floor of the submarine and began to flood from the rear in the direction of the engine room. Tom stared open-mouthed, a haunted look in the depth of his eyes, his gaze fixed on the gushing water now heading towards them.

'My God! We'll drown!' he bawled.

Seven or eight Japanese engineers charged away from the flooding aft compartments and entered the small chamber where the captives were held. They scrambled roughly over the reclining bodies not caring where they trod. A couple more, completely drenched, staggered behind them, horror mantling their faces as they shouted and screamed at the crew in the engine room.

With the control board reading all systems green, Tom could not believe that the rear engine rooms were flooding. He stared aghast at the scene as the water snaked towards them and was now only ten feet away. If the water reached the main engine room there would be no way the fault could be righted.

He tried to pull himself up from the floor but, with his hands and feet tied, the task was impossible. He swallowed hard and his heart pumped frantically in his chest. Was this the end?

Some of his colleagues started to cry out again, even louder now. Tom closed his eyes and sent up a silent prayer. And when he opened his eyes to the sound of a heavy crash, the rear door to the chamber shut tight, sealing the rest of the submarine against any further flooding. God must have heard him.

Tom stared and held his breath realising that the remaining Japanese engineers were trapped inside the rear engine room, lost in the flooded part of the vessel.

'They'll be goners, there's no doubt about it. But it's a miracle they've managed to seal us off,' he claimed, releasing the air and shaking his head in disbelief. But he calculated that, once they started their descent, the water in the rear of the submarine would drag them even further down, unless it could be released.

And then it happened. The weight of the water became too much for the ballast to compensate and the vessel began to plunge to the bottom at a fifty-degree angle. The men looked to each other, aware that if a submarine went down in this way, the crew were as good as lost. A cacophony of shouts and screams rang out.

The shrill voice of the captain, his statement

bald, his words clipped, rang in Tom's ears. What it was all about Tom could only guess. The captain's vicious verbal attack caused the crew members to panic. The savagery in the captain's eyes frightened them and they shrank back in horror. And now, seemingly touched by some sort of madness, he stomped towards one of his men, obviously the scapegoat for his own inefficient handling of the situation, and his eyes iced over as he raised his hand, bringing it back and swiping the sailor heavily across the face. The sailor lifted his hand to his face and turned away.

The stern of the submarine started to sag ominously, and the captives began to slide towards the rear door of the chamber. The vessel seemed to hesitate in the water and her descent was momentarily arrested. But then she continued her downward plunge and there was chaos all around them. Captives and crew were shouting and screaming. The crew in the engine room hung back staring vacantly at the levers. But the damage was done.

His face a solemn mask, Tom nudged the guy sitting next to him, one of *Resolute's* engineers. 'Are you all right, Ken?' he whispered, an anxious expression on his face.

'Apart from my arm.' It hung limply by his side. 'I think it's broken.'

Tom frowned. 'Did they do it?'

'I was testing a machine in the engine room when they burst in. I didn't get a chance to stop the machine before they dragged me away. My arm was caught in it.'

'Bloody sadists! Try to keep it as still as you can.' There was genuine concern in Tom's tone.

He sighed. 'I've no idea what happened after I was hit over the head. The next thing I knew I came round in here.'

'They took a number of us and threw us in the sub. And now this rapid descent.'

'A bit too rapid for my liking. Someone's made one hell of a blunder.' Tom shuffled backwards, making an effort to stop Ken from slipping any further.

'You can say that again! The vent operator must have opened the high induction valve by mistake. Either that or there's a fault on it.'

'That's at the rear of the sub isn't it?' He shook his head. 'But I don't understand. All the lights were green.'

'Were they? That says it all. The induction valve's the large air intake pipe next to the conning tower. If all the lights were green, there must be a fault somewhere.' Ken winced as he pressed his bent right arm close to his chest and held it there with his left hand. He closed his eyes and tears trickled down his face. He took in a deep breath. 'I think we've had it!' he claimed.

Tom was anything but optimistic but he tried to remain calm for the sake of his shipmate. 'Don't give in pal. It's not the end yet,' he maintained but he had no faith in the words he uttered. He lightened his voice. 'Is there anything I can do to make you more comfortable, Ken?'

'I don't think so. But thanks for asking, Tom. I'm trying to settle the arm into the best position to ease the pain. It's as well they haven't bound my hands together like the rest of you.'

'I'll say,' Tom agreed.

Ken nodded towards the engine room. 'It's obvious they meant to fill the negative tank to increase diving speed. I think someone might have hit the wrong lever and the water's flooded the main body of the sub.'

'I'm not surprised things have gone wrong the way the captain issues orders. He's a maniac. The crew are terrified of him.' Tom turned to Ken. 'What happens now?'

'God only knows. As I said, I think we're finished. I can't see any way out of this.'

Tom shuddered. The thought of a lingering death through suffocation in an icy steel coffin below the ocean's surface was not something he had contemplated when he joined the Royal Navy. He might have expected to be a target for enemy bullets, hand grenades, torpedoes, or even drowning quickly in a watery grave, but not this. He looked down at his hands. The ties were so tight his wrists were chafing now. But they were the least of his worries.

His attention was suddenly drawn to the voice of the Japanese captain who held what appeared to be a hurried roll call. Tom listened intently and counted twenty-seven replies from the Japanese crew. He had no idea what the full complement should be, but he knew for sure some of the men would have perished in the aft compartments.

From the heavy sway of the vessel, it seemed apparent the submarine was not embedded in the ocean's floor but still lingering in a suspended state, stern first. The captives, unable to maintain a grip on any part of the chamber, continued to slide backwards and forwards as the vessel pitched and rolled underwater. As they did so their bodies hit the rear and sides of the metal chamber causing even more pain to those already suffering. Some were so disorientated they vomited.

It was then the captain shouted yet another onslaught of orders to his men, but this time it seemed it was for the benefit of the captives. It appeared to Tom that either the captain felt guilty at their plight, or he had gone completely gaga. Two of his crew entered the chamber, grabbed the wrists and ankles of the captives and removed the ties.

The men stretched their arms and legs, and some tried to stand up, but the crew issued a tirade of verbal abuse and quickly pushed them back to the floor of the chamber. It was obvious the captives were not allowed to move about, not even within the chamber itself. But at least now they were free of the ties they could press their hands against the walls of the chamber and try to steady themselves.

Tom peered directly into the engine room where there was a flurry of activity. What the crew were up to, he had no idea, but when he listened to their voices, there seemed to be a smidgen of optimism floating around the place. But whatever it was, Tom could not conceive how on earth the captain could manage to get the submarine back to the surface. How could he release the water from the rear engine room and seal the sub when there would obviously be heavy pressure from the vast expanse of the ocean outside the vessel?

Tom looked up. The men in the engine room now appeared to be in conference. And then there was a massive surge and the vessel plunged downwards, hitting the ocean floor with a heavy thump. The men started to shout. The lights went out abruptly and darkness folded around them.

Tom shivered. The cold had started to penetrate. The captain issued further orders. Then came the sound of hurried movement about the vessel. Tom screwed up his eyes and peered through the blackness. The shadowy figures of the Japanese crew returned to their bunks and lay there in silence whilst someone issued them with blankets. But there were no blankets for the captives.

Tom was puzzled. Had the Japanese crew been ordered to rest, to conserve their strength? Or had they given in? If the latter had been the case, surely they would have committed hara-kiri by now. Only time would tell.

Chapter 7

1943

As he gradually gained consciousness, *Resolute's* Captain O'Neill opened his eyes. One of his men was bending over him and tapping him on the shoulder.

'Sir, sir! Are you all right?' His voice was filled with urgency.

The captain was puzzled to see the seaman staring down at him. For God's sake what was happening?

'I think so, Bates. But what's going on? Where are the others?' Shaking his head, he tried to pull his thoughts together. Within seconds it all came back to him. 'I remember now. The Japanese boarded my ship and I have a vague recollection that some of my men must have been captured. But why didn't they take me?'

'Most of the remaining crew are down below, sir but they have injuries, some quite severe. Coles and Dawson are doing their best to attend to them. Unfortunately the doc was taken with the others. At least the ones down below resisted the brutal bastards.'

'Absolutely, Bates.' O'Neill pulled himself up and looked around the deck. Roberts was still there and a couple of junior officers, but he was not sure if they were dead or alive. They were certainly still unconscious.

Bending over on his hands and knees, he tried to stand up. But the second he started to pull himself to his feet a searing pain shot through his ankle. It began to throb. He collapsed and fell back heavily, banging his head. Dazed he sat up wincing as he fingered his ankle with a gentle touch. He suspected it was broken. He certainly couldn't step on to his right foot.

'Sir, it would be better if you didn't move. You might do more damage to your ankle. I'll ask one of the first-aiders to have a look at you. I suggest you wait until one of them comes on deck to check you over. I'll go down below and have a word,' Bates offered before he disappeared.

Not to be deterred, O'Neill looked around searching the deck for something to take his weight. He spotted a short wooden post loosened during the melee. Stretching out he managed to poke at it with his fingers and after some strain the post rolled towards him. Placing both hands on top of it, he pushed himself to his feet and reached out for the ship's rail. Pain seared through his leg but he took a deep breath and glanced across the deck. Roberts seemed to be stirring.

'Is that you, Captain?' Roberts lay very still, his voice little more than a whisper.

'It is, Roberts. How do you feel? How badly are you injured?'

Roberts groaned. 'I think my back's broken. I can't move.'

'It sounds bad. Stay as still as you can. Don't even try to move.' O'Neill peered over the side of the ship. 'The sub has gone and some of my men with it. I can't weigh up why they didn't take us.'

Lieutenant Roberts sighed. 'They thought we were dead. They hit you across the legs and you collapsed.' He continued to groan, a heavy frown on his forehead. 'You must have banged your head on the deck. You were out cold.' He paused, took in several deep breaths and closed his eyes. 'I don't know what happened to me. I was still conscious when they took the others away. The little bastards kicked out at us and tried to stir us. You were obviously unconscious. I wasn't. I feigned it.'

'Feigned it?' O'Neill smiled. 'Good for you. That must have taken some guts.' He turned and pointed in the direction of the others. 'I'll check on those two and then I'll try to get down below.' He squeezed his hands on the post, gripping it so tightly his knuckles were white. He set off towards the two officers.

'I wouldn't try that, sir. You'll only make that leg worse,' Roberts called after him.

'It's only my ankle. I can't afford to hang around when my men are suffering.' He frowned. 'But I'm surprised they didn't blow us up, or set fire to the ship.'

'They wouldn't have done that. They'd drawn up alongside. It was a chance encounter I'd say. They obviously didn't know whether or not there were any more allied troops in the area. I reckon they'll use our lot to bargain, get some of their own men back.'

'Don't talk any more, Roberts. Close your eyes and rest now. Bates has gone down below. I'll ask him to send up Coles to have a look at you.' He glanced at the young officers and struggled to make his way across to where they were sprawled out on the deck. Easing his weight and leaning on the post he noticed that one of them was breathing heavily and the other had fluttering eyelids as though he was trying to pull himself around. 'We need a rescue operation and quick. I've no idea what happened to Morris and Crosby here, but they're both still alive. And you certainly need medical attention as a matter of urgency.'

He moved over to the steps and clasped his right hand on the top, but as he did so he jumped physically and almost lost his balance. What caught his eye was a cloud of red smoke in the ocean two or three hundred yards away. Seconds later an indicator buoy popped up and bobbed about on the surface. Startled he realised it was a distress signal, a call for help. But what could he do?

Filled with alarm, he shouted to the lower deck. 'Bates! Is Crossley down there?'

Bates came dashing to the bottom of the steps. 'Tom Crossley was on guard duty when the Japs came, sir. They took him.'

'Blast! That's all I need. Is the communication system still working? It looks as if the Jap sub is in trouble. They've sent up an underwater grenade. There's red smoke coming from it and an indicator buoy.' He pointed. 'I don't think we've any of our own subs around here. It's got to be the Japs – and with my men on board!'

'It might be an idea for me to get you down below, sir. I'm sure the switchboard's still OK.'

'Before you do that I need the first-aiders up here. Roberts is in a bad way. He thinks he's broken his back. There's also Morris and Crosby up on deck. Neither is fully conscious as far as I can gather.'

'I'll get at least one of them to come up, sir.' He turned and called out. 'Coles, Dawson! One of you is needed up here as a matter of urgency.' He made his way onto the top deck. 'How about making immediate contact with Commander Bradley now that we know the Jap sub is in difficulties. Not that I care about them. It's our own men I'm worried about.'

'I agree, Bates. You're right. I do need to contact him. It's crucial we get someone here – and quick!'

Bates backed down the steps slightly and Captain O'Neill stepped on with his good leg, gripped the rails tightly and slithered his injured leg down. With the help of Bates he struggled to the communications room where nothing appeared to have been disturbed. Before he checked out the remainder of the deck, he put out a call to Commander Ralph Bradley who was in charge of the fleet's lead vessel. O'Neill told him of the Japanese attack and the plight of the submarine.

'As a priority I need medical help immediately. The doc's been taken captive with the others and we're just about managing to cope with two first-aiders, but we're in desperate need of professional help.' He eased himself on to the swivel chair. 'And how about the sub?' He hesitated. 'I don't know whether it would help, but is there a rescue chamber in the area?'

'There is, but it's further south, I'd say roughly eight hours away and standing off Malaya with allied subs.' He paused momentarily. 'I wouldn't normally bring it away from our own, especially to try rescue Japs from a sub. But it's our men I'm concerned about. I'll have to take the risk and get it brought up here right away. Meanwhile I'll get one of the docs over to you. Are there any more foreign subs in the area?'

'Not to my knowledge. As far as I can gather from my men the attack was opportunist. It wasn't planned. That's why they only took a few of my men.'

'Leave it with me. I'll send the medics ahead.'

O'Neill pushed himself up from the chair and checked out the communal cabin where most of his crew were lying on bunks.

'Stay where you are, men, and well done for fending the buggers off. I've asked for help and it should be on its way pretty soon. There's little we can do until they arrive except stay calm.'

Inflamed by what had happened Cathy dared to confront Mum, an edge of anger in her voice. 'How could you do that, Mum, without talking it through with me first?'

Unfazed by her daughter's comment, Marjorie Ellis smiled. She was delighted the afternoon had been such a success. It was obvious Irene's boy adored Cathy. He couldn't take his eyes off her. Fair enough, Cathy had been sulky, but she would come round. Geoffrey was a nice enough young man and without any doubt he would be an excellent catch. Cathy should be pleased – and grateful.

'I don't know why you're making a mountain out of it, love. You could wrap Geoffrey round your little finger if you had the mind to.'

'I don't want to wrap him round my little finger thank you very much.' Her tone was mutinous. 'Listen to what I'm saying, Mum. I'm just not interested.' She spat out the words. 'I can't stand him!'

Frank roused himself. It was the same old story. The minute he picked up his newspaper he had all on concentrating for the racket going on around him. All he wanted was a little peace. He turned to his wife.

'Drop it now, Marj. Can't you see the girl's had enough for today? And if she's not struck on Irene's boy, leave it at that.' He shrugged in a familiar movement and looked away. God knows, wasn't it enough having to put up with Irene, Walter and Geoffrey Grant without all this. It was obvious Cathy was not impressed, and why should she be? Come to think of it Geoffrey didn't impress him either nor that wimp Walter. But as usual he had to play things along. He didn't want to upset Marjorie. She was trying her best for Cathy.

Reluctant to irritate Dad any further, Cathy made a huge effort to control her temper. 'That's right, Dad. You've got it in one. I'm not struck. And that's the end of it.'

But Mum was not prepared to stop at that. Later in the week she made an announcement.

'Guess what! Geoffrey's invited us all to attend the Charity Ball at City Hall. Sir Roland Brighton will be there as guest of honour. Geoffrey knows him well. Irene tells me Geoffrey has a great deal of pull when it comes to getting tickets for these functions. There'll be Dad and me, you and Geoffrey, Irene and Walter too.' She smiled and slipped her arm around Cathy's shoulders. 'I hope you're not going to spoil things.'

Cathy gave a bitter, mirthless laugh. In a gesture of defiance she wheeled round to retaliate, her face a mask of gloom. But Dad looked up from his newspaper and took hold of her hand.

'Come here, treasure. I know you're not happy about the arrangement, but your mother's organised it now. You know how she looks forward to these things.' He smiled. 'Put up with Geoffrey for her sake. It doesn't mean you have to dance with him all the time. Humour him. He'll soon realise you're not interested.'

I may as well give in, she told herself. She smiled.

'OK, Dad,' she replied, her voice surprisingly controlled. 'But don't expect me to get involved in any more arrangements. I think I've made myself clear. Geoffrey is just not my type.'

'Why is that, darling?' Did Mum ever give up?

'I don't like the way he thinks. I don't like his old-fashioned ideas. Fancy, expecting his future wife to give up everything to look after him!' A deep sigh trickled through her and a frown replaced her smile.

'But that's the way it is, Cathy. I gave up my job at the milliners when I married your father.'

'I know, and that was how it was in those days. That was then. This is now!'

'But that's the way it should be, darling, I don't care what you say.'

'Not in my book, Mum.'

'Are you saying you'd prefer to go out to work rather than run a home for someone kind and generous like Geoffrey?' she argued.

Cathy had no intention of pursuing this any further. 'Forget it, Mum. We obviously don't see eye to eye. I'll go to the ball; but it's definitely the last time!'

Marjorie took hold of her daughter's hand and squeezed. 'I think you might well change your mind when you get there.'

Cathy looked away and her face lost its tension. She knew beyond all doubt that Geoffrey Grant was not the man for her – he never would be. But, seeing the arrangement had been made, she knew she would need to prepare for it. A full-length ball gown was a 'must' for such an event even though formal balls were not her style. She much preferred having fun at Segar's and the *Trocadero* in the up-to-the-minute shorter dresses she'd made for herself. But what could she do? It was Dad she was thinking about. He always liked to keep the peace and she didn't want to let him down.

Mum's new treadle sewing machine was a vast improvement on the hand machine and, taking care with the cream taffeta, Cathy ran up the final seam of the gown. Mum hadn't told her who'd supplied the coupons for the fabric, but she guessed Irene Grant might have had a hand in it.

'There we go! And it had better be worth it.'

Cathy pulled a face and held up the dress.

'It's lovely. And don't worry; it will be worth it, believe you me. You'll look a picture in your new dress.' She took hold of the dress and gazed at it. 'Try it on and give us a whirl.'

Saturday evening came along. Dad ordered a taxi, a rare treat they couldn't afford. But they needed to get into the city and public transport wasn't much use when his two girls were wearing ball gowns.

Cathy felt overdressed in hers but she would be no different from the others once they mingled. And all eyes were on her as she followed her parents into the ballroom. The ankle-length sheath dress caught in a ruffle of folds at the waist fitted snugly around her curvy figure. Her glossy hair, fashioned in a sleek page-boy style, framed her lovely face and fell gracefully on to her shoulders. She followed her father to the reserved table at the front and close to the orchestra.

She stared vacantly at its occupants and she didn't recognise any of them. It was a pity there was no-one her age. They all appeared to be married couples, well into their thirties.

She pulled her thoughts together and then she blinked her eyes. Just as she expected! There he was, Geoffrey pontificating in front of his small group of guests. When he saw her he smiled, an easy confident smile, and he stood up to greet them. He had a distinguished air about him in his dinner suit and black tie as he gazed in admiration at Cathy, kissed her on the cheek and pushed a few strands of hair away from her eyes. He studied her at arm's length and she saw the delight leap into his eyes. In a moment of weakness, she almost felt sorry that she couldn't react in the same way. 'I do believe you're the belle of the ball, my dear.'

Cathy felt a flush spread from her chin to her forehead. 'Thank you, Geoffrey. It's kind of you to pay me such a compliment.'

He squeezed her arms gently and whispered. 'You know you never gave me those dancing lessons.'

Cathy smiled willingly. 'We hardly had the time. It's not long since you mentioned it, and we've both been busy.' Cathy was determined to keep her cool whatever he had to say. She had no wish to embarrass her parents by sulking again or by being too controversial.

Without removing his gaze from her face, he took her hand and led her to the dance floor. 'Let's see if I'm up to standard then.' He began to swing her around in the quickstep.

Surprisingly she found him quite a good dancer. She was impressed. He must have had lessons somewhere along the line. 'I'll give you full marks

141

for your quickstep. Where did you learn to dance like that? Not at Segar's that's for sure, otherwise I would have remembered.'

He laughed and shook his head. 'No. I didn't attend a formal dancing school. There was no necessity. It was when I was at boarding school. Strangely enough, it was part of the sports syllabus in our final year.' He pulled her close. 'I must say I wasn't keen at the time but the lessons have come in useful.'

The evening went with a swing. Cathy was relieved to see that Geoffrey seemed not to be too possessive, probably because he felt obliged to dance with the wives of some of his clients. That gave Cathy the opportunity to accept invitations to dance with other partners.

But Geoffrey was not impressed.

'I'm surprised you didn't stay loyal to me. After all you are my guest.' He drew in a deep breath and shook his head.

She looked him in the eyes and tried to grasp what he was on about. 'What are you talking about, Geoffrey? I don't know what you mean.'

His back stiffened. He checked to make sure no-one else was around and listening before leaning forward and lowering his voice.

'Flaunting yourself, that's what I mean, playing to the gallery, dancing with just about every man here!' He gave an awkward smile.

A bewildered expression in her eyes, Cathy stood her corner. Was she hearing things? 'Whoa! Hold your horses, Geoffrey.' Who did he think he was? 'I'm not in the habit of refusing to dance.' She almost snapped at him but she restrained herself.

'It's bad manners. That's the way I've been taught.'

'It's not bad manners as far as I'm concerned!'

His reaction irritated her and she tried hard to drive the anger out of her head.

'Sorry you look at it that way,' she replied, smiling, her words intended to sound conciliatory. And she refused to comment further.

Until this had happened Cathy had begun to unwind. Mum was right. It was much more enjoyable than she had ever anticipated. And maybe she would have accepted a future invitation, but Geoffrey had soured the evening and she was not prepared to put up with that kind of behaviour.

In the taxi home, Mum tried to appease the situation. For some unknown reason she was desperate to throw the two of them together. Maybe it was her close friendship with Irene Grant, or her admiration for Geoffrey and his status as Sylvania's bank manager. But neither of those reasons washed with Cathy and she was even more determined to steer clear of Geoffrey in the future.

The rescue chamber and a special unit of divers joined the main fleet seven hours later. Commander Bradley set out northwards towards the Burma shoreline, two tugs following in his wake. All night the *Nautilus* battled her way towards the position of her sister ship the *Resolute*, heavy spray sweeping across her decks and the wind battering the great rescue chamber which was lashed at the stern's fantail. And it was during the early hours of the morning when Bradley finally reached the southern tip of Burma. But the weather there was so bad that the ship struggled for hours to moor as close to the *Resolute* as possible.

Once anchored, the storm built up even more and the submarine's location was lost. But eventually one of the men spotted a smoke bomb. 'Over there!' he shouted. Another buoy was sent overboard to mark the place.

Realising their limitations, the commander sent in the two tugs.

'We need to know the exact location of the submarine before I'm prepared to send in my divers. I propose dropping grapnel down there and dragging the bottom. We need to get a hold on the vessel to act as a guide.' He signalled to his men and the fluked anchors were sent down in the hope that the hooks would latch on to the submarine. But the task was time-consuming, especially when the commander discovered that the area surrounding the vessel was full of debris and boulders. Eventually they located the submarine and the grapnel latched on to it.

Keen to get started with the rescue attempt, the divers leaned over the ship's rail, looking towards the spot where the buoy was bobbing on the ocean. Bradley did not hesitate in his choice of diver for the initial surveillance.

'Macintyre, I'd like you to make a general surveillance of the area. Let me explain.' He approached the diver, a Colossus of a man over six feet tall and known for his great physical strength. 'I am putting my trust in you to make the first dive. This is no easy task but I know if anyone can do it, you can. Try to make your way to the deck of the sub and let me know the state of things down there.' He was aware that the fate of the men in the submarine was now in Macintyre's hands and that he could not afford to fail.

'I'll do my best, Sir,' Macintyre replied as he prepared to dive. He climbed on to the diving platform and started to lower himself to the surface of the water.

O'Neill looked to Bradley, his eyes full of optimism, as the diving helmet disappeared beneath the surface. 'The wind's dropped. Let's hope the storm will abate now.'

The diver battled his way through the murky depths, catching his feet in weed and debris. But there was something heavier tangled just above the submarine. Luck was on his side and he landed carefully on the foredeck just a few feet away from the forward escape hatch, ready to make a preliminary observation. The tangled object was a cable hampering clear access to the hatch and Macintyre struggled for several minutes to free it before reporting back to Bradley.

'A salvage operation is possible, sir, and I suggest we make a start. Would you get the men to lower the chamber's downhaul cable to me?'

'That's great news, Macintyre. Well done! I'll get the cable down to you immediately.'

Whilst he waited Macintyre checked the hatch and managed to find the lug on which to fasten the cable. As soon as he spotted the cable swinging above him, he grabbed hold and shackled it to the hatch. 'Haul taut!' he instructed.

With the prospect of facing decompression before he saw the surface again, he knew he must start back up knowing his task was complete. The stage was now set for the rescue chamber to be lowered with two of his shipmates inside to carry out the rescue. His thoughts were on the men inside the sub and he hoped to God they were still alive when the chamber reached them.

Chapter 8

1943

Complete darkness settled around the men trapped in the submarine. Tom and the other British sailors spent hours huddled together in appalling conditions, some of them still crying out in pain. It was bone-chillingly cold and he estimated the temperature to be very little above freezing.

The Japanese were wrapped in blankets, probably damp ones, but the British sailors had no blankets at all and Tom couldn't decide which was worse. The bleeding close to his temple had stopped but his head continued to throb. Occasionally he felt himself drifting in and out of consciousness and his mind continually switched from pleasant thoughts of Cathy to the depths of pessimism. Had there ever been a successful rescue of seamen from a sunken submarine? Would they be the first, or were they destined to perish in this stinking hell-hole?

But then his mind became alert once more when he heard the 'putt, putt' of something up above. It sounded like an ocean-going vessel. And it was constant. The sound of the engine seemed to go on for hours. Something was happening up there. He hoped and prayed they were aware of the submarine lingering silently beneath them.

He turned to Ken. 'What do you reckon is happening up there? Do you think they might be trying to rescue us?'

'I pray to God they are. But we don't know if it's our lot up there or the Japs?'

'Whoever it is I can't wait to get out of here. If it's the Japs I'll suffer the consequences.' He closed his eyes and tried to remain calm. 'It's hard to breathe in here now the air's getting thinner. And there's a bloody awful stink.'

'What can we expect when we're all packed in like a tin of bloody sardines? And no fresh air! It reeks. It's obviously body odour but I can't help suspecting there's chlorine gas drifting around from the batteries as well. If they are trying to rescue us let's hope they're not going to be much longer.'

The sound of what appeared to be heavy lead boots clumping on the deck up above startled them.

'There's someone out there. Must be a diver,' someone called out.

The excitement mounted when they heard a vigorous tapping sound on the hull. The captives began to cheer. But their cheers were arrested when one lone voice began to sing out:

Abide with Me! Fast Falls the Eventide,
The Darkness Deepens: Lord with me abide!

As a couple more joined in, the Japanese crew sprang from their bunks and stared in amazement before charging to the bow of the vessel,

147

shouting and screaming. But the British sailors, undeterred, continued to sing.

When other helpers fail, and Comforts Flee,
Help of the Helpless, O Abide with Me!

Someone was out there. Someone was trying to rescue them. Tom didn't care who it was, whether the Japanese or the allied forces. Anything was better than the prospect of a slow burial they had all come to dread.

Commander Bradley pointed to the large steel rescue chamber now in close proximity to the *Resolute*.

'This is a first for me. I've never had to put one of these to use before. It's a modern version of the diving bell.' He smiled. 'But the men know exactly how it works. They've had plenty of practice, even though it's never been needed.' He turned to the remaining four divers, all experienced men. 'I need you to split the task between you, working alternately. Baines and Crabtree you two take the first dive, Wallace and Ingham the second. Take your time. There's nothing to be gained by rushing, provided you ventilate the sub as soon as you've established direct contact with the men. Let's hope they're still alive down there.' He stuck a thumb in the air. 'Go now. I have every faith in you.'

The two divers entered the upper compartment and the crew gently lowered the rescue chamber by cables until it reached the sub's escape hatch. At this point extreme care was needed. The rescue chamber's second compartment was open to the sea and, before the divers could make any sort of contact, they had to blow out the water with compressed air, making sure the compartment was completely empty. Once it was clear they sealed the rescue chamber to the escape hatch.

Crabtree blew out a heavy breath. 'Cracked it!' And when they heard the faint noise of the singing down below they looked at one another and smiled.

'My God. They're still alive!' Baines nodded his head. 'And it's our lot! Come on. Let's go.'

As the hatch swung open, Crabtree shone his torch into the dark fetid cavern and it lit up a sea of upturned faces, all of them Japanese. He nipped his nose. 'Phew! It stinks down here.' He turned to Baines. 'Selfish bastards,' he murmured. 'If they think they'll be the first to be rescued they've got another think coming.'

Having been trapped for more than thirty hours in almost complete darkness, the Japanese crew blinked in the sudden light before scrambling forward and jostling one another to be rescued first.

Crabtree called loudly and clearly, 'Get back!'

When they realised the rescuers were not Japanese, some of them shrank back in apparent disbelief. Whether or not they understood the diver's exact words was not clear, but his brusque tone would have indicated their meaning. The crew moved away and it seemed clear the prospect of being taken captive by the allied forces was shameful in their eyes. Tom hoped and prayed they would do nothing foolish to stop the rescue mission.

Crabtree then addressed the British seamen.

'Please stay back lads. We need to get you some

fresh air in there.' He connected a hose from the *Nautilus* compressors to ventilate the sub before the rescue could begin.

Meanwhile Baines shouted down the hatch.

'Hot food and drinks for you, chaps. Once we've renewed the air we want you to move forward to the hatch and prepare to leave. Brits first. You'll be leaving no more than eight men at a time. Are there any injured down there?'

'Yes. Some of *Resolute's* crew. We'll get them to the hatch first,' Tom replied and, despite the conditions they'd had to suffer, he now felt buoyant at the thought of being rescued.

'How many of you in all?'

'Fifteen.'

'We can take eight to start and then the remaining seven. The Japs will have to wait.'

'I should bloody well hope so too.' Ken smirked.

'We need to get the doc out first,' Tom announced. 'He must have had a heavy blow to the head. He keeps drifting in and out of consciousness.'

'Try pass him through. We're ready for him.' Baines promised.

Tom and an uninjured colleague lifted the doctor and carried him to the hatch but they struggled to thread him through. Fortunately the two men in the rescue chamber were ready to take hold of him.

'We can't take eight this time, probably just three or four of the injured to start. If they can't stand they'll take up more space. It may take a little longer but don't worry we'll get you all out.'

They led Ken to the hatch and helped him

150

through before approaching a crewman with a suspected broken leg. 'Come on Taffy. Let's get you up there. Grin and bear it.'

The seaman winced and tried to disguise the pain he was suffering as he was pushed through into the chamber. 'Talk about a bloody lame duck, quack, quack!' he joked. 'That's me right enough!'

'We're closing the hatch now,' Crabtree told them. 'But we'll be back.'

'What about you,' Ken called out to Tom, a look of concern on his face.

'I'm fine, pal. I'll be coming with the second lot. Get yourself up there and don't worry about me.' Tom's heart flipped in his chest. This was incredible. He would never in a million years have believed they would or could be rescued. He was so overjoyed he didn't care if he was the last to leave the submarine. They were safe now.

Once the first three casualties entered the chamber, the men sealed back the submarine hatch and, with difficulty, helped the captives into the upper compartment of the rescue chamber before climbing in themselves. They closed the hatch dividing the upper and lower compartments and once more flooded the lower compartment. Finally and silently the chamber gained positive buoyancy and started on its upward journey.

The men on board the *Nautilus* watched as the chamber surfaced. A loud cheer went up and when the hatch was opened it took some time for the survivors to be transferred on board the rescue ship. The applause continued and the survivors, tears rolling down their cheeks, weary after their ordeal and riddled with pain, struggled to put on a brave face. Cries rang out.

'I can't believe it!' Ken offered.

'Thought I was a goner down there!' Taffy pronounced, but the doctor, still unconscious, remained silent.

'How many more?' Commander Bradley was concerned there may be more injured men in the submarine.

'Thirty-nine all together,' Ken told him. 'Twelve Brits and twenty-seven Japs. Another four of our twelve have injuries, the rest seem to be OK.'

'Only twenty-seven Japs?'

'Some drowned in the aft compartment, sir.'

'Then that explains it.' He turned and addressed Wallace and Ingham. 'I must insist our men come first, starting with the four injured,' was the commander's reply. 'We must prepare for the Japanese, O'Neill. They'll be transferred to the *Resolute* and kept down below, locked in there if necessary. We don't want them trying anything on. You know what they're like.'

'Indeed I do, Commander.'

When Wallace and Ingham replaced Crabtree and Baines the crew lowered the rescue chamber once more. As the commander watched it disappear beneath the surface he turned to Captain O'Neill.

'I've had instruction from the war office the *Resolute* should return to Australia with the injured. Are you able to cope with a depleted crew?'

'Provided we don't encounter any more attacks I'm sure we can manage. I realise a lot of my men are injured but some of the injuries are superficial.'

152

'And what about you, O'Neill?'

'Don't worry about me. I can hobble and, of course I can give instructions.' He laughed.

'First of all we need to give the injured time to rest up before we start transferring them to the *Resolute*,' Bradley insisted. 'It's going to be a long, drawn out process.'

'I agree but it's for the best. It's going to be a few more hours before we have all the men on board.'

'I've instructed my men to bring up the Japs in threes. I know it'll take much longer but I can't afford for my men to be under threat.'

'You think they could attack? Surely there's nothing to be gained.'

'Yes, I realise that but we don't know how their minds work so let's take precautions.'

When the next group of injured were brought to the surface they included a man who had died through head injuries sustained when the Japanese had attacked the *Resolute*. When the rest of *Resolute's* crew discovered what had happened, they were in retaliatory mood. But Captain O'Neill soon put a stop to their plans.

'Calm down, men. The Japs will suffer more by being captured and kept imprisoned. There is more shame attached to that than if you were to dispose of them here and now.'

The men remained silent until the final *Resolute* captives arrived on board. Tom had opted to be brought to the surface with the last batch of *Resolute* captives. When he stepped onto the deck he shook the dizziness from his head. It was hard to believe they had been rescued from the hellhole that was nothing but a huge coffin lodged in the seabed. His pal, Mike, who had been down below in the *Resolute* when the Japanese invaded, had escaped capture. He dashed across the deck towards Tom.

'Thank God you're back, Tom.' He reached out and patted his friend on the back. 'I thought I'd never see you again.'

'Me too, pal. You kept out of the way of the buggers I noticed and I see you've no injuries, jammy devil!' He laughed.

'I shifted my arse sharpish when I heard them up above.'

They stood together watching as the remaining twenty-seven Japanese survivors were eventually brought to the surface. In a final descent, Macintyre cracked open the stern hatch. It was completely flooded. There were no more survivors.

Despite Geoffrey's persistence, Cathy turned down every one of his invitations. And there were plenty! Marjorie was not best pleased and she tried every technique she could to persuade Cathy to change her mind. She even tried to embroil Frank in her plans, but to no avail. Cathy made it plain to them all. Geoffrey was history.

The war in the Pacific continued to rage but still Cathy had no word from Tom. She had considered writing a letter addressed to him on board the *Resolute* in the hope that eventually he would receive it, but she was apprehensive on that score. The last thing she wanted was for him to think she was doing all the chasing. And it did of course cross her mind that he might write to her.

154

After Tom had left so hurriedly, Cathy realised it was inevitable his ship had entered the war zone. She shuddered. For all she knew he may have been killed in battle. But she was determined to think more positively in the future and she shook that morbid thought from her mind. She prayed he was safe but not back in Europe. That was too far away.

As time went by she couldn't get him out of her mind. Even at work she would sit and daydream. And she could barely whip up the enthusiasm to continue with her teaching either at Segar's or at the *Trocadero*. But she told herself the dance lessons would help to take her mind off Tom. After all, it was no good moping. That wouldn't bring him back. And dreaming didn't get the work done either. The best she could do was to throw herself into the day job and try not to think about him. But it certainly wasn't easy.

Her hard work paid off. Mr. Dallarup called her into his office. 'I'm really impressed the way you've tackled things, and in such a short space of time.' He paused momentarily. 'How old are you now, Catherine?'

'I'm almost nineteen, Mr. Dallarup.' She wondered why he wanted to check her age.

'I suppose you are a bit on the young side, but I've decided to promote you to personal assistant. What do you think? Can you tackle it?'

'But what about the secretarial side of things, letters and contracts?'

'Gloria can do that from now on.'

'She's older than me.'

'That's right, but she doesn't have your business acumen, and she's not as efficient as you.'

Cathy was puzzled. Why did he need a personal assistant? She wasn't replacing anyone. This was all new to her. But why should that concern her?

'I'd love the job. What exactly does it involve?'

'I've so much on my plate I need you to keep a check on things, especially those I might be inclined to overlook. The building trade is in the doldrums generally, but in some areas, especially those affected by the bombing, there'll be a lot of rebuilding needed,' Dallarup told her. 'I've been asked to go up to Brisbane. They need quotes for roofing. I think there may be contracts in Darwin and Broome too sometime in the near future, which means my business will be on the up again.' He folded his arms and leant on the desk. 'I'd like you to come with me to Brisbane. Get the feel of things. Find out what it's all about. What do you think?'

Cathy gasped. 'You want me to go too?'

'That's right. If you'd like to come along I'll have a word with your parents just to make sure they approve.' He handed over a sheaf of papers. 'There are the details. Read through them carefully and check out the requirements.' He smiled and flicked the back of his hand towards her. 'Off you go young lady and get cracking with the arrangements.'

Frank was not happy about the proposed trip to Brisbane. 'It's only eighteen months since the Japs bombed Darwin. It could happen again, mark my words. I don't want Cathy in any sort of danger.'

'I'm sure Mr. Dallarup knows what he's doing,

Frank. Don't spoil it for Cathy. She'll only be there four days. And there's been nothing since the nineteen forty two attack.'

'She'll be there for four days but what about getting up to Brisbane and back again. That'll take a couple of days or more. They'll be stopping off somewhere on the way up and coming back. Dallarup won't want to drive all that way in one day. It could be a nightmare.' He shook his head.

'Frank, there's been no mention of the Japs attacking so far down the coast. The allied troops would soon be onto them if they so much as ventured south. You've said as much yourself,' Marjorie argued.

'Well, yes I have. But MacArthur made it his Australian base. There's our lot and the Yanks in Brisbane. And they don't always get on. You know what the Yanks are like. Look at the trouble they caused in forty two fighting our lot. The violence lasted two days before it was stopped.'

'Who's to say the Yanks started it? Our lot can be as bad. And anyway Cathy is sensible enough to steer clear of that sort of thing. She's a sensible girl. She's not going to get involved with any of the troops. She's there on business.'

Frank shook his head. 'I suppose I am being pessimistic. But it still worries me.'

'It worries me too, love, but Cathy is growing up fast and we have to give her some leeway.'

Cathy knew Mum was right. Mr. Dallarup wouldn't have promoted her if he hadn't thought her mature enough to do the job, and she couldn't wait for the day to come. As a family, they hadn't travelled a great deal because it was such an

157

expense for Dad who was the only worker. When they were younger he'd taken Mum and the three of them to Bateman's Bay where they'd hired a chalet for the week. She had a vivid recollection of the kangaroos poking their noses into the doorway of the chalet. But the trip to Brisbane was different. She had never been up north before. And this was a business trip.

She thought about Rita's reaction later when she'd slipped out of the office and told her about the proposed trip.

'Good on you, but I'm really jealous, Cathy!' Rita laughed. 'Well, not really.' She patted her friend on the back.

'The exciting part is going up there in Mr. Dallarup's car. Apparently he's had it a few years, built early thirties Dad reckons, but it's in pristine condition. From what I can gather it's the boss's pride and joy.'

'Really! That must be a first travelling all that way by car.'

'Exactly.' She clapped her hands. 'I'm as happy as Larry. Dad gave his permission but I only hope he doesn't change his mind. He's not too rapt about it.'

'I can imagine. But he'll get used to the idea.' She took hold of Cathy's hand. 'Seriously though, I think it's great you've been promoted.'

'Thanks, Rita. But Gloria's not very happy.'

'Gloria's a bit behind the times. It's ability that matters, not age. And that's why you got the job and not Gloria.' Whatever happened in her life Cathy knew she could depend on Rita to support her.

And Mum was there at the forefront too living out her own dreams through Cathy. 'It's all happening, Cathy. First the dancing success and now this! I can't wait to tell Irene.' She considered her words. 'But on second thoughts, maybe not. It's too much like rubbing it in, especially when Geoffrey seems to be against women having any sort of career or even success.'

'There you go, Mum. I knew you could see through his old-fashioned ideas. He's proper Victorian.'

Marjorie laughed. 'I know, sweetheart but his prospects are good.' But despite her disappointment that she and Irene had not been able to secure the match between their offspring, Marjorie was elated. 'Would you like me to pack for you? I've found that small port you took to Bateman's Bay.' She reached behind her and waved the suitcase in the air. 'Remember this?' she asked.

'I do, Mum, and wasn't that a great time we had?'

'Yes, it was a very enjoyable holiday.' She lifted the suitcase in the air. 'I think it'll be big enough.' She placed it on the bed and opened it up. 'Now you must take some sensible shoes. You can't be walking about all day in your high heels. They're fine for the evenings when you go to dinner with Mr. Dallarup.' She was really getting into the swing of things now. 'And what about that nice navy suit? You've got to look business-like.'

'OK, Mum. Don't get too excited!' Cathy laughed. 'You'll burst a blood vessel.'

'Cheeky!' Marjorie joined in the laughter. 'I'll leave you to it then.'

When a black Austin Seven drew up outside the house the following day, Cathy knew it was Mr. Dallarup and she held her breath, hoping Dad wouldn't at the last minute put a stop to the trip. But by this time it seemed he was coming around to thinking perhaps he was being overly protective. Reluctantly, he gave his permission for her to accompany her boss to Brisbane.

Frank had taken a half day off work to see his daughter on her way when Dallarup arrived to collect Cathy.

'Don't worry about your daughter, Mr. Ellis,' he said. 'I'll take good care of her.'

'I'm sure you will, Mr. Dallarup. It's not that but it does seem soon after the bombing in Darwin. What worries me is that it could happen again.'

'I doubt it. I think our troops and the allies have the measure of the Japs now. They won't pull off a reconnaissance like the forty-two job. We were taken by surprise, Mr. Ellis. The harbour was crammed full of allied ships. And there were civil and RAAF planes at the airfields. Obviously, had we realised an attack was imminent, we would have been ready for them.' He shook his head. 'I wouldn't expect the Japs to come any further south. There's nothing to be gained by bombing Brisbane.'

'I don't know about that. The place is humming with our troops and the Yanks. And the Japs can be a sneaky lot.'

'But the allies are our defence. And they're a tough lot. Don't forget the Japs were trounced in the Battle of Midway.'

'Even so, some of the Queenslanders have been evacuated and sent further south.'

'That's right but only to release accommodation for the allies. And that's where we come in. We'll be there to make sure everything's secure building wise.'

Frank didn't argue further and Dallarup didn't make any more comments. He'd said enough on that score and he swiftly changed the subject.

'On the positive side my company is expanding and that means Cathy will be needed more than ever,' he said before placing her suitcase in his Austin Seven.

'Fair enough,' Frank replied but not without a heavy sigh. He turned and shook hands with Dallarup. 'By the way, nice little number,' he added, smiling and patting the bonnet of the Austin Seven.

'Yes. I've had it several years now and it's very reliable.'

'Well at least that's reassuring,' Frank kissed his daughter on the forehead. 'Take care, precious,' he concluded.

'Will do, Dad, and stop worrying.' She gave him a hug. 'I'll be back before you know it for goodness sake,' she added before waving him goodbye.

When Dallarup opened the car door for her to step inside she whispered, 'Dad's quite a worrier.'

He nodded. 'Well, young lady, I appreciate that in a man. It's better to care about his daughter than to be blasé about the trip.'

Chapter 9

1943

Seven hours later they stopped at Nelson Bay and spent the night in a little guest house there. Their next stop was Port Macquarie, three hundred miles from Sydney and it was early evening when they arrived. The hotel Cathy had booked was small and reception was nothing more than a desk in a narrow corridor. She hoped this wasn't a reflection of the size of the two single rooms she'd booked.

There was no-one on duty when they entered and Dallarup, looking weary, stared ahead frowning heavily.

'There doesn't seem to be anyone around.' He rang the bell and let out a heavy sigh. 'It's been a tiring journey but as long as I have a good night's sleep that's all that matters.' Turning to Cathy he added, 'Have you travelled north of Sydney before, Catherine?'

'Never. The furthest I've been is down south on the train to visit an aunt in Merimbula.'

'Then this is a first, but I'm sure it won't be the last. If we manage to scoop the contract in Brisbane I'm sure there'll be more to come. As I mentioned earlier we may have work in both Darwin and Broome later in the year, that's if we manage to pull this one off.'

'Then the company will definitely be on the up.' Cathy claimed, smiling.

An elderly woman bustled through and extended her hand.

'G'day, sir. You must be Mr. Dallarup from Sydney,' she said, smiling brightly.

He nodded. 'That's correct.'

'Perhaps you would give your details and sign in when you've taken your cases to your rooms.' She handed over two keys. 'These are for rooms four and five. They are up the stairs and to the right. Breakfast is from seven until nine.'

'Thank you, Mrs...'

'Corby,' she offered. 'You've had a very long journey I gather. Would you like a cup of tea?'

'That would be lovely,' he replied, turning to Cathy and handing over one of the keys. 'There you go, Catherine.' He turned to Mrs. Corby. 'We'll be down shortly.'

Mrs. Corby pointed to the door behind her. 'Come through into the dining room when you're ready.'

They took the stairs and Dallarup placed Cathy's small suitcase outside her door before opening his own and taking a brief glance inside the bedroom.

'You've done well,' he continued. 'I wasn't expecting anything lavish but this looks a comfortable little place, an improvement on last night's guest house.'

'Last night's was a last minute's arrangement of course. We weren't sure how long the journey would take.'

'I realise that but it was adequate.'

163

Once in her bedroom Cathy too was impressed. Both the room and the bed were bigger than the one she slept in at home and there was a small bathroom just two doors down the corridor. This was luxury as far as she was concerned.

She placed her suitcase on the bed, opened it up and took out a cotton dress she'd decided would be suitable for the evening. Placing it carefully on a hanger she hung it over the wardrobe door before going downstairs to the dining room. Dallarup was already there and Mrs. Corby was setting a small table in front of the window with a teapot and a cake stand full of freshly baked scones.

'There you go. A little tucker to revive you both,' she offered. 'I don't do evening meals but I can give you the name of a café along the road.'

Dallarup beamed, rubbed his hands together and pointed to the table. 'This looks good, Mrs. Corby. Thank you so much,' he said politely. 'It's very thoughtful of you.' He pulled out a chair. 'Come, Catherine, sit down.'

Twenty minutes later and suitably refreshed they returned to their rooms having arranged to meet downstairs at seven to find the little café Mrs. Corby had recommended. Cathy lay down on her bed and rested but her mind was still buzzing. Where would Tom be now? What would Mum be doing? She smiled to herself. Bragging to Irene no doubt.

The café Mrs. Corby had recommended was only minutes away. It was basic but the food was good and Cathy chose red snapper for her main course. 'This is delicious,' she maintained. 'It's

164

equally as good as the fresh fish Dad brings home from the market.'

'I'm pleased you've enjoyed it,' Dallarup replied.

As soon as their main courses were over the waitress came up behind them. 'Would you like a pudding?' she enquired.

'Not for me, thank you very much.' Cathy placed her napkin on the table.

'Nor me. But compliments to the chef. The steak was delicious.'

The minute the waitress collected their dishes and took them away Dallarup stood up and paid the bill at the desk before turning to leave. He covered his mouth as he yawned. 'Do excuse me,' he added as they set off back to the hotel. 'I need an early night after all the driving. But I'd like to be off around eight-thirty in the morning. How about breakfast at seven thirty?' he suggested.

'That suits me, Mr. Dallarup. It's my usual time.'

'Then, good night, my dear,' he said as he opened the door to his bedroom. 'I'll see you at breakfast.'

By the time Cathy slipped into bed it was after nine. She snuggled into the sheets but she didn't drop off to sleep for some time. Her mind was still alive. The trip to Brisbane was so exciting and although she missed being with Mum and Dad she couldn't wait to tell them exactly how things had gone.

She was awake by half past six the following morning and after an early breakfast they left for Port Macquarie and headed for the spare ground behind the hotel where the car was parked.

'I had an excellent night's sleep,' Dallarup

announced. 'At least I feel refreshed now and ready for the next stage of our journey. Did you sleep well, Catherine?'

'Like a log and, as you said, the place was lovely and comfortable.'

'Let's hope your next choice is as good,' he offered before going to the front of the car, bending down and heaving the starting handle several times. The engine fired into action and he quickly slipped into the driving seat and set out for Brisbane.

They sat in comfortable silence for some time, Cathy's mind once more focusing on Tom and his possible whereabouts, her boss concentrating on the road ahead. But when they came to a crossroad Cathy stared at the almost desert-like wilderness stretching before them.

'There's not much around here,' she observed, 'no buildings to be seen, nothing but a long dirt track that seems to go on forever.'

'That's right but once we come to the end of this stretch it shouldn't take long before we arrive in Brisbane. The overall distance from Port Macquarie to Brisbane is not too long,' he told her, 'and with luck we should have time to check out the whereabouts of the factory before we head for the hotel. That should save us time in the morning.'

Cathy opened her mouth to reply but she didn't get the chance before Dallarup put a finger to his mouth and shushed her. 'What's that noise?' he muttered, listening intently. 'Do you hear a hissing sound?' The noise was coming from the front of the car.

'Yes,' Cathy replied. She pointed to the bonnet and frowned and, as she continued to stare ahead, she saw steam issuing through the sides of the bonnet. 'I think it must be coming from the engine.'

Dallarup pulled off the road and drew to a standstill.

'It seems I spoke too soon, Catherine,' he continued as he slid from the seat. 'It looks as though the engine's overheating but I can't afford to take a look, not until it cools down. It appears we've run out of water. I'm sure the steam is coming from the radiator.' He looked around. They were now on that lonely stretch of road, and there were no vehicles in sight. He placed his hand over his mouth and, sighing heavily, he shook his head. 'It's entirely my own fault. It was chocka when we left Sydney but I should have known after all that distance. It was foolish of me not to have checked before we left Port Macquarie.' He paused for a moment or two. 'We haven't passed a garage or a petrol station so it looks like I'll have to search out a billabong, hopefully one still containing unpolluted water.' He poked his head inside the car. 'How do you feel about staying in the car while I go off and look for some?'

'I'm sure I'll be fine,' she replied, lifting her voice and trying not to pass on her apprehension. Although she felt nervous at being left stranded in the car in such an isolated area it seemed they had no alternative.

For something like twenty minutes not a single car passed the Austin but then a truck came along and stopped. The driver jumped down and came towards her. As he neared the Austin she noticed his unkempt appearance. There were heavy dark stains on his pants and his shirt was filthy and badly creased. She didn't like the look of him and her heart began to beat wildly. She turned her head away. He scared her.

When he knocked on the window at the driver's side her stomach churned aggressively.

'Broken down, lady?' he asked.

She nodded.

'What seems to be the problem?'

She was about to tell him the engine had overheated but the words seemed to stick in her throat. She pointed to the bonnet of the car.

'What's it worth?' he continued, grinning inanely. But she barely took in his words before he turned and walked to the front of the car still grinning. 'I'll have a look and then I'll take my payment.' He lifted the bonnet and, as he did so, a cloud of pressurised steam rose from the radiator and flooded the air. Although his reaction was quick and he drew back in an instant, the vapour must have hit his face. Unfortunately he let go of the bonnet and it fell heavily onto one of his hands.

'You bitch,' he screamed his face crimson. Releasing his hand he rubbed his fingers and advanced towards her. But this time he aimed for the passenger side. 'You deliberately didn't tell me!'

Terrified now, Cathy shrank back into her seat.

'What the hell's going on?'

The stranger, startled by the voice of Dallarup, turned and stared before dashing back to his truck. It was only seconds before he started it up and drew away. They both stared after it.

'What happened there, Catherine?'

'He said he'd check out the problem and he lifted the car bonnet. I think the steam scalded his face a little but then he trapped his fingers in the bonnet when it fell down.'

'That's really bad. At least he was trying to help,' he continued. 'But why was he shouting at you?'

'He seemed to be blaming me for what had happened. I think he thought I was an easy target. He said he wanted his payment once he'd sorted out the problem.'

'My God. If that's the case I was back in the nick of time,' he said frowning. 'You know even though his clothes were in a filthy state I could swear his pants were khaki. I've a feeling he could be a deserter.'

'Not one of ours, I hope.'

'Looks like it, and the vehicle he was driving was very much like one of our army trucks. Pity we didn't get the number.'

'I was too shocked to think about that, Mr. Dallarup.'

'Of course you were, Catherine. But sorry you were put on the spot. Believe me it won't happen again. I shouldn't have left you here alone.' He took the billy can and filled the radiator with the water he'd managed to find. 'The radiator is partially full now. Let's hope I can get her started and we can get on our way. We might make it in time to check out the factory after all.'

Cathy thought about the promise Mr. Dallarup had made to her mum and dad. They would be furious if they knew what had happened.

The journey seemed to drag but eventually they reached Brisbane. It was late-afternoon and they headed towards one of the suburbs, noting the whereabouts of the factory before checking in at the hotel.

'At least we've sussed the place out. I shall rest my bones until it's time for the evening meal. Feel free to do as you wish until then my dear. I'll see you at the front door seven o'clock sharp.'

Cathy wasn't in the mood to hang around in her room and she decided to take a look around the city. After all it was her first visit to Brisbane. Tomorrow business would begin and Mr. Dallarup would expect her full attention when they visited the factory.

Her room was smaller than the one in Port Macquarie but it was adequate and, after unpacking her navy suit and a couple of dresses she decided to take a stroll.

It was almost four-thirty by the time she left the hotel and wandered down towards the river walkway. After her ordeal with the deserter she made sure there were several other people passing by. She gazed across the river at the mangroves growing there and watched the little boats bobbing up and down on the water. It felt good to stretch her legs after being cramped up in the car for so long.

When she looked up at the clock on the church spire it was almost half past five and she realised she needed to return to the hotel. But by this time the roads were still quite busy with evening traffic, mainly army trucks and big, flashy cars, and she stood on the pavement for a couple of minutes waiting to cross the road. She stuck out a foot ready to step off the pavement when she felt a tap on her shoulder. Startled she looked around.

It was Andrew. He stood there facing her, bell bottoms fluttering in the breeze. He was breathing heavily and he took hold of her shoulders.

'I thought it was you, Cathy,' he said, catching his breath. 'I saw you from a distance and I ran like a maniac to catch up with you. I can't believe my luck.' He leant towards her and kissed her on the cheek. 'It's so good to see you again.'

'Andrew! This is a surprise,' she replied, still taken aback. 'What are you doing here?'

'The *Victor* is anchored further down towards the mouth of the river. We're here for a couple of days and then we're back up north. But more to the point what are you doing here?'

'I'm here with my boss. We have a job on the outskirts of the city. I was promoted to Personal Assistant a few weeks ago and here I am.'

'Personal Assistant, eh? What does that entail? Nothing too personal, I hope.'

Cathy laughed. 'Not at all. Mr. Dallarup is very much the gentleman and he's very polite.'

'Are you likely to have time to yourself whilst you're here?' he asked.

Cathy shook her head. 'It's out of the question I'm afraid. We're at the factory tomorrow to start the job and it'll be a pretty intensive four days before we leave for Sydney. I can't afford to take any chances by leaving the hotel without telling the boss where I'm going, just in case I'm needed. I don't want to lose my job, Andrew.'

'No of course. I understand. But that's a pity. It would have been like old times meeting up tomorrow.'

'I know. Sorry about that. But it's been great seeing you again.'

'How about a drink before you leave? Half an hour. That's all I'm asking.'

'I think I can manage that but then I need to get back. I'm having a meal with my boss at seven.'

'How about that little café across the road?' he said, pointing. 'Let's not waste time,' he added, taking hold of her arm and escorting her across once there was a gap in the traffic.

'I've never seen as many cars and trucks. Some of them are a bit showy,' Cathy observed, staring back as they reached the pavement.

'The cars belong to the Yanks, the higher ranks I'd say,' he laughed. 'Our lot have nothing so over the top. But the trucks are both yours and the Yanks.'

They found a table in the corner of the café close to the window and sat down. 'What would you like?' Andrew asked.

'I'd like a flat white, please,' Cathy replied as Andrew stood up and went to the counter.

When he returned he stared intently into her face and, tentatively, he took her hands in his.

'I can't help myself when I say this, Cathy but you're gorgeous,' he told her. 'I wish I could take you back to Scotland with me. You must realise I've fallen for you!' His face indicated the urgency of his words and Cathy felt the heat rising from her chin to her forehead. This was not what she wanted. She liked Andrew but only as a friend, nothing more. And she was afraid her blushes had given him the wrong impression.

'Thanks for the compliment. But it's probably nothing but a crush.' She tried to laugh off his serious comment. 'After all we haven't spent much time together, you and I. And you guys must get very lonely.'

The coffee arrived and she thought perhaps she could quickly change the subject to save her any more embarrassment. But Andrew continued.

'It was love at first sight,' he clichéd somewhat self-consciously before taking his cup of coffee and drinking. 'It's a pity we couldn't have had more time together.'

'But that's how it goes, I'm afraid. And as for leaving my precious Australia I couldn't do it.'

'You won't forget to write to me will you?'

'Of course not.'

'If we're down in Sydney again I'll look you up. You don't mind do you?'

Cathy smiled. 'I'll still be there!'

'Maybe you'll come over and see me in Scotland sometime once I'm back home.' He grinned. 'But look at you, probably set for the top the way things are going, the boss's PA before you're even twenty! But you will need a holiday at some point. How about Scotland?'

Cathy laughed but she didn't answer his question directly.

'You said it, Andrew,' she replied. 'You never know what the future holds do you? Maybe you're right.' Cathy wasn't used to blowing her

173

own trumpet but she had to get out of this sticky situation.

Her mind was constantly on Tom and there was no substitute.

'But I won't be in for another promotion if I don't get myself back to the hotel,' she continued, looking at her watch. She drained her coffee cup. 'I must go now,' she stressed, hoping to get away without any more emotional scenes.

He led her outside, stopped and took both her hands in his before drawing her towards him. 'Just a little reminder before you leave,' he begged and kissed her gently on the lips. 'I'll savour that kiss until I see you again. I hope this is not the end,' he added before Cathy said goodbye, squeezed his hands and left him standing there staring after her.

It was early evening when HMS *Resolute* docked at Sydney's Garden Island. Captain O'Neill announced they would be there for six days.

'We'll spend the days running up to Christmas in Sydney but come Boxing Day we're back to the conflict area.'

The first to leave the ship were the injured crew, stretchered off and taken to the waiting ambulances. The Japanese prisoners, wailing and shouting in their foreign tongue, were escorted ashore but not without a struggle. Finally the ship's jubilant crew followed.

The temperature was in the thirties when Tom stepped onto dry land and his first intention was to make his way to Cathy's house in St Peter's. He couldn't wait to see her. But he hadn't thought it through and he soon realised she would still be at work.

'It looks as though we'll have to wait until tonight to see the girls. I'm hoping they'll be at either the *Trocadero* or Segar's.'

'You could be right. Surely we'll bump into them at some point,' Mike replied. 'How about taking a ferry to Bondi? We could take in the talent,' he suggested, laughing, 'have a swim and do a spot of sunbathing. What do you say?'

'Sound idea, Mike but I'm not interested in the talent. Cathy's the only one I'm keen to see.'

'Only joking, pal. Cheer up! Come on let's get moving.'

The ferry journey from Circular Quay didn't take long and they managed to find a space on the beach. Mike wiped his forehead.

'It seems strange it should be so hot when it's almost Christmas.'

'I'll say,' Tom agreed. 'Our lot at home will be togged up in thick coats, scarves, caps and probably wellies too.'

They rolled up their bell-bottoms and paddled in the ocean. But after spending an hour or so at Bondi Tom was anxious to return to Circular Quay.

'I can see you want to get back,' Mike said nudging his friend. 'But we won't see the girls until tonight don't forget. Come on, we may as well take the next ferry. Are you satisfied now?'

Tom laughed. 'You can read me like a book!'

'It's not just that, I'm as keen to get back as you are and hopefully see Rita.'

'There you go, it's not just me.'

When they returned to the harbour and Circular Quay they ordered cold beers and sat outside in the sunshine. But time seemed to pass slowly for Tom and he had the urge to surprise Cathy and meet her outside the office where she worked. He put his suggestion to Mike.

'She told me the name of the company and I know it was somewhere on the outskirts but I can't quite remember the name of the suburb. It's apparently a tram ride to the centre and one out to the suburb so it's at the opposite end of town to St Peter's.'

Mike shook his head. 'Hold your horses, Tom. Even if you did find out the exact whereabouts don't you think you're expecting too much of her?' he pointed out. 'You don't know what sort of welcome you'll get after all the time we've been away. You know you could be disappointed. I think you'd be better to stick to your original plan.'

Tom sighed. 'I suppose you're right but I hope she hasn't met someone else.' He tried to cast that possibility from his mind. Surely even after the short time they'd been together she had feelings for him. 'OK. Let's start at Segars. If she's not there we'll try the *Trocadero*. What do you think?'

'A much better idea, pal. And with any luck I could bump into Rita again, although I don't know if she'll still be keen to see me.'

'I know what you mean. Cathy seemed happy enough to be with me the last time we were here. But if someone else steps in and tries to take over, especially the Yanks, we'll be out in the cold.'

Excitement and apprehension led to disappointment when the girls didn't turn up at either

176

Segar's or the *Trocadero*.

Disillusioned, they were about to leave the *Trocadero* when Mike went across to one of the dance teachers. He returned looking glumly towards his pal. 'Something must have happened for neither of them to be here. I asked one of the other girls and she told me they hadn't been here for over a week.'

'That does it. Tomorrow I'm going to St Peter's. If Cathy's not there her parents will surely tell me where she is. They seemed friendly enough when Cathy introduced me to them.'

'Lucky you. I've never met Rita's lot. She seemed a bit guarded when I walked her home.'

'To be honest so did Cathy, at least I think that's the way it was. I was only invited in because her dad came to the door to see who was outside.'

Despite Tom's bravado his nerves almost got the better of him the next day when he took the tram to St Peter's. But he took a deep breath and knocked at the door. Cathy's mother answered it.

He held out his hand. 'Tom Crossley, Mrs. Ellis. Remember me? I'm on leave again for four days and docked in Sydney.' She frowned and ignored his hand. 'I wondered if Cathy was around.'

'She's away on business, young man and she won't be back for a day or so, certainly not before you leave Sydney.' Her voice had a sharp edge to it and although she smiled Tom was aware the smile lacked sincerity. 'And to tell you the truth I do believe she's spoken for, a friend of ours. But I'll tell her you called.' She closed the door.

Spoken for? That was a blow. And it was obvious Mrs. Ellis was not about to invite him in.

Shoulders slumped he made his way down the garden path and set out for the tram. He couldn't believe it. When he was last in Sydney she seemed keen to pursue their friendship. But he supposed it was to be expected. She probably thought she'd never see him again especially after he'd had to leave suddenly and been forced to stand her up. Any girl would take the huff if that happened.

What bad luck. It looked as though he would be leaving Sydney before she returned from her business trip. And that was another thing. Cathy had told him she was a secretary and secretaries don't normally take business trips.

Mike was waiting at Circular Quay when Tom stepped off the tram and headed towards him. He shook his head.

'No luck I take it,' Mike said.

'There's no chance I'll see her this time, maybe never again. It's worse than I thought. Apparently, according to her mother, she's already spoken for.'

'Chin up, pal. It's not the end of the world. But I must say I'm disappointed. It looks as though Rita's out of the picture too. They usually come as a pair.'

'You're right.' Tom gave a heavy sigh. 'I can't believe I probably won't see Cathy again. I'm going back to the ship, Mike. I've lost all enthusiasm for going to the *Trocadero* or anywhere else tonight.'

'I'd hoped you wouldn't give in so easily. There's still time. And what's the point in going back to the ship and moping? It's not worth it, pal. And if you go back it means I'll be on my own at the Troc.' He placed a hand on Tom's shoulder. 'If you come with me and I happen to meet up with Rita we could ask her what's going on. Find out exactly where Cathy is, when she'll be back and if she really has taken up with another chap. Her mother might be laying it on to get rid of you. You know what some mothers are like, controlling. And especially if they think of us as foreigners.'

But of course Tom didn't know what some mothers were like. He didn't even know what his own mother was like. She certainly wasn't controlling or protective, not like Mike was making out. But enough of that.

Mike patted him on the back. 'But if you're set on going back to the ship I'll go it alone.' He turned to leave Tom behind.

'No, wait!' Tom spun around quickly. 'Don't dash off, Mike. I will go with you. You're right. As you suggest Rita might be there and she'll surely know what's going on with Cathy. We'll check things out once and for all.'

Chapter 10

1943

Dallarup completed the work in less time than he'd anticipated and after their final visit to the factory they returned to the hotel.

'I must say, it's a bonus completing so soon, Catherine. But I couldn't have done it without your help.'

'But I only did as you asked, Mr. Dallarup. I don't see that I made a great deal of difference.'

'Oh but you did. You took down all the details without my having to break off and make notes. It makes a tremendous difference.' As he set off up the steps leading to the front door of the hotel he turned and added, 'I suggest we stay back at the hotel for our meal tonight. I don't know about you but I'm dog tired. I need an early night if we're to get away promptly in the morning.'

After the evening meal Cathy moved into the guest lounge and took out a notebook from her bag.

'Don't linger too long, Catherine,' Dallarup urged. 'We need to feel refreshed for our journey tomorrow.'

'I'm not going to be long but I need to write up my notes before I turn in for the night,' she replied.

'Couldn't they wait until tomorrow when we arrive in Port Macquarie?'

'I like to check my shorthand whilst things are fresh in my mind and make sure I have all the details down correctly.'

'I must say you're conscientious. But of course that's why I promoted you.' He patted her on the back and smiled. 'I'll see you tomorrow,' he concluded.

Before retiring for the night Cathy went through her shorthand and made copious notes ready to check things out with Mr. Dallarup when they were back in Sydney.

It was another half hour before she climbed into bed. Her immediate thoughts were of the earlier meeting with Andrew and how coincidental it was that they should bump into each other in Brisbane of all places. But it didn't take long before her recollections triggered off thoughts of Tom. Would she ever see him again? She hoped with all her heart that his ship would dock in Sydney at some time in the future.

Now she reprimanded herself for not trying to contact him. At least she could have written and marked the envelope with the name of the ship. It would have been worth a try. Some time ago she had considered doing just that but her pride had denied her from carrying it through.

Her sleep was fitful although eventually she did fall into a deep slumber. But it seemed like only minutes before she heard Mr. Dallarup's voice.

'Catherine! Catherine!' There was a light knocking on her bedroom door. 'It's seven thirty. You are up, aren't you?'

Cathy awoke with a start, rubbed her eyes and grabbed her watch from the bedside table. She checked the time. Mr. Dallarup was right. She'd overslept.

Jumping out of bed she called out, 'Yes. I'm coming,' as she threw off her pyjamas and stepped into her navy skirt. 'I'll just be a few minutes, Mr. Dallarup.' She dashed over to the washbasin and quickly splashed her face with cold water before dragging a comb through her hair. Scrabbling through her small suitcase she took out a fresh white blouse, smoothed it out and slipped it on, tucking it carefully into her skirt. There, she was as ready as she could be in such a short space of time.

After breakfast Cathy packed her few belongings into the suitcase and set off downstairs. Mr. Dallarup was already at the door waiting for her. He smiled. 'Ready are we?'

They were heading for the long isolated stretch of road on their way to Port Macquarie when, in the distance, Cathy spotted something unusual. She screwed up her eyes and tried to peer more closely.

'That's strange. There wasn't anything to be seen the last time we came along this track but now there's a small tent pitched on the scrub.' She pointed it out. 'It seems an odd place to pitch a tent.'

Dallarup shot a brief look in that direction. 'Yes I can see it now. How odd. And there's also a truck parked nearby.' He took a second glance. 'If I'm right in my assumption it looks very much like one of our army trucks.'

When Cathy looked more closely she spotted the truck. 'I think you're right,' she replied but what she saw sent a shiver through the whole of her body. Someone was crouching beside a fire. She took a deep breath and covered her mouth with her hands. 'I'm sure it's him,' she gasped, 'the man you thought was a deserter.'

Dallarup kept his eyes on the road. 'If that's the case we need the truck's registration. If you can see it, would you write it down? I'm not prepared to stop but I'll slow down. Even a part of the registration will indicate if it's an army requisitioned vehicle or not.'

He took his foot off the throttle as they neared the truck. The man looked across and pulled himself up from his haunches, making as though to advance towards them. His gesture appeared threatening. Cathy shuddered.

Dallarup glanced across and when he saw the look on Cathy's face he was obviously aware she was upset by what she saw.

'Take no notice, Catherine. I'll speed up once you have it.'

Cathy peered more carefully through the window and struggled to focus but she did manage to pick up the registration and she hastily scribbled it down. 'Got it,' she said. 'What now?'

Dallarup put on speed and left the man staring after them. 'I intend calling in at the police station in Byron Bay. This matter needs nipping in the bud,' he maintained.

'You mean you're going to dob him in?' Cathy asked in surprise.

'Absolutely! He's a menace to the public. Remember how he threatened you only a few days ago.'

'I do and he scared me.' She began to rationalise in her own mind and agreed with Mr. Dallarup's words. 'My two brothers are in the army, both in the war zone. Why should a waster like him get away with it? He's not only a deserter and that's a military offence but he was about to commit a criminal offence too when he threatened me.'

'You're quite right there, Catherine. Your brothers are fighting for their country. That scoundrel is a coward and thinking of no-one but himself.'

When they stopped off in Byron Bay to report what they'd seen Dallarup pressed the bell and

183

waited in reception for someone to deal with the problem.

'They're a bit slow but it's worth waiting,' he whispered. 'The deserter needs to be caught.'

Minutes later an officer appeared. 'Sorry for the wait but we're a bit short-staffed today, sir. What can I do for you?'

Dallarup explained and the officer scribbled down the details before checking out the registration. 'Well spotted. It sounds as though you were right. The registration is definitely military issue. There's no doubt about it, the digger you saw must be a deserter. We'll contact the army,' he reassured them. 'They'll know the exact ID of that no-hoper. They'll track the culprit down.'

'That's reassuring,' Dallarup offered before they left and set out on the road again.

When they arrived in Port Macquarie and booked in once more with Mrs. Corby they sat in the dining room whilst she served tea and cakes. The wireless was on in the background and as they listened Cathy turned to her boss.

'There you go, Mr. Dallarup. We were right to dob him in. The man is a deserter and he's been on the run for eight days, staying low wherever he could.'

Dallarup jumped up from his seat and twiddled with the knob of the wireless to increase the volume. Mrs. Corby looked puzzled and appeared to be on the verge of commenting when he put a finger to his mouth. The announcement continued.

When questioned he admitted he'd holed himself up in the outback and stolen food from farms to stay alive.

'We foiled his daring plan to get back home

that's for sure. He took a step too far when he foolishly approached you, Catherine,' Dallarup maintained. 'It'll be a court martial for him,' he suggested before turning to Mrs. Corby. 'Sorry to appear so rude, my dear but we had a hand in his arrest so to speak. If he wanted to stay on the run he might have had a chance. He might have continued to live rough if he'd not threatened Catherine here,' he told her. 'We wouldn't in normal circumstances have thought there was anything untoward. We wouldn't have taken any notice when we were returning from Brisbane and saw the fellow camping out. But Catherine here recognised him.' He put Mrs. Corby in the picture about the earlier event when the man had approached Cathy.

'Well, well, Miss Ellis,' Mrs. Corby replied addressing Cathy. 'I'd say you've had a lucky escape.'

Their subsequent journey direct from Port Macquarie back to Sydney took less time than Dallarup had reckoned. The roads were quieter and when he dropped Cathy off at St Peter's shortly after half past six he thanked her.

'I'd say we've had a successful trip, Catherine,' he told her. 'Take the morning off and I'll see you tomorrow afternoon.'

'Tomorrow afternoon?' she repeated. 'Are you sure I won't be needed in the morning? We have a lot of paperwork to sort.'

'That can wait. I'll be in the office late morning. I'm not prepared to break my neck. I need some time with my wife and I'd like to see the children before they leave for school. And of course, with Christmas coming up we'll need to start thinking about presents.' He handed over her suitcase, climbed into his car and said 'See you tomorrow, Catherine,' before moving away.

Cathy smiled to herself. She hadn't pictured Mr. Dallarup with a wife and small children. He always seemed so business-like, so super-efficient. But when she thought seriously about his possible age she supposed he was no more than fifteen years older than she was.

The minute she entered the house Dad dropped his newspaper, stood up and gave her a hug.

'You're back, and so soon treasure.' He held her at arms' length. 'How's it gone?'

'We've had a busy time of it but it's been interesting, and enjoyable. Mr. Dallarup said he couldn't have completed the work so quickly without me. How about that?'

Marjorie came in from the kitchen. 'I've said it all along, darling. You'd be an asset to any man.'

Not that again, Cathy thought. The 'any man' she was probably referring to would no doubt be Geoffrey Grant. She quickly changed the subject. 'And I don't need to go into work until tomorrow afternoon.'

'My, my, you must have done a good job. Good on ya!' Frank sat back down. 'By the way we had a visitor for you earlier today. Isn't that right Marj?' he called through into the kitchen where his wife was now making a pot of tea.

Marjorie appeared at the living room door shaking her head. 'Let the girl tell us the important things first, Frank,' she said, pulling a face at her husband. She turned to Cathy and smiled. 'I'd love to know all about the business trip. How did it go?' she said before pointing a finger in her husband's direction. 'And don't you start going on about something and nothing, Frank.' She folded her arms and waited for a response from her daughter.

But Cathy recognised the falseness of her mother's tone and she became suspicious.

'How do you mean, Mum? Who was the visitor, and why is it "something and nothing" as you call it? I presume you mean it wasn't important.'

The response her mother received was apparently not what she'd expected. 'Not in my book,' she replied, dashing back into the kitchen. She didn't tell Cathy who the visitor was or why, to her, it seemed irrelevant. 'The kettle's boiling,' she added and Cathy knew she wanted to skirt over the business of the visitor. 'I'll make the tea.'

But realising it was a deliberate ploy to withhold the information, Cathy didn't intend letting her mother digress. She needed to know who had called to see her and she needed to know right now. Hands on hips she followed her mother into the kitchen. 'Come on, Mum. Spill the beans!'

'It was only that young man, Tom I think his name was, the pom. He called today. I told him you were away on business.' She began to pour the tea.

Cathy couldn't believe what she'd heard. 'Tom's back here?' she asked.

'That's what I said.' Her reply was brusque.

'I can't believe it.' Her heart started to pound. 'How long is he staying here in Sydney? Did he say?'

'Just a few days from what I could gather.' She

didn't look up from what she was doing.

'And what else did you tell him? I hope you didn't put him off.'

'Not at all. I just said you wouldn't be back before he left Sydney, nothing more.'

'But I am back, Mum. And you did put him off. You weren't going to tell me, were you?' Cathy took a deep breath and sighed.

'Of course I was, if you'd given me a chance. And how was I to know you'd be back early?'

'But I *was* back early and you deliberately tried to put off telling me.' She frowned heavily. 'It was only when Dad mentioned it that I knew anyone had been.'

'Don't you start getting on your high horse with me, madam,' Marjorie told her.

'But I'm right, Mum. And if he's here for a few days I might see him if I go down to the Troc.'

'Not tonight, darling, surely,' Marjorie continued, now trying to appease the situation and slipping an arm around Cathy's shoulders. 'You must be tired and you've had nothing to eat. It's already seven o'clock.'

'I can be ready and round at Rita's by half past.'

'Really, you surprise me! If you go dashing down there tonight he'll think you're chasing after him.'

'Yes, mother, and you're right. I am – chasing after him I mean.'

'That's so cheap, Catherine, flaunting yourself like that! I'm disgusted.' Marjorie shook her head.

'But if he can chase after me I can do the same. What's the difference?'

'It's just not done.' Marjorie tutted loudly. 'I'm ashamed, Catherine.' She turned away.

'So you think I should let him go back to the ship and sail away never to be seen again?'

Frank pulled himself up from his chair and threw the newspaper down on the floor. 'Marj! Leave the girl alone. Can't you see she's jacked off? She's had a busy few days. She's entitled to some time off with her friends.'

'Friends you call them. She's only seen the lad a couple of times. She hardly knows him. And he's a Pom into the bargain. I don't want Catherine getting involved with him. She could end up at the other side of the world.'

'Marj, love! Don't you think you're jumping the gun? She only wants to see the lad. He hasn't asked her to marry him for goodness sake.'

Marriage! Cathy giggled at the very idea. That possibility hadn't even crossed her mind.

Marjorie huffed and continued to pour out the tea. 'I'm going to be pushed to have a meal ready before you leave, Cathy,' she said, shaking her head.

'Anything will do, Mum. Beans on toast if you like.'

'Beans on toast?' she repeated raising her voice. 'I'm not having people thinking all we can afford is beans on toast, young lady. You'll have what I make.'

Dad and Cathy exchanged a secret grin. They both knew how to get round her.

When Cathy eventually got away Rita had already left. But Cathy was confident she would find her friend.

Tom didn't hold out any hope of meeting up with

189

either Rita or Cathy. He'd already knocked that idea on the head. But he felt obliged to accompany Mike who was the closest pal he'd ever had. He neither wanted to let Mike down nor disillusion him.

It was still early and Segar's was almost empty when they arrived. Should they leave and head towards the *Trocadero* or should they hang around in the hope that Rita would eventually arrive? That was their dilemma.

'I'm sure it's Tuesdays when Cathy and Rita teach. That means Rita should be free tonight,' Tom said recalling the night he first visited the dance hall. 'And if you remember we arranged to meet at the *Trocadero* on the Wednesday when the girls were free. I think we'd have more luck there than here. What do you think?'

'I think you're right. I remember it was the night we set sail and we had to let them down. If we can find Rita she might be able to tell us when Cathy's due back.'

'Righty ho! Come on, pal. Let's get moving.'

The lights were dimmed and it was quite dark except for the coloured lights flashing from the glitter ball in the centre of the ceiling.

'I don't see either of them in here,' Tom moaned, tapping his foot impatiently. 'I think we're on a wild goose chase.'

'You're not giving it a fair crack of the whip, Tom. Have some patience,' Mike demanded. 'There's plenty of time for them to arrive. It's not even eight o'clock yet.'

Tom was in a mood. He looked down at the floor knowing he should lighten up but he was so disappointed. He'd been looking forward for months to seeing Cathy again and now when the opportunity had arisen she was away.

Mike poked a finger in his arm. 'Hang on, Tom!' He shot a look to the far end of the dance floor. 'Would you say that was Rita?' He pointed.

Tom pulled his thoughts together and, with a glimmer of light in his eyes, he stared to the spot Mike was indicating. 'I think you're right. But we'll have to wait until she's finished dancing with the Yank.'

'I don't know about that. Why should he try to work his charm on her? Let's at least go over there.'

Tom sensed his pal was flooded with jealousy. He followed Mike to the far end of the dance floor and they waited for the dance to come to an end. Eventually when it was over the American airman escorted Rita to the other side of the hall and held on to her.

'That makes it a bit awkward.' Mike stared across at them, a look of annoyance on his face. 'And I don't think she's seen us.'

'Let's move over to where they are and stand as close as we can. Surely if she sees you she'll excuse herself and come over and talk.'

'I don't know about that,' Mike replied sullenly. 'They could be together. But I suppose that's the best we can do,' he agreed.

The American airman had his arm around Rita and seemed to be talking non-stop. He had his back to them and all they could see were Rita's feet.

'He's all mouth,' Mike whispered obviously

resenting the American. 'He's nothing but a show off if you ask me.'

Tom sensed Mike was getting more and more rattled and the last thing he wanted was for his pal to cause a skirmish. But it was a tricky situation. He cringed when, seconds later, Mike plucked up the courage to approach Rita. He watched and hoped there would be no trouble as Mike passed by the airman and turned to face Rita.

Tom still couldn't see Rita's face but he saw two arms stretch out to greet Mike. And what a relief! At least she hadn't shunned him. But the American airman spun around, an angry look on his face. 'Hey you! Can't you see she's with me?'

Before Mike could make any sort of response, Rita stepped in. 'But, Joe. Mike is a friend of mine,' she said smiling up at him. 'And remember, you don't own me!' She took hold of Mike's arm and they moved away, the American airman still scowling after them.

Tom hung back for a while, giving the two a chance to talk in private. He was also intent on keeping an eye on the airman. The last thing he wanted was for a fight to break out. In a situation like this things were quick to flare up and they could do without trouble.

When he finally caught up with Mike and Rita he discovered the full story about Cathy's promotion and her trip to Brisbane.

'She should be home tomorrow,' Rita claimed, 'but whether she'll be out tomorrow night, I don't know. She could be tired after the journey back. But it's for sure she'll let me know as soon as she's back. There's not much I don't know about Cathy.' She laughed.

Tom was on the point of asking about the guy Cathy's mother had mentioned. He didn't have the guy's name but if there was any truth in Mrs. Ellis's suggestion no doubt Rita would know all about it. But he ran off the idea of asking. It wouldn't be fair to put Rita on the spot. It wouldn't be right to spoil it for Mike and Rita when they seemed to be hitting it off so well. And it occurred to him that, with any luck, he might see Cathy after all if Rita could persuade her to meet up with them the following night.

'Do you think you could get her to come down here tomorrow, Rita, that's if she's back? We've only a couple of days left and I'm so looking forward to seeing her again.'

'I'll try, Tom. It means I'll have to go round to their house after work and let her know you're here. Although I should know whether or not they're back. I'm sure Mr. Dallarup will call in the office before he goes back home.'

Tom was swamped with relief. If only Rita could pull it off, it would be a dream come true.

But there was no reason for him to stay at the dance hall now that he had the full story about Cathy's business trip. He was still worried about the other guy, the one with whom Mrs. Ellis had intimated Cathy was going steady. But surely, had there been any serious relationship, Rita would have been more guarded in her reply.

All he could do now was stay positive. After all, things had perked up since earlier in the day when he'd been given to understand Cathy wouldn't be back until after HMS *Resolute* left for the war zone.

'Then I'll leave the two of you together. I'm sure you've a lot of catching up to do. I'll get off back to the ship if you don't mind, Mike, now that you've found Rita, you lucky blighter!'

Mike grinned. 'Fair enough, pal. Let's hope your luck will change and you'll see Cathy tomorrow.'

'I'll say! See you later.'

Cathy took the tram into the city and in her haste she almost tripped on the cobbles in her high-heeled shoes as she headed for the *Trocadero*. She thought about Mum's version of Tom's visit. It had seemed garbled as though Mum hadn't paid attention during the conversation and it was obvious she still had her plans for Cathy to get together with Geoffrey. And although Mum had said Tom would be leaving in the next day or so, Cathy worried that he may have already left.

She was only yards away now from her first port of call, the *Trocadero*. She hoped upon hope that Tom would be there, but if he wasn't she'd decided to dash back to Segar's. Hopefully she would catch up with him at one of the two places.

There was a queue of servicemen when Cathy arrived and she waved to Flo in the ticket office and made her way through into the dance hall. She searched the floor for her friend but didn't spot her. It wouldn't have surprised her if Rita was already up dancing. The two of them had taught so many of the forces that, even on their nights off, they were constantly in demand.

The music stopped and Cathy was surprised

when she spotted Rita but she wasn't dancing. Cathy took a second look. Surely that was Mike beside Rita. But Tom didn't appear to be around. Her stomach churned. Don't say she'd missed him, worse still Mum had probably said something to put him off. Don't say he'd left with someone else. She sighed heavily. But she was sure if he'd taken the trouble to call at the house he wouldn't have deserted her, not so quickly. She tried to lighten up and she moved towards her friend, pulling her thoughts together when she heard Rita's voice.

'Cathy! I didn't expect you back until tomorrow.'

Cathy smiled. 'We completed everything a day early. I didn't arrive home until half past six.' She paused. 'Mum told me the ship was in. Apparently Tom called but I think she must have misled him, told him I wouldn't be back before your ship left Sydney.' She frowned.

'That's an understatement, Cathy. Mike here told me she said you were *spoken for.* Tom assumed you were more or less courting.'

'What?'

Rita began to laugh. 'That's what she told Tom. Isn't that right, Mike?'

'He was really disappointed when she told him that,' Mike assured her.

'I bet she still has hopes for you and Geoffrey,' Rita offered.

'You're joking! But, more to the point, where is Tom now?' Cathy looked around the hall.

'He left about five minutes ago.' Mike looked at his watch.

'Five minutes ago? I don't believe it. Why didn't I see him leaving when I came in?' She shook her head. 'Just my luck.'

Mike turned to Rita. 'I'm not leaving but I'll see if I can catch up with Tom.' He took her hand in his. 'Stay here won't you? Don't go away,' he begged.

'Don't worry, Mike,' Cathy replied. 'We're not going anywhere.'

Chapter 11

1943–1944

Mike dashed from the *Trocadero* and out into the open. There was no sign of Tom but he carried on running. When he turned the corner into Circular Quay he could see his pal making his way to the ferry ready to be taken across to Garden Island and the *Resolute*. Mike cupped his hands, put them to his mouth and shouted at the top of his voice. 'Tom! Come back.' But there was a strong wind blowing from the ocean and it was clear that Tom hadn't heard his call.

Now only yards away from the ferry Tom walked briskly along the jetty ready to board. Mike began to panic. If he didn't look sharp he'd miss Tom and that would complicate matters. He couldn't afford to board the ferry in case it pulled out of the harbour and yet he couldn't afford to leave Rita and Cathy hanging around waiting for him – yet again! He put on an extra spurt and almost fell as he neared the little jetty. When he heard the engine spring into life he realised the ferry was on the point of moving away.

'Quick! Don't go! Cathy's here,' he bellowed.

This time Tom heard Mike's cry. He turned and saw his pal rushing towards the ferry. It took a few seconds for the fact to register but if he'd heard the words correctly Cathy was mentioned. Filled with desperation to disembark he headed towards the ramp. But by this time a crewman was about to pull it away from the jetty. Tom stumbled towards him.

'I need to get off,' he said, raising his voice above the sound of the engine. 'Sorry but it's urgent,' he added and he dashed across the ramp towards Mike.

The crewman stared after him and shook his head. 'Crazy!' he called out.

Tom would have agreed. He'd almost fallen into the brink but as soon as Mike's words had sunk in, he just had to get back to dry land.

'Did I hear you right? Did you mention Cathy?'

'I did, Tom, and she's waiting to see you,' Mike offered, panting and trying to catch his breath. 'She turned up at the *Trocadero* minutes after you left. Thank goodness I've caught up with you. I couldn't afford to jump on the ferry and leave them behind.'

'I'll say,' Tom replied, a huge grin on his face. 'I'm glad you caught me,' he added and he patted Mike on the back. 'Thanks for that.' He swallowed. 'I can't believe my luck. How did she seem? Do you think she'll be glad to see me?'

'Slow down, pal!' Mike put an arm around Tom's shoulder. 'I'll tell you what. She was disappointed you'd left. She was almost in tears.'

'Really!'

'I'm not kidding you, pal. She can't wait to see you.'

'Did she mention the other guy?'

'She didn't get a chance. As soon as I realised she'd come down specially to see you I knew I had to do something about it. I made them promise to wait for me and I charged out of the place.'

By the time they left Circular Quay and set off at a run towards the *Trocadero* Tom's heart was beating double time, but not through the effort he put in to get to the dance hall at full speed, rather through his anticipation at the prospect of seeing Cathy again. And his heart began to race even faster when he spotted her at the other end of the dance hall. He couldn't believe his luck. All his hopes and dreams had come true in a flash. The minute she saw him heading towards her she ran into his arms.

'Tom! I thought I'd missed you,' she offered, laughing with absolute joy.

'I know what you mean, Cathy. I thought I'd missed you too.' He hugged her close. He desperately wanted to kiss her but not there. It was too public and the last thing he wanted was to spoil his chances. 'Let's go outside for a breather,' he suggested and Cathy knew without another word what his intentions were. She wouldn't have told him to his face but, after being apart for such a long time, she was looking forward to their first kiss.

As they passed through to the exit Cathy motioned to Flo in the ticket office that they would be back. She led Tom outside and round to the back of the hall. When he took her in his arms and pressed her against the wall his lips met hers. The kiss was soft and gentle to start but then it became more urgent and she sank into his embrace relishing the feel of his arms bound tightly around her and his whole body pressed up against hers. This was bliss. This was what she'd been waiting for over the past few months.

Tom relaxed and drew slightly away from her, holding her at arms' length. 'You don't know how much I've looked forward to that.' He placed his hands on her cheeks. 'You're my angel! I was worried you'd ignore me after what happened the last time we were together. I've spent months wondering if you'd understand and hoping I'd see you again to explain. Our ship was called out on an emergency and we had to leave for the war zone.'

Cathy looked into his eyes. 'I did understand eventually but not at first. I was disappointed and, to say the least, very much put out. But once we realised your ship had disappeared from the harbour we came to that conclusion realising it must have been something urgent for you to leave so quickly.' She smiled up at him. 'I've missed you, Tom,' she whispered shyly.

Tom sighed heavily. 'That's a relief. I thought when your mother mentioned you were more or less spoken for – a close friend she said – I was mortified.'

Cathy gasped. 'Mortified? I should think you were. How dare she make such an insinuation?

What exactly did she say?'

'Just as I said. You wouldn't be back before I left and her exact words were that you were spoken for by a close friend. I assumed she meant a family friend.'

'Wait until I see her!'

'If what she told me isn't true it might be better if you ignore it,' Tom suggested. 'I wouldn't like her to think I'd been stirring things up.' He paused and shook his head. 'I honestly don't think she's too keen on me, Cathy. She was quite abrupt when I called.'

Cathy frowned and blinked her eyes. 'I can imagine she would be abrupt. She's been trying to fix me up with her friend's son, Geoffrey for some time now. They've been cooking things up between them to try and get us together. He's a bank manager with prospects according to Mum, but talk about square. I wouldn't consider him if he was the last man on earth. And to top it all he's years older than I am.'

'Thank goodness you've rejected him.' Tom patted his chest. 'I was dreading the truth but now you've reassured me.' He slid his arms around her and held her close.

'Don't worry about Mum appearing to dislike you,' she whispered. 'It's probably because you're English. She'll get used to the idea.'

Used to the idea? Tom smiled to himself. What did that indicate? That things were looking up. Cathy obviously had her sights set on some sort of future together and so did he. But then a thought occurred to him. What would happen when he received his demob papers? Would she be willing to leave her family and return to England with him?

But he told himself to stop procrastinating. Things would be sure to pan out when the time came.

'Shall we go back inside?' Cathy asked him. 'I'd like a word with Rita if you don't mind.'

'Sure.' He kissed her forehead. 'That's fine now that we have things out in the open. I can't tell you how relieved I am that you still want to see me.'

'Of course I want to see you. My only hope is that you'll come back safe and sound when the war comes to an end.'

'Don't you be worrying about me, sweetheart. I know how to take care of myself,' he told her, thinking about the time he was captured by the Japs. He didn't intend telling her about that. She'd worry herself silly if she knew. It was best kept under wraps until the war came to an end.

They went back inside and Rita gave her a knowing look. 'I take it you've caught up,' she asked.

'Of course and we've cleared the air about Geoffrey,' Cathy replied, laughing.

Rita joined in the laughter and Mike turned to her.

'What's the joke?'

'Just something between Cathy and me about her intended so to speak,' Rita told him with emphasis on the word *intended*. 'Nothing important. The guy's a joke!'

Tom and Mike both grinned knowingly. 'OK then,' Mike offered. 'The music's just about drawing to a close. How about if we walk you home?'

'We'll have to think about it,' Rita joked but Tom had already put an arm around Cathy's shoulder and drawn her close.

They took a tram to St Peter's and as they neared Cathy's house she began to wonder if she'd done the right thing allowing Tom to come all the way with her.

'It might be an idea if you leave me at the end of the road, Tom. It's better if Mum doesn't see us together for now. I will have a word with her but I won't mention what you told me. I need to keep her sweet. I need her to be on my side. You do understand, don't you?'

'Exactly. I'm sure it would be better if we took it a step at a time.' They stopped and he kissed her once more before asking her about arrangements for Christmas. 'I don't suppose I'll see you during the holidays,' he asked.

'You'll see me on Christmas Eve if you and Mike are off duty. I can get you tickets if you let me know tomorrow night.'

'You mean I'm seeing you tomorrow?'

'If you'd like to.'

'If I'd like to? You're joking. It's a bonus seeing you two nights on a trot.'

'The *Troc* isn't open Thursdays but how about if we go to the pictures?'

'Good idea. Anything good showing?'

'There's Errol Flynn and Olivia de Havilland at the local in *Robin Hood*. That should be worth seeing.'

'Sounds great. It's a deal. Where do you want to meet up?'

Cathy didn't answer and he guessed she was toying with a possible meeting place.

'How about here at the end of your road?' Tom

asked tentatively.

Cathy nodded. 'I know it sounds a bit furtive not calling at the house for me but in view of Mum's negative comments I think it's a good idea if you don't call just yet.' Tom was aware her voice held a note of relief. 'But I'll work on her don't worry.' Cathy laughed in embarrassment realising it wasn't the way either of them wanted things to turn out but they needed to be comfortable with their relationship, and now wasn't the time to push things.

'That's fine by me, Cathy. I understand completely. I can't wait to see you tomorrow. And then Christmas Eve is my last day ashore. Christmas Day on the ship and then we head up north.'

'I can't bear the thought of you leaving, Tom.'

'Nor me, my angel. But I'll keep in touch.'

He wrapped his arms around her and kissed her soundly before turning and making his way back to the tram stop.

Cathy couldn't hide her excitement at seeing Tom again but she tried to curb her over-exuberance and stifle her grin when she entered the house.

'You're back at last,' Mum announced looking up at the clock on the mantelpiece. 'And not before time.'

'How do you mean, Mum? You seem to forget how old I am.' Cathy was adamant.

'Don't forget we're still your legal guardians.' She stuck her nose in the air and huffed.

'Come off it, Mum. I bet you weren't a saint when you were my age.'

'You know full well I was married when I was

203

your age.'

'There you go. You were married and I can't even have a boyfriend, unless it's Geoffrey Grant of course.' She folded her arms and threw out the challenge.

'There's no need for that attitude, Catherine. Your father and I had been courting for some time, hadn't we Frank?' she said aiming her question at her husband.

Frank nodded. 'That's right.'

'Then don't you think it's time you let me choose who I want to go out with?' Cathy shook her head. 'I'm not going astray, Mum if that's what you're thinking.'

'I didn't say you were. It's just that it's rather late coming home at eleven when you have to be in work early tomorrow.'

Cathy smiled to herself. Mum had certainly backed down after she'd challenged her about her own relationship at twenty. But then she started up again.

'I suppose you've been to that *Trocadero* place. I've heard it's quite rough. I don't know why you can't stick with Segar's.'

'How can you say that about the *Trocadero?* You're taking someone else's word for it. How would you know about any of the places when you've never been there?'

'It's the reputation of the place, that's all I'm saying.'

Cathy had heard enough. She'd been on the verge of mentioning the business of Mum intimating Geoffrey Grant was her 'intended' but she knew that would not be for the best, especially when she'd made Tom a promise.

She climbed into bed and she couldn't stop thinking about him. It had all happened so unexpectedly and so soon after she'd arrived back from Brisbane. But she must try to get off to sleep. It was important to be fresh and alert for work the following day ready to complete the report and the estimates. She was looking forward to the new challenge and she decided not to take the morning off. There were lots of things to get through and more organising to be done for Mr. Dallarup before the Christmas break.

The day went well and her boss was delighted with the report. But she needed to stay over a little later than normal to catch up on some of the work she'd left behind when they set out on the business trip.

By the time she'd finished and tidied her desk she realised time was passing by. Having arranged to meet up with Tom that evening it was important she arrive back home in sufficient time to change into something suitable for her date.

There was a long queue for the tram when she arrived in the city centre. If she'd thought things through carefully she would have made a move earlier and left some of the work until the following day. But her decision had been made and it was unfortunate she'd caught up with the employees of Mortimer's wool warehouse flooding towards the tram queue. Twenty-five minutes later she managed to climb aboard a tram and, with standing room only, she was the last passenger to squeeze inside.

Eventually the tram came to her stop. She

dashed along the road and waved when she saw Mum looking out of the window.

'You're much later tonight, Cathy,' was her mother's greeting. 'But we've waited until you were home before we had our meal together.'

'Thanks Mum. I've been trying to catch up on the work load I left behind when we went up to Brisbane. But I should have left a little earlier. I didn't account for the workers from Mortimer's. I should have remembered they left an hour after my usual time. The thing is I'm going out tonight.'

'You'll be worn out dashing about like you do, my love. Why not have a night in. We could relax and listen to the wireless together.'

'Sorry but I've made arrangements,' Cathy informed her before quickly changing the subject. The last thing she wanted was to have to admit she was meeting up with what her mother termed as *the Pom!*

Tom was waiting for her at the end of the road just as they'd arranged. Cathy looked around to make sure she was out of sight from Mum's inquisitive eyes before she ran into his arms.

'Glad you could make it sweetheart.' He looked at his watch.

'Sorry I'm a little late, Tom but things didn't quite go to plan.'

'Don't say you've had more grief from your mum,' he asked, a frown appearing on his face.

'No, nothing like that. I worked late and then I ended up queuing for the tram. It's been quite a rush but at least I've made it.'

'Don't worry. I would have waited all night as long as I thought you'd turn up.' He kissed her.

'How far away is the place you mentioned?'

'The Odeon? It's just around the corner. The film starts at eight.' Cathy looked up at the church clock. 'It's only a quarter past seven. There's a soda bar next door. How about if we call in and have a drink?'

'Good idea.' He took her arm. 'Come on, angel. Lead the way.'

Frank looked across at his wife. 'What are you making now, Marj! Surely it's not another dress for Cathy.'

Marjorie held up the delicate pink circle of crochet work. 'Nothing like that. But it is for Cathy; it's for her glory box. I'm making a set of mats for her vases and ornaments.'

'A set of mats for Cathy?' Frank questioned. 'But she has no vases and ornaments.'

'Not yet, Frank. But she's bound to get married sometime in the near future. Don't forget she's going on twenty now. She needs to make a start on her glory box.'

'But it was only the other day you were more or less insisting we were still her legal guardians and she should do as we say. You insisted she didn't stay out late and she didn't go out with that nice English lad. Let's face it, Marj, don't you think you're jumping the gun?'

'Not at all. And I meant every word I said. I wasn't the one who called him that nice English lad. That's your description. And for a start, how do you know what he's like? I don't want her going out with people we hardly know.' She picked up her crochet work. 'I'm not expecting anything too soon, Frank but I am making a start and getting things ready for her. Having said that I do hope she picks the right man in the end,' she insisted.

Frank smiled to himself. The *right man* was no doubt that dag, Geoffrey Grant, a right egocentric prig who hadn't an ounce of personality. He picked up his newspaper, sat back and began to read.

'It looks as though the war in Europe's coming to an end, love. All I can say is that it's a good thing. The trouble is it's all at our end now and it won't be over until we defeat the Japs. That'll be the day we can celebrate.'

'I'll celebrate when the boys are back home and the sooner the better as far as I'm concerned.' Marjorie didn't look up from her crochet work.

All was quiet for several minutes, the two of them sitting in comfortable silence and Frank continuing to read his newspaper. But their peace was disturbed by a knock on the back door.

'I wonder who that is?' Marjorie put down her crochet work, went through into the kitchen and opened the door.

What she saw startled her. Her mouth dropped open and she stood there staring at the young uniformed man before looking in horror at the envelope he was about to hand over to her. It was a telegram.

'Mrs. Ellis?' the young man said. 'For your husband,' he added and offered her the envelope.

She took it and turned it over in her hands. 'Thank you,' she mumbled before closing the door.

'Who is it, Marj?' Frank called through from the lounge room.

Completely dazed, Marjorie stumbled through the kitchen and stood in the doorway, 'It's a telegram, Frank.'

Frank jumped up from his chair and rushed over to her.

'Now stop worrying, treasure. We haven't opened it yet.' He took the envelope from her, slit it open and read the message in complete silence. When he looked up Marjorie could tell there was something wrong. She started to whimper.

'Calm down, love,' he offered, placing a strong arm around her shoulder and pulling her to him. 'It's Danny. He's been badly injured. He's in military hospital and they're operating tomorrow.' He swallowed hard. 'They may have to amputate one of his legs.'

'Oh my God! I can't believe it, Frank.' Marjorie burst into tears. 'Is he going to die?'

'Come on, treasure. Keep your pecker up. They're going to keep in touch with us.'

Marjorie looked up at her husband and then she slowly sank to the floor in a faint. Frank bent over her and struggled to lift her onto the sofa. He patted her on the cheek. 'You'll be fine, love,' he whispered. 'And you know what Danny's like. He'll never give in. He won't let anything get the better of him.'

Marjorie opened her eyes. 'I'm sorry I went to pieces, love.' She shook her head. 'It's such a shock.' She took a deep breath. 'And yes. You're probably right. I know exactly what you mean. Our boy will fight it.'

Frank took a handkerchief from his trouser pocket and dabbed the tears from her eyes. 'Come on. Let's be positive. He'll be out of the woods before we know it.'

Marjorie sat up. 'Let's hope so, Frank. Let's hope so.'

The film was about to start when they took a double seat on the back row of the cinema. Tom leant across and kissed her lightly on the lips.

'It's so good to be together, sweetheart. I didn't expect to see so much of you, especially with Christmas coming up.' He gazed into her eyes. 'What am I going to do without you? Three days and that's the end.'

'Let's not think about that, Tom.' Although Cathy knew she would feel exactly the same when he left for the war zone, she was looking forward to savouring their time when they could be together.

'But I can't help it. You know how I feel about you. You're on my mind day and night.'

When he put an arm around her shoulder she snuggled into his chest and she wondered what her mother would think if she saw them together like that.

When the lights were dimmed he turned her towards him, cupped her chin and tilted her face to his, pressing his lips to hers. The kiss started slowly and leisurely, continuing with no hint of desperation.

For Cathy things seemed to be happening in slow motion. It was a new experience. She'd never felt like this with anyone before and she closed her eyes, sinking into the kiss. It was the start of their emotional togetherness. Her senses were suddenly so alive and they spent most of the time completely wrapped up in each other.

When the final credits appeared on the screen Tom gently eased his arm from around her shoulder and turned to her.

'Great film!' he whispered.

Cathy started to giggle. She had the gist of the film but nothing more. 'Yes, I bet it was.'

He took her hand and led her out into the foyer. She blinked her eyes in the harsh light as they left the cinema walking arm in arm.

'By the way, what's the score for tomorrow?' Cathy asked him. 'Are you relieved of duties?'

'Fortunately, yes.'

'I'll ask Rita to pick up four tickets for the *Trocadero*. She has the day off tomorrow.'

'That'll be great,' Tom replied. 'But what now?' he asked, turning towards her. 'I take it I'll be leaving you at the end of the road.'

Cathy shook her head. 'Why should you?' she replied in rebellious tone. 'I don't see why we should carry on being furtive. Come on, Tom. Walk me home, right to the gate.'

'Are you sure? It won't cause any trouble for you if they see me will it?' Tom added, a concerned look on his face.

'It's not as bad as you think. Dad's OK about it. He likes you. He said so right from the first time he met you. Mum likes you too but she's frightened I'll get involved with someone who'll take me miles away from her. It's a joke isn't it, Tom?'

Tom nodded his head and returned a tight

smile. And Cathy could tell by the look on his face she was making light of their relationship whilst it was obvious that for him it was no joke.

'I didn't mean it the way it came out, Tom. I know it's not a joke as such, but Mum thinks too far ahead. Who knows what might happen in the future?'

'I know what I'd like to happen, Cathy.'

She looked puzzled. 'How do you mean?'

'I'm going to be truthful with you.' He stopped, turned her towards him and looked into her eyes. 'You're the one I want to marry at some time in the future. There's never been anyone else in my life like you. I love you, Cathy.'

Cathy felt the heat rising from her chin to her forehead. She was stunned by his words and, momentarily, she was stuck for a response.

'That's floored you hasn't it, sweetheart?' Tom smiled. 'I suppose I'm living in dreamland.'

'Don't say that, Tom.' She swallowed hard. 'I love you too.'

Tom threw his arms around her. 'You do? I'll never forget those words as long as I live.'

Chapter 12

1943–1944

The Christmas Eve celebrations at the *Trocadero* would be the last time they'd see each other until Tom was back in Sydney. Cathy would be spending Christmas Day with her family and there were plans for Tom and his pals to spend the day on board the *Resolute*. The ship would be sailing for the northern war zone on Boxing Day, and the thought of their separation continued to be a source of worry to Cathy. But there was nothing to be gained by agonising; negativity would cause even more anxiety, and she told herself it was time she accepted the fact and enjoyed what was left of their time together. She tried hard to cast all thoughts of his departure to the back of her mind and, although she knew she should be concentrating on the present, it was difficult.

With that in mind she cleared her head of those depressing thoughts and she drew strength from the positives. Hadn't Tom told her he loved her and hadn't she admitted she loved him too? Deep down, she rejoiced. In fact, she was so elated she had it in mind to tell her parents of her relationship with Tom. It was time they knew her feelings towards him. She loved him. She had nothing to hide.

She skipped up the garden path, determined to

213

take the plunge and let them in on her news. With a beaming smile on her face, she threw open the back door and bounced through into the kitchen.

But she stopped abruptly when she took in the picture of Mum and Dad sitting at the kitchen table, facing one another. From the grave looks on their faces Cathy knew something was wrong. Were they waiting to reprimand her?

It went through her mind that normally it was fathers who were strict, but Mum was the disciplinarian in their house. Cathy glanced at her watch. She wasn't late. And Dad was usually in bed by nine. It must be something serious for him to be up at this time. Perhaps she should put on hold her plan to tell them about Tom.

'I'm not late, Mum. It's only half past ten,' she announced.

Dad stood up and came towards her, placing an arm around her shoulder. 'It's not that, treasure,' he replied, a heavy frown on his face. 'We've had some bad news. Come and sit down.'

Cathy's stomach began to churn and she began to panic. Dad had mentioned bad news but surely it wasn't one of her brothers. Her eyes filled with tears at the very thought that something might have happened to one of them. On the other hand it could be Gran, although the last time Gran visited she seemed so lively and she could certainly talk for Australia.

Cathy held her breath waiting for Dad's explanation. 'What is it, Dad? What's wrong?'

'We've had a telegram. It's Danny. He's been badly injured. He came out of an aircraft into the ocean, shot down by the Japs. Mum and I are worried the surgeons may have to amputate one of his legs.'

Cathy fell to her knees in front of him and tears trickled heavily down her cheeks as Dad took hold of her hands.

'Oh, Dad. I can't believe it. Not Danny.' She shook her head. 'He was fine the last time we had a letter from him.' She jumped to her feet and stretched across to Mum. 'You must be out of your mind with worry, Mum.' She hugged her. 'This is exactly what we've all dreaded isn't it?'

Unable to hold back her tears, Marjorie nodded. She dabbed her face with a handkerchief and clung onto Cathy.

'What are we going to do, cherub? I can't bear hanging around waiting for them to get back to us. I need to know what's happening.' She turned to her husband. 'Can't we go and see him, Frank?'

'I doubt it, Marj. He's in Darwin. We all know the place is a danger zone.'

'But surely not now. That was some time ago. Two years or more.' She shook her head and sniffed. 'Don't you think it'll be safe to go up there after all that time?'

'It was a while ago. You're right. Point taken, love. And the allies are constantly on the lookout.'

'Then why can't we go?'

'There's more to take into account.'

'But you told me they've put a net across the harbour.'

'I know it's good protection against Jap subs entering Australian waters but Darwin is still a key port for the allied troops. Let's face it the Japs are still on the prowl. They'll stop at nothing.

What's to say there won't be another attack? An air attack.'

He shook his head and pondered. 'There's no way we'll be allowed to go up there, not with the government controls these days. Why do you think we've taken in evacuees from the Northern Territory? It's still a danger zone. They say controls are stricter than they've ever been.'

'But what about Danny? Where does that leave him? He can't defend himself.' Marjorie started to cry again.

'Look at it this way, Marj love. They'll do what's necessary and, as soon as Danny's out of danger, they'll fly him down here, I'm sure. There's nothing to be gained in keeping injured servicemen in a danger zone. There's a military convalescent home just outside Sydney,' he reassured her.

'All I want is to see him.'

'We all do, Mum. But we'll have to bear with it until we find out what's happening.' Cathy took hold of her mother's hands and squeezed them. 'And you know what Danny's like, Mum. He won't be beaten.'

'That's just what Dad and I have said.'

'There you go.' Cathy eased herself up from the floor. 'Right, Mum. Is there anything I can do? How about a cup of tea? That might calm your nerves.'

'Good idea, treasure,' Frank volunteered. 'And then we'd better get off to bed. It's no good moping around.'

Once they'd turned in for the night Cathy began to put things into perspective. Perhaps she should cancel her Christmas Eve ticket for the *Trocadero* and stay with Mum and Dad to give them moral support. She felt the tears spring to her eyes. From a selfish point of view it would be devastating missing Tom on their last evening together. She loved her brothers dearly but why did this have to happen just when she'd been so hyped up and looking forward to the Christmas Eve celebrations?

She was still undecided as to what she should do when she left for work the following morning. If there was no further news of Danny when she arrived home in the evening it wouldn't be right for her to go out celebrating whilst Mum and Dad were sitting at home worrying.

She tried to stop thoughts of her brother and the possibility of an amputation from constantly flashing through her mind. But it was no use guessing what might happen. She would find out when she finished work and arrived home. The main thing now was to make a determined effort and concentrate on her work. Her final report was almost complete when she felt a tap on her shoulder. It was Mr. Dallarup.

'Come along now, Catherine. You've done enough for today. There's nothing that can't wait until after the Christmas break. Get off home and see how things are.'

'Thank you, Mr. Dallarup,' she replied. 'I'm grateful for that, but I've almost finished this report. I can have it completed in a couple of minutes and then I'll leave.'

'That's fine but don't start anything else. Leave the report on your desk and I'll collect it later. You know, Catherine, family should always be your priority. Give my regards to your parents and tell them I'm sending up a special prayer for your brother.'

'That's very kind of you. I hope you enjoy the break with your family. I'm sure the children will be excited on Christmas Day and enjoy opening presents. A Happy Christmas to you all and I'll see you in the new year,' she added.

She collected her bag and left the office the minute the report was complete and, as she waited in the queue for the tram she couldn't take her mind off the dilemma she faced. She still hadn't decided whether or not she should cancel her evening with Tom at the *Trocadero*. But she must stop dithering. Mr. Dallarup was right. Family should come first. It was disappointing having to cancel but perhaps it would be for the best if she stayed back with Mum and Dad.

Decision made but the problem now was how to let Tom know she couldn't make it? The only solution would be to get back home and check out with Mum and Dad if there was any more news before going to Rita's house. Assuming Rita hadn't cried off going to The *Trocadero* herself without Cathy, she would ask her to pass on the message to Tom and tell him why she couldn't make it.

Her stomach churned at the thought of Tom eagerly standing there waiting for her. He'd be disappointed when she didn't turn up, she could vouch for that. But these things happen and at least he had said he would write to her. Cathy sighed. It would have been such a bonus if they'd been able to meet up for the last time before his ship sailed.

Frank finished work at lunchtime, the usual routine each year on Christmas Eve. Although it was traditional for him and his men to celebrate the festive season with a schooner of beer at the bar close to the market, the men didn't pressurise him into joining them knowing that he would be waiting for news of his son.

Both he and his wife were on tenterhooks all afternoon and it wasn't until sometime later when they had a visitor to the house that they heard more about Danny's condition.

There was a knock at the front door and, this time, Frank went through the lounge room and into the hall, pulling back the bolts and unlocking the heavy door. An officer from Danny's regiment was standing there. He held out his hand.

'I take it you're Mr. Ellis, father of Aircraftman Daniel Ellis?' he enquired briskly.

'That's right,' Frank replied warily taking the officer's outstretched hand.

'Warrant Officer Mackay,' he announced. 'I have an update on your son.'

'Do come in, sir.' Frank led the officer through into the lounge room where Marjorie sat nervously waiting for any snippet of news.

Mackay sat down and smiled. 'Don't worry, Mrs. Ellis,' he reassured her. 'It's rather better news than we anticipated.'

'Tell us more,' Frank said eagerly.

'As you know your son was shot down in the Andaman Sea by the Japanese but fortunately he was rescued by the allies.' The officer took a notebook from his top pocket and opened it up. 'Bear with

219

me will you? He wasn't the only one rescued from the sea that day and I need to make sure I have the correct details for your son.' He flicked through the pages. 'Fine, here we are. Aircraftsman Ellis. Your son has a very badly crushed foot and ankle and, considering the ligaments and the muscles themselves were very badly torn and some of the bones of the foot, ankle and lower leg were either broken or splintered, the medical team thought initially that his injuries would be irreparable. Your son has had an emergency operation. The surgeon has made a start, worked on the injuries and he's managed to put things back together on a temporary basis.'

He turned over the page. 'But there is more to do. I'm sure you'll understand the difficulties. In layman's terms we all know the foot is a mass of tiny bones and the ankle is a complex joint, all of which are likely to present difficulties. However, at the present time, the decision to amputate mid-calf has been put on hold.'

He referred once more to his notebook. 'To keep you fully in the picture I want you to know we've transferred your son closer to home where he'll be constantly monitored. The orthopaedic surgeon down here, a foot and ankle specialist, is to perform a second operation later today, hopefully with more permanent results if that's possible. Professor Bates is a top surgeon, he knows his stuff, and there isn't anyone better in the whole of Australia.'

Marjorie perked up at the news pulled herself up in the chair. 'That's good to know. But where is Danny now?' she asked. 'Will we be allowed to visit him?'

'He's in the military hospital on the outskirts of Sydney. Give us a couple of days and we'll be in touch again. It'll probably be Boxing Day before he's settled and ready for visitors.' He smiled. 'I'm sure you'll be relieved to know his condition may not be as bad as we thought and hopefully the amputation can be avoided.'

'Thank God for that,' Frank replied. 'I take it you'll let us know when we have permission to visit.'

'Indeed we will, Mr. Ellis.' He stood up and tapped Marjorie on the back of her hand. 'Keep your chin up, Mrs. Ellis.' He smiled and went through into the hall.

Frank and Marjorie followed him through.

'Thank you so much, officer for coming here and letting us know what's happening,' Marjorie offered, now looking much brighter than she did before the officer arrived.

'It's all part of the job, Mrs. Ellis and I can tell you it's not always pleasant. But this time we need to stay optimistic. Let's hope the amputation isn't necessary.' The officer nodded as he opened the door and stepped outside. 'You can be sure I'll be in touch,' he concluded.

Frank closed the door behind him, heaved a sigh of relief and put an arm around his wife. 'There you go, Marj love. It's not as bad as we thought.'

'I know Frank but judging by what the officer told us, Danny will be lucky to even walk again.'

'Don't get too downhearted.' Frank squeezed her shoulder. 'As the officer explained we have to be optimistic. You know I have a gut feeling

Danny will be fine as long as they can save his leg. He might have a bit of a limp but he'll work on it, and that's better than losing your leg. We all know how strong he is and we can't dispute the fact that he's a fighter.'

Marjorie put on a brave face and smiled. 'I know, love, I know.'

Cathy stepped off the tram and hurried along the road. Her spirits rose when she came towards the house and passed the front window. Mum was looking out, probably waiting for her return, and it seemed she had a smile on her face, a weak one but it was there.

Dad was waiting for her in the kitchen when she opened the back door and stepped inside. 'I'm glad you're back. It's better news, treasure,' Dad told her, a spark of optimism in his voice. 'Your Mum has the colour back in her cheeks after what the officer told us.'

'The officer?' Cathy repeated.

'That's right. Warrant Officer Mackay called to see us this afternoon.' Dad slipped an arm around Cathy's shoulder and led her into the lounge room.

'Come and sit down. We'll tell you all about it.'

Cathy had to admit Dad was right when she saw Mum. Looking one hundred per cent better than when Cathy left for work that morning, Mum sat with her hands folded on her knees. 'We're so relieved he might not need the amputation,' she told Cathy and, between them, they spelt out their conversation with the officer.

Eventually Dad said, 'Let's hope all goes well in

the next forty-eight hours.'

'Now that he's back down here we'll be able to visit,' Mum added. She kept a straight face but she lifted her voice as though to acknowledge the inevitability of it. 'But not tonight. It'll probably be Boxing Day before they'll allow us in there.' She stood up and went into the kitchen. 'We'll have a cup of tea and try to relax,' she offered. But then she turned and frowned. 'I only hope our prayers will be answered.'

'We'll stay positive, Mum,' Cathy responded, 'and by the way,' she called through into the kitchen, 'Mr. Dallarup sends his regards and says he'll be saying a prayer for Danny.'

'Now that's really kind of him,' Mum asserted. 'I've always thought he was such a gentleman.'

'That's right, Marj. We thought just that when he called to ask permission for the Brisbane trip.' He turned to Cathy. 'I expect you've made arrangements for tonight. You can't let Christmas Eve go by without some sort of celebration. Not at your age.'

Cathy was surprised at his comment. 'I had arranged to go to the *Trocadero* with Rita but I thought maybe you'd like me to stay back in view of what's happened.'

Mum came in from the kitchen shaking her head. She seemed to have pulled herself round considerably. 'You'll do nothing of the sort. We don't want you missing out, cherub. Don't worry about us. We'll be fine. The last thing we want is to stop you from having a night out with your friends on Christmas Eve.'

'But, Mum, are you sure?'

'I am sure,' she stressed. 'There's nothing more we can do now until we hear from the officer again.'

'Your mother's right. You get off out and enjoy yourself.'

Cathy took a deep breath. She had to come clean. And now was the time. She couldn't hold back her feelings any longer.

'I had arranged to meet up with the English sailor, Tom Crossley.' She looked across at Mum. 'I know you're not keen, Mum but he does think a lot about me and I like him too. And he's not like some of the forces. He's really considerate.' That was a weak description of their feelings for each other but it was an indication of their togetherness. She held her breath and waited for Mum's reaction.

Mum didn't start or look up in dismay, nothing like that. She handed her a cup of tea. Cathy was stunned. She'd been waiting for the usual insults about Poms.

Mum took a sip of her tea before she commented. 'After what's happened to Danny, life's too short to have grudges my love. You go and enjoy yourself.' She paused, placing her cup and saucer on the little coffee table. 'But tell the lad he'd better not get any ideas about taking you back to England with him!' She smiled but Cathy knew she meant what she'd said.

Cathy put down her cup and threw her arms around Mum. 'You're a star, Mum. You know I would have stayed back if you'd wanted me to.'

'Yes I do,' she replied. 'And I know Danny's not out of the woods yet but things do seem more promising. Let's hope for the best.'

'We know how much you think of your brothers and how much you care. Make the best of Christmas Eve, treasure. And let us do the worrying.'

After the conversation with her parents and in the knowledge that the evening out wasn't scuppered after all, Cathy went into her bedroom. Whilst she dallied in her preparations to be ready on time for her evening with Tom she hadn't decided what she would wear. She opened up the wardrobe and picked out the pale blue strapless dress with matching bolero, the one Mum had made for the work's Christmas party the previous year. The dress had a fitted skirt that crossed over in a flounced drape from the waist down and showed off her curvy figure. She checked her appearance in the mirror before she left and the thought went through her mind that it still looked good. And the bonus was that Tom hadn't seen her in it before.

Now much more relaxed and ready to leave she seemed to be in a dreamy state. The image of Tom in his full uniform floated before her and a delicious tingle bombarded her from head to toe. But she took a steadying breath and managed to infuse some control into her body before leaving her bedroom.

'Rita's Dad ordered us a taxi,' she said as she stood looking out of the front window waiting for it to arrive.

'That's real kind of him,' Mum announced.

The taxi turned up at seven o'clock sharp and Rita was sitting in there smiling and obviously excited. When Cathy left the house Mum and Dad stood at the front door waving them off.

'Enjoy the celebrations,' Mum called after her but not without adding her usual comment, 'but don't be too late will you, Catherine?'

Cathy nudged Rita. 'Wouldn't you know it,' she whispered, replying to Mum, 'Of course not, Mum.'

She told Rita the news about Danny. 'I thought I'd have to cancel. I was going to come to your house and ask you to give my apologies to Tom. Fortunately Mum and Dad felt I should stick to our plans.'

Rita gave a heavy sigh. 'That was nice of them. I'm really glad they did. It would have put me in a bit of a predicament going on my own. Dad wouldn't have liked it, especially when he'd ordered the taxi for the two of us. But I'm really sorry to hear about Danny. I hope he pulls through.'

'Me too. And I know what you mean about going on your own. But we're lucky the way it's worked out.'

When the driver pulled up outside the *Trocadero* Cathy took a deep breath, opened the taxi door and stepped out. Her gaze went to the front of dance hall and the first person she saw was Tom standing there waiting. He rushed towards her and when they came face to face his eyes lit up to an azure glow.

'You look absolutely gorgeous,' he said and by the hungry look on his face, he was obviously taking in every curve of her body.

She shot a measuring glance in his direction and

her lips trembled. 'You're looking good yourself in your uniform.' She smiled up at him adoringly.

'Thanks for the compliment,' he said jokingly and laughed. But seconds later he appeared rather pensive and a frown furrowed his brow.

'Are you all right, Tom?' Cathy asked.

'I'm fine,' he returned, now smiling. 'Just something that came to mind.'

He was probably thinking the same as she was thinking, about his departure in a couple of days' time. But then he took her hand and led her towards the foyer. Rita and Mike followed.

The dance hall was already busy when they entered and Tom led her to one of the small tables down the side.

'What would you like to drink, Cathy?'

'I'd love a Babycham,' she replied.

'Sit down and I'll order.'

He came back from the bar with the drinks and when their eyes met he held her gaze for several seconds. She couldn't believe how her heart began its rapid tattoo when he stretched out his hand and placed it over hers.

'You have no idea how much I've been looking forward to this moment.'

'Me too but I nearly didn't make it.'

'Why's that?'

'It's my brother, Danny. He's in the RAAF. We had a telegram yesterday telling us he'd been badly injured. Worst of all they added that they may have to amputate his leg mid-calf.'

'Oh no! What a nightmare for him! And for you and your parents too. It's terrible news and such bad luck.' He shook his head and frowned at the gravity of the situation. And when he saw her eyes shiny with tears he added, 'Are you sure you should be here with me?' He paused. 'Obviously I don't want you to leave, but I would understand.'

'That's kind of you. Tom and I did offer to stay back with Mum and Dad but they wouldn't have it. They gave me their blessing and said they wanted me to try and enjoy the evening despite the bad news. I did tell them about us, you and me. I was surprised when Mum said it was all right but she added the proviso that you mustn't even think of whisking me off to England.'

Tom began to laugh. 'Not that again.' He pondered. 'But you must agree it will need serious thought when we decide to marry. You realise I've left my sister and younger brother behind. I would like to see them again and make sure they're comfortable. After that, I don't know what to think.'

It was Cathy's turn to laugh. 'I see. You've already decided to ask Dad for my hand in marriage I take it. It's not *if* but *when* we decide to marry.'

'That's right. I'll go down on bended knee as soon as I'm demobbed.' He took her hand in his.

Cathy continued to laugh but she knew Tom was right. They would have to come up with a mutually agreeable decision at some point in the future. But not just now. She supposed she was burying her head in the sand. She knew how Mum would react if they chose to move to England. In fact, despite his explanation about his sister and younger brother, Cathy wasn't sure she wanted to move so far away and yet...

She dithered. 'Is that so,' she said, trying to sound lively. But the very thought of being with him for life had her legs turning to jelly. She pulled her thoughts together and, unable to stop herself from becoming excited at the idea, her mouth curved into an embarrassing smile. 'You certainly know what you want, Tom.'

'I do although I was being spontaneous, nothing more. I haven't even thought things through seriously myself,' he added. 'But you're right, angel! All I know is that I want you.'

And Cathy wanted him too, that was for sure.

'How did it go at work today? I suppose it was difficult to concentrate knowing your brother was injured.'

'I coped but I couldn't help thinking about Danny. I thought about us too and wondered if I'd ever see you again. I was in a dilemma, that is until they told me an officer came to the house late afternoon and gave them more hope.'

'You mean an officer from Danny's regiment?'

'Yes. He told them they'd moved Danny nearer home. The good news is they may not need to amputate after all. It's a waiting game. We'll just have to pray they can sort his injuries without having to resort to that.'

'I must say that's a better outlook.'

'That's the way we're looking at it. Fortunately Mr. Dallarup gave me permission to leave at lunchtime. He said there was nothing urgent and that I should get off back home and find out how things were. He's really kind. I left but I felt really tired.'

'Probably the stress and the worry. But we

don't have to do every dance if you don't feel up to it.' He grinned.

Cathy smiled at his response. But after a couple of drinks her tiredness seemed to drift and when the resident orchestra played a waltz Tom turned to her.

'This is a slow one. I'm sure it won't be an effort for you.' He grinned. 'How about it?' he asked and, before she had the chance to reply, he pulled her into his arms and swept her on to the floor, lifting her hands to his shoulders and wrapping his own around her waist. She felt him drawing her close, pulling her to the full length of his body. She could feel his heat permeate hers and her excitement soared as she inhaled the masculine scent of his skin. When she rested her head against his chest she became lost in the sensation, the feel of the hard planes of his body and the very maleness of him. They kept in time without speaking but unspoken messages seemed to drift between them. And when the dance ended they held hands and sat down at the table again, gazing into each other's eyes. It was such a heavenly sensation just the two of them together, Cathy never wanted it to end.

Tom had the urge to take her in is arms right there in the dance hall. But he was aware he must control his feelings and keep them on the surface. Otherwise things would get out of hand. He smiled to himself. At least they were in a public place where nothing could come of those unruly thoughts chasing through his mind and the reckless desires flooding his veins. The more he tried to control his feeling the more he realised he needed to rein in his emotions completely. The last thing he wanted was to embarrass Cathy.

When the celebrations were coming to an end, despite his heavy heart at the thought of their separation Tom took her hands in his and said gently, 'I haven't enjoyed myself so much in a long time.' He looked away wistfully before adding, 'I need to get you back home now. It's Christmas Day tomorrow and we both need a good night's sleep – separately of course.' He laughed and rolled his eyes exaggeratedly. 'I'm joking,' he said after seeing the naive look on her face.

'I know you are,' she replied and he was aware she had accepted the fact that he was merely trying to amuse her, and that was his intention, his way of teasing her. 'But it's not like when we were kids is it and we had to be in bed early because we'd be up at the crack of dawn next morning eager to open our presents,' she added, grinning and trying to make light of the situation before they parted.

Tom laughed. 'I know what you mean. We would sneak downstairs at some ungodly hour to see what was waiting for us under the Christmas tree.' His mind went back to those early days when he was a kid. The three of them accepted they were poor and didn't expect much. 'There wasn't much in our stockings, maybe an apple and an orange for each of us, a Dandy Annual for me, a toy car for Billy and gloves and scarf, knitted by Grandma of course, for Dorothy. Yet it was exciting. The annual was usually getting dog-eared by the time I'd read it time and time again before I went back to school after the Christmas break.'

His mind flicked back to the present and when they reached the gate to Cathy's house they stopped. Cathy turned to face him. 'Thanks for a lovely evening, Tom. I'm so sad it's come to an end.'

Cathy saw that look appear on Tom's face but only fleetingly and she knew he felt the same. He took her hands in his and drew her close. When she looked into his eyes his intent was clear to read. It was then she felt the first brush of his lips against hers, his kiss light at first but it lasted for some time. As it became more intense a floating sensation came over her and she felt she could lose herself in his arms his kiss had affected her so much. No man had ever kissed her like that and she'd never felt this way about anyone, that is until Tom came along.

She opened her eyes and returned to reality, gently pulling away. After swallowing hard she tried to hold back her tears. 'I can't bear to see you go. I'm really going to miss you, Tom,' she confessed.

He wrapped his arms tightly around her and kissed her for the final time.

'Me too, precious,' he told her. 'Let's hope the war will come to an end, and soon.' He looked into her eyes. 'I'll be back, don't worry,' he promised. 'You will wait for me, won't you?'

'You know I will,' Cathy declared, but letting him go wasn't easy. She clung to him and, when he turned and left her standing there she was speechless with tears. The one thing she couldn't bear was the thought of anything happening to him. And her mind was filled with turmoil when he walked away. He didn't turn around and she stared after him until he disappeared.

All she could do now was try to fill the emptiness until she could feel his closeness again. She sent up a silent prayer. *Please, God keep him safe!*

Chapter 13

1943

Misery seemed to surround them once they were on board even though Christmas Day was looming and more celebrations would be underway. But the men had been ordered to stay on board. They would be leaving early the following day and it was crucial everything went to plan.

Some of the guys were late boarding the ship and Roberts reprimanded them but the captain gave some leeway in view of the season of goodwill.

But that didn't help Tom. He couldn't stop himself from moping the minute he left Cathy standing at the gate. He wanted to run back, take her in his arms and whisk her away. He could cheerfully have absconded with her. But he was no deserter and he disciplined himself. He didn't look back again.

He wasn't the only guy on board the *Resolute* who looked down in the dumps. Mike and many of his pals were no better; they were pining for the girls they'd left behind in Sydney.

'How did it go, Mike? Cathy was in tears when we parted and quite honestly I wasn't much better. I had to pull myself together sharpish or else everyone on the tram would have thought I was a bit of a cissy!'

Mike laughed at his words. 'What a picture, you roaring your head off on the tram! But I know what you mean, pal. Rita was upset but she cheered up when I asked her to marry me,' Mike whispered. 'It went down better than I expected.'

'You've asked her to marry you?' Tom shook his head in disbelief. 'You've actually proposed to her? And so soon?' he replied, unable to take in the news.

'What could I do? I had to make sure she'd wait for me. You never know what happens when you leave. But I look at it this way, as long as they know you're coming back for them and they've given a promise, they're not going to entertain anyone else surely.'

'I take your point, Mike. I hope you're right. But has she agreed?' Tom added.

'Not only has she agreed, she's coming back to England with me when the war is over.'

'Wow! You've got onto that quickly enough. Do her parents know?'

'Not yet, and I've a feeling she won't mention we're engaged. Hopefully if the war is over soon and we're ready for demob, she'll be going on twenty-one. She can make her own decision then.'

'Believe it or not I've done the same but not officially. I told Cathy one day I'd like to marry her but there was nothing formal about it and she didn't give me a reply.' He pondered wondering if he'd made a mistake by not making it an official proposal just the way Mike had done. But on balance it was early days and he thought it might have been premature. One thing at a time he told himself. It was only a couple of days since she'd mentioned to her parents she was seeing him. And he hadn't completed his National Service yet. The one thing he was confident about was that Cathy was sincere when she promised to wait for him.

When he thought about the issue of where they'd live he felt uneasy. That could be a sticking point, a major problem. As far as he could gather England wasn't exactly where she'd choose to settle.

He shut his mind to that eventuality. There was no knowing what the future might hold. And in a way he felt Mike was jumping the gun asking Rita to go back to England with him. What if she couldn't settle? But that was their business, not his.

When the men assembled on deck on Christmas morning it seemed strange that the temperature was over thirty degrees and the sun was shining. Back home it was always cold outside but if they were lucky they occasionally had a white Christmas.

There were two envelopes for Tom when the purser distributed mail to the men.

Mike looked across at Tom. 'You lucky blighter! There's just the one for me.'

Tom smiled. He couldn't wait to open them. He knew one was from Dorothy but he couldn't make out the handwriting on the other. It was neatly written in a young person's style. He opened that one first and smiled when he saw it was a Christmas card from Billy. The words inside the card read:

Happy Christmas Thomas. Looking forward to seeing you soon. Love from your brother Billy. Xxx

The envelope also contained a school photograph of Billy. Tom stared wide-eyed. He couldn't believe how his brother had grown. But thinking about it, Billy would be eleven now.

Tom couldn't help himself. A tear sprung to his eye and he quickly wiped it away. Now he knew he must see both Dorothy and Billy once his time in the navy was over.

He stuck his thumb under the flap of the one from Dorothy and read it through quickly at first before reading it more carefully.

Dear Tom,

I wanted you to know the good news and I thought Christmas would be the best time to surprise you. George and I are getting married soon and we have chosen the end of March so that George would benefit from the tax relief. It seems to be the done thing these days for couples to marry before the end of the tax year 5th of April. We've booked St. John's Church where Mam and Dad married, but of course unlike them we're hoping our marriage will be permanent.

(It had been two years since Dorothy had told him George Swanwick had proposed to her and that they were getting engaged.)

We've saved up enough for both the wedding and for some pieces of furniture that we can call our own to replace some of the old stuff left by Mam and Dad. I don't think theirs was new when they bought it and if you remember it was quite shabby even when you left home but we've decided to take it to the second hand shop up the road in the hope someone might be desperate. We'll not only be getting rid of it but who knows we might get a few bob for it even though I must admit the stuff is ancient. George says he'll decorate the living room if he can get his hands on some decent wallpaper. He's decided to flush the doors too when we have a bit of money to spare.

Auntie Alice had saved up some clothing coupons for me so that I can have a wedding dress made up. Do you remember Lilian Baxter who was in your year at school? They reckon she's quite a whizz at dressmaking and she's promised to make the wedding dress for me.

Billy is doing really well at school and working hard. You wouldn't believe the difference in him since Dad passed away. We told him he'd have to pull his socks up and you know he's always looked up to you Tom. Well, he passed his scholarship to go to grammar school and what do you think? George bought him the uniform. He looks a proper Bobby Dazzler in it. You'll realise he's the only one of us to have brand new, not like when we started school and had to have second hand.

The weather here is cold and they say we may have snow at Christmas. Billy will love that. He's looking forward to sledging on the moor.

There isn't a great deal more to tell you from our end. We all hope things are going well for you and that you're keeping safe. We do worry about you, Tom and it would be lovely to see you again, and the sooner the better.

I know you must be in the thick of it over there but

if you get a chance, please get back to me. We're all wondering where you are and what's happening at your side of the world.
All our love,
Dorothy, Billy and George

So Dorothy and George were finally going to marry. At least Billy would be well cared for, and it was certainly a turn up for the book George Swanwick buying the school uniform. Tom had always regarded George as a bit of a penny-pincher. At least he had that reputation. All he could think was that George must be so besotted with Dorothy that he wanted to impress by spending money on Billy. On the other hand he could be totally wrong in that direction. Perhaps he was being small minded labelling George as a skinflint. And Billy was a likeable kid. George probably thought a lot about him. When all said and done Tom had to admit to himself it was good of George.

Before he took the envelopes down to the cabin he read the letter through a couple of times and it gave him a good feeling inside. He put the card on display together with the photograph of Billy which he proudly admired. It was a pity the mail hadn't arrived a couple of days earlier when they were still docked at Garden Island. He would have enjoyed showing Cathy the photograph of his young brother.

The captain was all for letting his men relax as much as possible on Christmas Day, although Tom still had to take a shift manning the communications room. And when it was time for the evening meal the galley steward excelled himself and did them proud by serving a traditional Christmas dinner of roast turkey with all the trimmings followed by Christmas pudding and rum sauce. It went down wonderfully well even in those high temperatures. But it was Christmas and that was their traditional way of celebrating. The men sang, told jokes and generally tried to pull themselves out of the depression they'd felt when they'd boarded the ship the previous day.

When Cathy let herself into the house after leaving Tom behind she was relieved that all was quiet. Mum and Dad had gone to bed although she could hear someone moving about. They were probably restless and that was understandable. Until they'd visited Danny at the military hospital and spoken to him they would still be worrying. And of course they may have been listening for her to return from the *Trocadero* before they could settle down for the night.

At least she didn't have the third degree about how the evening had gone. Worse still she might have burst into tears when she told them Tom had returned to the ship for the final time, destined once more to head up north to the war zone. But realising either Mum or Dad might wander into the lounge room to make a final check she hastened into her bedroom and closed the door behind her.

Tiredness must have come over her quickly because no sooner had she slipped into bed than she fell into a deep sleep. But when she awoke on Christmas Day her stomach began to churn. The

239

first thing that sprung to mind was Tom's imminent departure from Sydney.

She tried to cast the thought from her mind especially now that she could hear someone up and about in the kitchen. It was Mum who knocked on her door and came into the bedroom with a cup of tea and a biscuit.

'Happy Christmas, cherub! There you go.' She gave a heavy sigh. 'I know we're all waiting to hear about Danny but Dad reckons we have to try and carry on as normal. It won't help any of us to get through it if we go around with long faces all day. So I reckon we'll open our presents as soon as you're up and about.' She bent over and kissed Cathy on the cheek.

'Thanks, Mum. Happy Christmas to you too. I know how you must be feeling and it's good of you to put on a brave face. I'm looking forward to opening our presents. I'm sure it'll take our minds of things and cheer us up,' Cathy replied, lightening her voice so that Mum wouldn't suspect how depressed she felt not only about Danny but about Tom's departure too.

Cathy drank her tea and tried to ease her depression by having a soak in the bath. When she went into the lounge room Mum was busy in the kitchen. There was so much happening later in the day. Gran and Mum's sister were due to arrive and Mum had food to cook.

'Happy Christmas, Dad,' Cathy offered.

'And to you, treasure,' he replied and to Cathy's relief he only asked a cursory question about Christmas Eve. 'I take it you had a good night,' he continued.

'Yes. The *Trocadero* was just about packed, Dad. I enjoyed it very much.'

Mum came in from the kitchen. 'We didn't wait up for you because I knew I'd have a lot on my plate what with Gran and Auntie Doris coming for the day. But we heard you come in and lock the door,' she said. 'I've just about prepared everything so let's open our presents.'

'I didn't expect you to wait up for me, Mum. Did you have a decent night's sleep?'

'I slept on and off but I won't be at ease until I've seen Danny.'

Cathy nodded. 'I know, Mum but try and settle down today. I'm sure we'll be able to visit tomorrow.'

They sat in the lounge room and Mum passed Cathy a parcel.

'This is from me and Dad. I do hope you like it,' she said, smiling and eagerly waiting for Cathy to open it.

The present was a lovely hand embroidered blouse in lilac which Mum had obviously made. Cathy was delighted. 'Wow! This is gorgeous, Mum. It'll go a treat with my mauve skirt.' Mum beamed proudly. 'I'll wear it tomorrow for Segar's,' Cathy told her. 'Rita's going to be so envious when she sees it. Her mum doesn't sew, knit or crochet. Her gran does but she's not up to date. Not like you, Mum. You're more a trend setter.'

'I suppose she's a bit like Gran. And thank you for the compliment, Cathy but I'd hardly say I'm a trend setter.'

'You do accept the new fashions, Mum. And I remember exactly what Gran said about short

241

skirts and dresses.' Cathy said laughing and Mum joined in the laughter.

'Well she is in her eighties, love, so we'll excuse her.'

Cathy took a couple of small parcels and gave one each to Mum and Dad.

'There you go.'

She'd bought Mum chocolates as a special surprise having saved her coupons especially. For Dad she'd bought cigars, the ones he always chose for celebration days like Christmas. Her second gift was an ornament Mum had been admiring for months in Bailey's shop a few streets away.

'You know exactly what I like, cherub. I'm going to enjoy these chocolates. And the figurine is lovely. It's funny because I've been hoping it didn't sell. I was disappointed when I passed the shop the other day and noticed it wasn't in the window.'

'Ha-ha Mum. You didn't suspect I'd bought it then?'

'Not at all but I will treasure it.'

Dad's second gift was a silk tie Cathy had had her eye on for ages. He slipped it around his neck and tied a Windsor knot in it to show her how it looked.

'There you go,' he said, posing dramatically.

'You are funny, Dad but yes, it looks good.'

He folded the tie and put it back carefully in the box. 'I'll wear it this afternoon when Gran and Auntie Doris come, and after that only for best,' he told her. He turned the box of cigars over in his hands, admiring it. 'And I'll smoke one of these after the meal.'

When Cathy opened her second present from Mum and Dad she almost burst out laughing. She pulled away the tissue paper. It was a set of place mats in a delicate pink colour.

'For your glory box,' Mum insisted. 'You have to start somewhere.'

Wasn't it coincidental that Mum had crocheted the mats for her glory box when Tom had said he wanted to marry her? Was that an omen? Not that Mum knew anything about that. But when she made the mats the idea of a glory box probably triggered off thoughts of Geoffrey, certainly not Tom.

'These are just what I would have chosen, Mum. And as you say I have to start some time.' She looked admiringly at the mats. 'You do me proud.' She leant over and kissed Mum and Dad before taking the presents into her bedroom, placing the blouse on a coat hanger ready for Boxing Day.

By late morning Gran arrived accompanied by Mum's sister, Doris and her husband Albert.

'It's been a treat coming in Albert's car, Marjorie,' Gran said pointedly doing her usual comparisons and giving Dad a withering look.

But Cathy knew Dad could take her comments with a pinch of salt and she giggled when he winked. Although Mum always defended Dad when Gran made these pointed comments, she merely shook her head and went back into the kitchen. This wasn't the right time to be causing friction.

She had the meal ready by mid-afternoon and they feasted on jumbo prawns in a delicious sauce, a large tossed salad with a tasty dressing and baby new potatoes.

'You certainly know how to cook, Marj,' Doris offered, forking a prawn and lifting it to her mouth. 'I've always said so. You never fail to come up with something tasty.'

'Thank you for the compliment, Doris. Yes, we thought it might be nice to have the prawns. And it is traditional on Christmas Day. Frank has a mate in the fish market. They help each other out when things are scarce. That's the advantage of being in charge you know,' Marjorie bragged.

'I know what you mean, Marj. Albert does the same with Walter Gibbins down at the yard. It's tit for tat you know.' She paused, frowning. 'I didn't like to mention it because I know how upsetting it must be but we were sorry to hear about Danny. When do you think you'll be visiting?'

'The officer said probably tomorrow but we'll have to wait and see.'

'Tell him we're thinking about him won't you, love and hope he has a speedy recovery.'

'I will, Doris,' Marjorie offered. 'I'm trying not to think about it too much.'

When Mum and Dad went into the kitchen to wash up after the meal, Doris leant over and whispered in Cathy's ear, 'Betty told me she'd spotted you outside the *Trocadero* last night canoodling with ever such a handsome Pom. I'm surprised, Cathy. Do your Mum and Dad know?'

'Yes, they do know about Tom. But I didn't realise Betty was at the *Trocadero*,' Cathy replied. 'I certainly didn't bump into her, although the place was just about full to capacity.' She tried to stop herself from sounding irate and she frowned, annoyed her cousin had misled them. 'And it wasn't anything like canoodling,' Cathy protested. 'Tom had his arm around me, nothing more.' But it was obvious that by the look on Aunt Doris's face that she believed Betty's version rather than Cathy's. It was to be hoped Aunt Doris didn't try to dob her in to Mum and Dad with her twisted version.

When Mum came through from the kitchen she went to the cupboard and took out a pack of cards. 'Game of cards anybody?'

Dad, Doris and Albert joined Mum and played cards whilst Gran listened to the wireless. By this time Cathy had heard enough of the four of them trying to out-brag one another and Gran chipping in with irrelevant comments. She was also still seething at the comment Aunt Doris had made.

'If you don't mind I'll go to my room. I'd like to start reading the book Gran bought me for Christmas.' Once she started reading the book, *Little Women* by Louisa M Alcott, she managed to free her mind of Tom for a while. And she was so engrossed in the story she didn't hear Mum calling out to her. But then the door to her room opened.

'Didn't you hear me, love? Rita's here to see you,' Mum said popping her head around the door.

Cathy jumped off the bed. They didn't normally see one another on Christmas Day. It must be something important, hopefully nothing depressing. It was always a family day. Cathy was puzzled. 'Would you mind asking her to come in, Mum?'

When Rita entered the bedroom she was all smiles and it was obvious to Cathy she was wrong. 'Come on,' she said smiling back at her friend. 'I know you've got something up your sleeve.'

'I couldn't wait to tell you' Rita whispered. 'I had to make an excuse to come and see you. I told them I'd left something in your handbag last night and I wanted to collect it.'

'Oh dear. That's naughty of you.' Cathy put her hand to her mouth and giggled. 'Don't be putting off telling me. What is it?' she asked excitedly.

'Mike has only gone and asked me to marry him.' Rita's eyes shone with delight. 'He's given me a ring.' She held out her hand. 'The stone is quite small but he says he'll buy me a better one when he has a chance to look around. But I told him I didn't want another one. I love this one. It's one his grandma gave him for good luck and he wore it on a chain round his neck. I feel so honoured that he's given it to me. I only hope his luck doesn't run out. What do you think?'

'It's beautiful, Rita and so dainty. What did your mum and dad say?'

'I haven't told them. Not yet. And they haven't seen the ring.'

'You mean you're only wearing it to show me?'

'I hang it on my silver chain when I'm home.'

'I presume you've said yes!' Cathy continued.

'Of course.'

Cathy threw her arms around Rita and hugged her. 'That's a lovely Christmas present isn't it?'

'I'll say,' Rita offered.

'But where will you live, Rita? I hope you're not going to settle in England. You're not going to leave me are you?'

'I have said I'll go back to England with him,' Rita confessed.

'Your mum and dad will go spare.'

'I know but look at it this way. When I'm twenty-one I can make up my own mind.'

Cathy didn't mention that Tom had talked about marriage. She didn't want to spoil the occasion for her friend. And he hadn't made it official. He hadn't actually proposed. But what worried Cathy most of all was the thought of leaving Australia.

Chapter 14

1943–1945

On twenty-sixth of December the *Resolute* left Garden Island and sailed north to join the Eastern Fleet. They anchored and waited for further orders. When British aircraft carriers came into the area the allies carried out a series of air strikes against oil targets in Sumatra. The *Resolute* provided air-sea rescue facilities during those bomber attacks.

'How long do you reckon we'll be here?' Mike asked Tom. 'You seem to get a whiff of things before anyone else.'

'It goes with the job as you know. I'm not supposed to hear but sometimes I get the gist of what's happening.'

'Have you heard anything?'

'From what I can gather reading between the lines we'll be here a few weeks but I'm not exactly sure and I don't know what the orders are. I've a feeling we'll be moving closer to Burma afterwards. The allies over there are up against the Japanese. The buggers are everywhere.'

'I know and it doesn't surprise me, not after what happened before with the sub.'

'We were lucky on that occasion,' Tom said. 'Surely nothing like that will happen again.'

'Let's hope not. I was luckier than you. At least I didn't have to put up with the ordeal,' Mike replied.

'It sure was an ordeal. I thought I was a goner all right. We were lucky to be rescued.'

Once they were anchored the weeks seemed to pass slowly. Tom was right in his forecast. The crew of the *Resolute* remained in the area and picked up British and American airmen shot down by the Japanese. Some of the airmen had unfortunately died before they hit the water, but others had ditched their aircraft and were still alive. They were transferred to another hospital ship and when the *Resolute* eventually left and embarked on the passage closer to Burma they were met by hostilities and ordered to stand off once more.

'At least the Japs have launched air attacks,' Tom announced. 'Let's hope there are no subs in the area.'

'I doubt it.'

It was an air-sea rescue effort. More victims were transferred to the hospital ship before they left on their next passage when they headed for Palau Island in the Pacific Ocean off the east coast of

The Philippines. This time it was a different story.

'There's an American Base there and they need allied forces for search and rescue,' the captain informed his men. 'The waters might appear beautifully calm but we're up against Japanese submarines in the area again. You know the score. You'll all take shifts on watch duty and be particularly vigilant.'

But despite the men's extra caution when they were on lookout duties a torpedo hit the *Resolute* before they reached Palau Island and they were left limping to the nearest small island where they hid in a quiet cove. On inspection the engineers concluded the ship needed urgent repairs.

But there was another major problem too. When the captain entered the communications room, the grave look on his face told Tom they were in big trouble. And he knew the reason why. He'd been trying to get through to the rest of the fleet for the past seven hours but to no avail. The ship had unfortunately lost all communication.

'Unless we can get the lines fixed, Crossley, we can't move from the cove. We're stuck. We need to know what's happening out there. We don't want another torpedo hitting the ship.' He pondered. 'Can you think of anything else we could try to get communication back? I know it's a tall order but if we're completely out of contact with the rest of the fleet there's no knowing what might happen.'

'I'm aware of that, sir but I've had no joy so far.'

'The trouble is that the bilges are gradually filling. Although the hole in the hull is quite small it won't take long for us to become unstable. We need to get somewhere pretty soon and get it fixed before it causes more problems.'

'I think it might be an idea to get Scottie to help. Maybe we can fix the switchboard between us,' Tom offered.

'That's the ticket, Crossley. I'll get Duncan down post haste.'

Tom and James Duncan, the ship's electrician nicknamed Scottie, worked tirelessly and after hours of trial and error tactics they managed between them to repair the switchboard.

'Hallelujah,' Scottie cried out when they made contact with the fleet. 'We've done it. Two brains are better than one.'

'That's great. I know the lines are still a bit shaky and the conversation tends to break up but at least we've made contact.'

Once they were convinced they were out of reach of the Japanese submarines, they left the cove and managed to continue slowly to the American Base on Palau Island where the ship was finally repaired.

They were still in the area in June when the Imperial Japanese Navy was defeated. Their losses were heavy and by September the *Resolute* was deployed for diversity operations close to the Nicobar Islands.

'Surely it's going to end soon,' Mike ventured.

'Let's hope so. We've gone nine months without a break!'

Frank and Marjorie had no plans for Boxing Day except that they were waiting to hear from the military hospital to find out if they could visit Danny. It was late morning when Cathy saw a military vehicle draw up outside their house.

'I think there's someone here now, Dad,' she called through into the kitchen.

Frank dashed into the lounge room and looked through the window. 'That's him. That's Warrant Officer Mackay right enough.'

When the officer knocked on the door Cathy answered.

'Do come in,' Cathy said, opening the door wider. The officer stepped into the hall and remained standing.

'Sorry to be so late, Mr. Ellis but I'm doing the rounds,' Mackay informed them. 'We have three patients who live in Sydney but it so happens their families are at opposite ends of the city.'

'Isn't it typical,' Frank said as he invited the officer into the lounge room. 'Do sit down, sir,' he said.

'Would you like a cup of tea,' Marjorie offered.

'Thank you but I can't stay. I have another visit. But I wanted to let you know your son's operation has been successful. He's pulled through and it seems there are no complications. The professor is extremely pleased with the outcome. So let's keep our hopes up.' He turned towards the hall ready to leave.

'Are we allowed to visit?' Marjorie asked seemingly holding her breath.

'Sorry, I thought you would have taken it for granted, Mrs. Ellis. But yes. Visiting is three o'clock until four.'

After the officer left Marjorie busied herself making lunch and then she dashed into the bedroom to change ready for the visit.

'He was a bit late letting us know,' she announced, shaking her head. 'We'd better make a move otherwise visiting will be over by the time we arrive.'

'Stop fussing, love. We've plenty of time.'

'But there's a limited tram service on Boxing Day. They're only running every two hours.'

'Is that so?' Frank replied. 'If that's the case, we'd better get a move on.'

Marjorie was right and fortunately the tram was a couple of minutes late otherwise they would have missed it.

But by the time they reached the city centre Marjorie was shaking.

'I'm so worried Frank. What if the doctor decides Danny needs the amputation after all? I can't imagine how he'll feel. He's so used to being active.'

'You're jumping the gun again, Marj. As far as we know things are going well,' Frank assured her.

'Dad's right, Mum. Stop whinging. Everything will be fine. And we don't want Danny thinking we're worried, even if we are. So let's try to cheer up.' Cathy linked her arm through Mum's.

'Mum's not whinging, Cathy. She's naturally worried.'

'I know, Dad but I'm trying to lighten things. Worry gets you nowhere.'

Mum squeezed Cathy's hand. 'I suppose you're right, Cathy. I'll pull myself together and try to put on a brave face.'

They had the best part of a mile to walk after they left the tram behind and most of the way it was uphill. Cathy strode on ahead whilst Marjorie, who'd recently put on a little weight claiming it to be 'middle-age spread', clung on to Frank.

'I didn't think it was this far, Frank,' she said slowly coming to a halt and catching her breath.

'We're nearly there,' Frank replied doing his best to coax her along.

Once at the hospital the sergeant approached them. 'Sorry, sir, but it's my duty to vet all visitors,' he said. 'I need some sort of identification.'

'That's fine, sergeant,' Frank replied as he handed over the telegram they'd received informing them of Danny's injury. 'Will this do?'

The sergeant nodded and waved them through.

Danny was in a side ward and at first they barely recognised him. His face was badly swollen and Cathy's first impression was that everything about him looked damaged. But she told herself it wasn't surprising. He had come out of an aircraft and he would have hit the ocean with some force. She gulped in air knowing the three of them had to be strong. She gave Mum a warning look that told her she must compose herself and put a rein on her emotions.

It seemed Mum got the message. 'We're here, darling,' she whispered, smiling and taking his hand. 'It's so good to see you. We'll stay for as long as they'll let us.' She swallowed hard.

At the sound of her voice, Danny opened his eyes, stared hard and scowled. 'Don't bother putting on a show on my account,' he said, his voice raised as he stared up at Marjorie, obviously detecting the wariness in her eyes. 'I can do without your false smiles, Mother. And I'm not in the

253

mood for visitors.' He sighed heavily. 'I didn't want you seeing me like this.' A shutter came down over his eyes and he turned his face away.

Cathy had the impression anger was coursing through him and she was disappointed at his reaction. A cold fist clenched inside her and squeezed when she thought about what had happened to Danny. He must be feeling so weary after his ordeal. But she was reluctant to accept his words. They were insulting especially to Mum.

Cathy told herself she must stay calm, for Mum's sake more than anything and, although she wanted to speak her mind, tell him he was being rude, she took his hand and whispered.

'You know you want to see us, Danny. We're your support team, always have been.'

Mum took his other hand to her lips and kissed it. 'We were desperate to see you – after all you've gone through.' She rubbed the back of his hand now. But he tugged it away again.

Cathy kept her gaze on his. It seemed fury was still bubbling up inside him despite her words. He glared back wide-eyed before staring up at Marjorie and mumbling through clenched jaws. 'You don't know shit,' he exploded impatiently, his voice distant and amazingly cold.

'Look here Danny, you can stop that language in front of your mother, I won't have it!' Frank's mouth trembled but he remained calm. 'You've never used it in front of any of us before and this is not the time to start.'

Cathy's head was aching fit to burst and her stomach felt raw from all the churning. But she was determined not to give in. Mum and Dad were so caring and Danny had no right to be rude to them.

'That's not very nice when all Mum and Dad have been thinking about over the last couple of days is you,' Cathy stressed pointing a finger towards him, 'and only you.'

'Well they needn't have bothered.'

Mum seemed to calm her nerves and assert herself.

'You can't get rid of us like that, darling. We're sad and upset, but you're still our son and we love you with all our hearts.' She bent over him. 'All we want is to get you back home so that we can look after you.' Her eyes were trained on his. The shadows of pain in his eyes were clear to see.

He shrugged and then he scowled at her before looking away. 'You would say that wouldn't you – just to try and make me feel better,' he scoffed. 'But it doesn't cut with me.'

Cathy stepped forward again and, with a determined effort, she scowled back and continued, matching his acid tone.

'You can stop that right now. Mum and Dad deserve more. All you're doing is feeling sorry for yourself.' She trembled slightly. She wasn't used to reprimanding anyone, especially her older brother but she needed to be strong and firm.

'Yes I am feeling sorry for myself! So what?'

Cathy braced herself. 'That surprises me, Danny. You've had the best surgeon in the land and your operation has been a success and here you are moaning. If we'd known you were going to be so grumpy we would never have come.'

He closed his eyes. 'Well you know what you

can all do!' he shouted. 'You can bugger off.'

It seemed however they approached him he couldn't snap out of the mood. Marjorie stared in disbelief and opened her mouth to speak but Frank interjected.

'I'm not going to tell you again, son. We're not here to put up with your language. You can either pull yourself together or we will leave. And it'll be the last time we'll visit,' he threatened.

'You can't say that, Frank,' Marjorie cut in.

'I've just said it, love and I'm not backing down.' He turned back to Danny. 'Now, son, what exactly happened and what are your injuries?' His voice was firm.

'You must have been told I was shot down,' he replied sulkily, 'and I've had an operation on my foot and ankle. And if you must know the pain's killing me. Whether I'll ever walk again without a limp God only knows.' He looked his father in the eyes. 'Any more questions?'

Aware that, for today, there was nothing more they could do, Frank decided to call Danny's bluff. Surely he'd come round eventually.

'If that's the way you want it, fair enough. We'll leave you to it.' He beckoned to Marjorie and Cathy, tipping his head towards the door of the ward. Reluctantly he turned, tight-lipped and left. Marjorie and Cathy followed. And once they were far enough away Frank turned to them. 'He'll come round just you wait and see.' He smiled a brave smile. 'We'll come again tomorrow. He'll soon change his tune.'

Cathy looked across at Mum who had that hurt look about her.

'Come on Mum,' she offered. 'I suppose that's how they all react after what they've gone through. It's obvious he's frightened he won't walk again without a pronounced limp. But we know the stern stuff he's made of. He'll pull through.'

'Cathy's got it in one,' Frank said as he placed an arm around Marjorie's shoulder. 'He's plenty of time to think about what he said. He'll regret his words. And apart from the swollen face and a few bruises I'm sure he'll cope fine.'

Frank smiled to himself when the ambulance drew up outside the house. Danny had spent less than a week in the military hospital and already he was being discharged. He struggled with two crutches and the medics gave him no help but they followed him up the few steps and into the lounge room.

'There you go, Ellis,' one of the medics said to him. 'It might be a struggle to start with but you've got the hang of the crutches now. We'll be back for you next week for physio. Keep it up. We want to see an improvement by then.' His voice was firm. 'And don't forget you're needed back with the unit so don't be getting any ideas about settling down and giving in.'

They left and for a while Danny remained quiet. But then he shook his head. 'I suppose they're right. That's the only way I'm going to beat this.' He looked up at Frank and grinned. 'And I will beat it don't you worry.'

'That's the ticket, Danny. We knew you'd fight it.'

Within the next two months Danny was back walking without his stick. He was determined to work hard to try and disguise the limp.

Cathy was proud of her brother. 'I'll tell you what, Danny. No-one would ever know you'd been shot down and survived through your injuries. You've made a wonderful recovery.'

'I couldn't let Dad get away with thinking I was a wimp, could I?'

Frank laughed. 'I never said you were a wimp, son but I can use a bit of that psychology stuff or whatever it's called. I think Cathy takes after me.' He turned to Marjorie. 'Don't you think so, Marj?'

'I'll say, and not only that she's really matured in the last few months. I know you've always thought of her as your little girl but she's a woman now Frank.'

Frank sighed. 'I know love but she'll always be my little girl.'

'That's until the right man comes into her life and she has her own little girl, or little boy of course.'

'I'm still enjoying life too much, Mum, to think about getting married,' Cathy retorted smiling to herself and knowing what Mum was thinking. But all Cathy could think about was Tom. Would he ever come back into her life again?

Cathy occasionally stayed in bed for an extra hour on Saturday mornings whilst Mum was out shopping. And now she lay there thinking about Tom and she began to fret. Six months had gone by and she hadn't heard from him. She'd written more than a dozen letters but up to now she'd not had one reply. At the back of her mind was the fear that something sinister might have happened to him. But surely if that were the case and her letters had reached his ship, someone would have opened one of them and contacted her. The other possibility was that the ship might have sailed back to England in which case it would be some time before he could afford to make his way back to Australia, if that was his intention. But surely he would have written to her.

She needed to get up out of bed. All she was doing was adding to the confusion by allowing these possibilities to flash through her mind and trouble her. She walked through into the bathroom and decided to take a quick bath before breakfast. Maybe afterwards she'd call in at Rita's house to make arrangements for the evening.

She'd been up for about twenty minutes and was having breakfast when a knock on the front door startled her. She stared at the clock. It was not yet nine. She peered through the window but all she could see was a shadowy figure standing inside the porch. She went through the lounge room and looked through the glass door panel. The person standing there was surely Jim Warrender from the market. That was strange. What did he want? Her hand froze when she took hold of the doorknob, and a ripple of concern appeared on her face. The light fluttering that began in her stomach quickly became a heavy churning sensation when she took a deep breath, opened the door and saw the look on Jim's face. Something was wrong. His face reflected both gloom and sorrow. Her heart jolted in her chest.

'Is your mother in, Catherine?' he asked, his voice wavering slightly.

'No,' she stuttered in no more than a whisper, anticipating his words with a feeling of dread. Was it about Dad? Had he been involved in an accident?

'When will she be back?' he asked.

'I'd say she'll be home in the next half hour. Is there something wrong, Mr. Warrender?'

'I really need to speak to your mother. Can I come in and wait?' Without a word, Cathy opened the door wider. He stepped inside and followed her into the lounge room.

'Sit down, Mr. Warrender. Mum won't be long I'm sure.' By now Cathy knew it was something serious. She was disappointed Jim didn't think fit to tell her. She resented the fact that he probably still regarded her as a child. 'Would you like a cup of tea?' she asked him.

'That would go down a treat, Catherine,' he replied.

The next couple of minutes seemed like a couple of hours as she put on the kettle and waited for it to boil. Just as she was pouring the water into the teapot Mum came blustering through the back door with a heap of shopping.

'What a lovely surprise to be met with a cup of tea! You must have known I was on my way.' She plonked the basket on the kitchen table and let out a heavy sigh. 'Well I'm glad that's over and done with. You know...' she started but Cathy interrupted her.

'Mum, sorry to butt in but Jim Warrender's here. He's in the lounge room. I think something's wrong.'

'How do you mean?'

'I think we'd better go through and ask him.'

Cathy carried the cups of tea on a tray and Jim stood up when the two of them went through into the lounge room.

'Sit down, Mrs. Ellis,' he said gently. 'I'm afraid it's bad news.'

Bad news! The words clawed at Cathy's brain. She was so on edge she could hardly mutter a word. She placed the tray on the coffee table.

'I'm sorry to have to tell you this,' Jim paused and cleared his throat, 'but Frank's had a heart attack. He's down at the infirmary. I don't know how bad it was. All I know he collapsed when he was supervising the unloading.'

Cathy tried to swallow but a lump gathered in her throat and slammed it shut. Devastated, she slipped her hands over her face and pressed her fingers over her eyes. Surely not Dad! He was as strong as an ox. And now, dreading Mum's reaction, she couldn't bear to look up. But she must try to steel herself and overcome her emotions. She had to be strong for Mum's sake. Her heart was racing now as she tried to brace herself for the worst before he continued. She turned to Mum who was staring ahead blankly and didn't seem to be taking in Jim's words.

There was an ominous silence before, rigid with tension, Mum sat down heavily on the sofa. Stiff-backed, she perched there on the edge. Still no words came from her lips but then her body began to shake, anxiety filling her eyes and the colour gradually disappearing from her already pale cheeks. It seemed she couldn't maintain control.

'Don't panic, Mum,' Cathy said. 'We don't know the extent of it. Come on we'll go down and see what's going on.'

Mum's face was a mask of shock, terror and disbelief. Rubbing her hand over her mouth hysteria took over. And before either Jim or Cathy had the chance to continue, Mum opened her mouth. What started as a squeak developed into a full-bodied scream. 'No, no.' Her words echoed through the room followed by harsh sobs. Her legs buckled beneath her and she staggered forward, reeling and slipping from the chair. She went down hard on both knees.

Jim took hold of her and helped her back on to the chair before bending over and gripping her shoulders. 'Breathe!' he implored. Cathy stood there motionless whilst Mum sucked in air and exhaled. 'One more time,' he said, still holding her and angling his head so that her eyes met his.

Tears began to steal down her cheeks. 'Is he going to die?'

Cathy took a deep breath knowing Mum was sensitive and worried so much, always thinking the worst. She reacted in exactly the same way she had when she heard about Danny's accident.

Jim crouched down on his haunches until his face was level with Marjorie's. 'Fortunately he is still alive, Mrs. Ellis, and I'm sorry I can't give you any more detail.'

But Mum seemed too desperate, too unhappy to listen to reason and Cathy, her stomach was now tied up in knots, wondered if Jim was covering up the truth. She watched Mum swallow hard, her eyes wet and red now.

Jim turned to leave. 'I'd better get back now. Why don't you get yourselves down there and find out exactly how Frank is?'

Mum grimaced and replied in between sobs. 'Sorry, Jim, but it was such a shock when you told us. We'll get ready and go to the infirmary. Thank you so much for coming.' She tried to calm herself. 'All I want is to see him.'

'I'm sure you do. Take care, Mrs. Ellis. And let's look on the bright side,' he urged, patting her hand. 'Hopefully with your help he'll make a full recovery,' he added, now trying to lift his voice and emitting a tone of optimism.

Cathy closed the door behind him, staring into space and rubbing away the tears with the heels of her hands.

'Jim said Dad was still alive, Mum. That's the main thing. We need to keep that thought in mind and not dwell on anything else,' she said. 'He'll be fine,' she added, trying to convince herself of that.

It was late morning by the time they arrived at the infirmary. Having made enquiries at reception they followed the corridor to the cardiac ward. Cathy knocked on sister's door and it opened almost immediately. The ward sister, a middle aged woman with a cheerful smile asked if she could help.

'My husband, Frank Ellis was admitted early this morning. Is it possible for us to see him?' Marjorie asked.

'Of course, my dear, but do come in and I'll explain what's happening.' She waved her hand and invited them through into the office. 'Do take a seat,' she offered.

Aware that Mum was feeling nervous, Cathy took hold of her hand as they sat down opposite sister.

'First of all let me tell you that Mr. Ellis has improved dramatically since we admitted him. The consultant reckons the people at your husband's workplace did the right thing when they realised there was a major problem. They had the common sense to call the ambulance immediately and that meant we were able to start treatment.'

'That's a relief, Sister,' Cathy replied. 'As you can see Mum's been beside herself with worry.'

'I can imagine but, of course, there are no guarantees that it won't happen again. But it wasn't a major heart attack and, with a change of lifestyle, the odds can be improved.' She pondered. 'Tell me, Mrs. Ellis, has your husband been under a lot of stress recently?'

'I'll say. We've all been stressed after what happened a couple of months ago. Our son who's in the RAAF was shot down from his aircraft and he landed in the ocean. Fortunately he was rescued but he was badly injured. Worst of all we were very worried he might need an amputation.'

'Oh my goodness, Mrs. Ellis, you have been through the mill.'

'But going back to what you were saying earlier, Sister, what do you mean by a change of life-style?' Marjorie enquired.

'First of all he needs to lighten the load, physically I mean. He tells us he's a supervisor and he starts work at five in the morning and finishes sometime around one o'clock. That's fine but

264

apparently he's recently stayed behind and done extra hours in addition to some of the physical work, lifting and carrying, which is quite a strain on the upper body and which he tells us is not part of his contract.'

'We've been telling him that for months but he takes no notice. He laughs it off.'

'I've a feeling he won't be laughing it off any longer. The consultant has told him in no uncertain terms that it must stop.' She paused and smiled. 'You see he's at a vulnerable age, Mrs. Ellis.'

'Is there anything else we can do to help?'

'There certainly is. Your husband is slightly overweight. He needs to cut down on some of the fatty foods. Don't worry we'll give you a diet sheet.' She stood up. 'Now I suppose I'd better let you see him. Follow me.'

Sister led them down the corridor and into the ward. Cathy spotted Dad straight away and she dashed over to his bed.

'I don't know Dad, Mum's been a bundle of nerves worrying about you. As though we haven't had enough with Danny and now you.' She smiled and kissed him on the cheek.

'Oh Frank, it's so good to see you. We've been worried sick.' Marjorie took his hands and kissed him gently. 'But I'll tell you what; you're going to do exactly as I say once we get you out of here.'

'I see, and what makes you think that?'

'We've had our instructions from Sister.'

'She can be a right old battle-axe!' he chipped in but his smile told her he was exaggerating for effect.

With a sense of relief Marjorie sighed. At least Frank was back to his old jokey self, an indication that surely he was on the mend.

Chapter 15

1945

It was the end of February 1945 and the *Resolute* was still in the Pacific but there was less activity now that the Japanese Navy had been defeated. Tom was becoming more optimistic by the day that the war would soon end in victory for the allies. And although the sense of fear amongst the men was slowly diminishing during their time in the Pacific, the captain reminded them that the war was not over yet.

'We've been warned that Kamikaze aircraft have damaged some of our British Pacific Fleet ships.' He took a long pause. 'And those ships have sustained casualties. Some of our men have been killed. In view of these spasmodic Japanese air attacks we need to stay vigilant. Don't forget the war still remains to be won,' he stressed.

After the announcement there was a buzz of activity amongst the men, some discussing possible tactics, other forecasting what the future might hold. And when Tom was relieved from duty he went up on deck. He lit a cigarette and pondered over the captain's words. Like the rest of the men he felt the war had gone on too long and he couldn't wait to make his life his own once more, especially knowing Cathy was waiting for him in Sydney.

When he looked up he noticed Mike leaning over the rail, obviously taking a break after a long spell in the galley. Mike turned and came up beside him. 'It's so good to get a breather after being cooped up down there,' he admitted.

'I'm sure it is. I don't know how you can stand the heat in the galley. It's bad enough down in communications,' Tom replied, patting him on the back.

'You get used to it after a while.' He frowned. 'I'm longing for the time I'll be with Rita again. I was beginning to think we were in the clear. It was a shock hearing about the Kamikaze attacks. Have you heard anything more?' he asked.

Tom looked around to check no-one was listening and then he whispered, 'I've heard it on the grapevine that after our attacks on the Japanese oil installations, there's a massive fuel shortage. After the allied blockade they reckon the Japs have no chance. But that was just the captain talking with some of the other fleet bigwigs.'

'I suppose he could be right but we still need to watch it. You never know with the Japs what the buggers are up to,' Mike replied.

'You're right there. I know the captain mentioned the Kamikaze air attacks in his announcement but if there is a shortage of fuel surely it's going to put a stop to their invasions.' He shrugged and shook his head. 'But I think the captain's given us the hard word to stop us from being complacent. I realise we have to be wary and all I'm telling you is just what I've overheard. But I have to admit it does make me feel easier knowing things will have to stop without fuel for their aircraft.'

'I'll say...' Mike's words were interrupted by the purser.

'Lightowler,' he called. 'Mail,' he added, handing Mike a bundle of letters.

Mike stared hard and grinned. 'And not before bloody time.'

'You lucky blighter,' Tom said looking enviously at the bundle of mail.

But then, turning to Tom, the purser passed him an even thicker wodge of mail.

Tom stared hard at the envelopes, his face reflecting absolute delight.

'Bloody hell. It's Christmas all over again if you ask me,' he replied as he hurriedly flicked through them and, in his haste, let a couple fall to the deck. His immediate reaction was to stick out his foot and step onto them, stopping them from blowing overboard. He put his hand to his chest and let out a sigh. 'My God. Just in time. I nearly lost them,' he gasped as he bent down to retrieve them. He pulled himself up, staring avidly and smiling.

He couldn't believe his luck. 'There must be all of ten letters here and I think most of them are from Cathy. But I'll soon see.' He flicked through them. 'Three or four of them are from Dorothy.' He stubbed out his cigarette with the heel of his shoe and sifted through the letters trying to put them in some sort of order. 'These range back from months ago,' he continued, taking in the postmarks. 'It's not surprising though. We've had no mail for ages. I think the last letter I received was the one from Dorothy at Christmas.'

He chose the first letter he believed to be from Cathy and tried to slit open the envelope but in his intense anticipation and excitement he almost tore the letter itself, his hands were shaking so much. He couldn't believe that at last she'd made contact but he hoped upon hope it wouldn't be a 'Dear John' letter. He shook his head. He was being stupid. She wouldn't have sent him so many follow-up letters had that been the case. He read the letter slowly.

My darling Tom,

(His heart skipped a beat. All this time he'd been wondering if she'd still maintained her promise to stay true to him, and here was the proof the way she'd addressed him!)

I hope this letter doesn't take too long to get to you but I waited a couple of weeks to give the ship a chance to reach its destination.

It didn't seem the same without you after Christmas Day. All I could do on Boxing Day was to think about your ship leaving for the war zone again. I know it's not long since we met but you've no idea how worried I felt when I thought about you being so far away. And I can't stop myself from wondering what's happening. Although we've really only known each other a few days I've missed you more than I can put into words, certainly more than I ever expected.

I've been really busy at work. We've had a request from a company in Darwin to quote for repairs to war

*damage at their factory. I have a feeling Mr. Dallarup
will want me to go with him again, although Mum
and Dad are certainly not happy about a trip to Darwin. But Mr. Dallarup believes there'll be no more
trouble up there and I'm determined to persuade them
it will be fine. I am looking forward to going.*

*I have to say that has kept my mind off things to
some extent – although when I'm alone, especially
when I'm in bed at night, I do have the chance to think
about you and what you said to me before you left.*

(He guessed she was referring to his comment
about wanting to marry her someday)

*I hope you are being careful and not taking too
many chances. I want you back safe and sound – and
I mean that. Please, please come back soon. I'm dying
to see you again and to know that you're safe. If you
find out when you might be back on leave in Sydney,
please let me know and I can plan to have some time
off so that we can be together.* (It gave him a
particular thrill to read those words.)
*Of course the worst that could happen is that you'll
go straight back to England when the war is over but,
fingers crossed, I will see you again.*

Take care my darling.
Lots of hugs and kisses. Cathy

He stared at the letter. Whatever happened he
must go back to Sydney. How he'd get there or
when, he had no idea but that was his goal.

When he finally came to the last letter he realised
lots of things had happened in Cathy's life whilst
he'd been away. He was particularly pleased to

know her brother had progressed well and the surgeon hadn't had to carry out the amputation.

Kamikaze activity slowed down in the area they were anchored off the coast of Japan and Tom had serious thoughts about the war coming to an end. But at the beginning of March the *Resolute* joined the American forces in their preparations for an invasion of the large Japanese island Okinawa which the allies intended using as a base for air operations. The *Resolute* still continued its air-sea rescue function and, after a long campaign of island-hopping supported by amphibious and tactical air forces, in early April the allies approached Okinawa.

The fighting became ferocious, the Kamikaze attacks intense and the Battle of Okinawa lasted for eighty-two days until Mid-June.

Shortly afterwards and during a quiet period the captain made an announcement. Glum-faced and still in pessimistic mood after the length of time they'd been in the Pacific, the men assembled and listened carefully.

'The *Resolute* is due for a refit after the torpedo damage she sustained a few months ago. The work carried out in Palau Island was nothing more than a quick-fix job to get us back on course.' He paused and then a smile touched his lips. 'I'm sure you'll all be pleased to know we shall be returning to Sydney in two days' time.' A loud cheer went up from the men, their faces now wreathed in smiles. The captain put up a hand to stop the noise. 'A special team will start work on the refit which shouldn't take more than three weeks. That gives us time to take a period of recuperation until the ship is ready to set sail again. I'm sure we all deserve a break.'

The men couldn't contain their excitement and there was a buzz of comments and laughter. But the captain continued. 'After that we'll be needed back up north to resume our air-sea rescue operations.'

He left the men cheering loudly and Tom joined in, thrilled to know he would soon see Cathy again. And although she had asked him to let her know if they were due to return to Sydney at any time in the future, it was too short notice to send her a letter. That meant he could surprise her. He shook himself. He'd worried that the ship may never return there. Yet here they were ready to set sail in a couple of days' time. What a bonus!

Each day Cathy dashed up the path and checked the mail box fixed to the garden gate. Each day she was disappointed that after months there'd been nothing from Tom even though she'd written to him every week since he left Sydney on Boxing Day.

It was the first day of April, a new month, and when she unlocked the mail box and slipped her hand inside retrieving a single brown envelope, her stomach churned. Nothing but another bill for Dad.

Totally dejected now she turned and walked slowly back towards the front door absently turning the envelope over in her hands. She was about to go inside when she looked down at it. Her heart skipped a beat. She gasped and her mood changed from depression to excitement. She had been too hasty in her assumption it was merely a bill. Her luck had changed. The envelope had the British forces stamp on it and her expectation soared. A letter from Tom! What a wonderful surprise.

She ran inside the house. Dad had left much earlier for the market and Mum wasn't around. Relieved she didn't have to explain she headed straight into her bedroom, eager to read the contents of the letter in private. She slipped it from its envelope and opened it up. There were two pages to it and she ran her fingers over the flimsy sheet touching Tom's neat handwriting and feeling warm inside that he had at last made contact.

My darling Cathy

I must be careful what I include in my letter in case the mail gets into enemy hands but I have to tell you how much I've missed you since the ship left Australia behind.

There's very little I can say about our time up here. All I can reveal is that we've been north of Australia for the past three months and we're now in the Pacific. It's been quite an eventful time and I'll fill you in with the details if we're lucky enough to return to Sydney at some time in the near future.

You must be wondering why I didn't write to you earlier but I'm sure you'll understand it's been difficult for the ship's purser to pass on mail in view of the circumstances. I was thrilled to bits when I received a bundle of letters from you only a few days ago. You can imagine my reaction. I didn't think you'd deserted me but I kept on wondering if there was anything wrong at your end.

I was relieved to hear that your brother had made a good recovery. It must be soul-destroying watching someone who is normally so active struggling with a disability but, as you say, he made an excellent recovery and he must be ready to go back to his unit by this time.

Mike told me the good news about the engagement and you confirmed that Rita is excited about it too. I told Mike what you'd said in your letter and I think he felt reassured.

I'm very much looking forward to seeing you again. I know we're gambling on the ship returning to Sydney but I'm determined to see you whatever happens.

I hope you enjoyed the trip to Darwin with your boss and I'm looking forward to hearing all about it when I return.

All my love my darling Cathy
Yours ever Tom

Cathy read the letter through several times. Tom had said he was determined to see her again which reassured her and, if he did propose to her as he'd intimated, there was nothing she would like more. But the question of their return to England together was still on her mind and it worried her.

She opened the drawer of her bedside cabinet and took out a pen and notepad. She must write back immediately and let him know she'd received his letter.

My darling Tom
Just a short note to tell you how overjoyed I was to receive your letter and I look forward to hearing all

about your time up north when I see you again.

When I didn't hear from you I was really worried. Having seen the news reports I began to wonder if you'd been injured – or even worse. But I tried to stay optimistic. What more could I do?

Wouldn't it be great if you returned to Sydney? As far as I'm concerned, the sooner the better. All we can do is hope and pray that the war will be over in the very near future and then things can get back to normal.

The trip up to Darwin went really well and Mr. Dallarup is pleased with the outcome. He's talking about expanding the company because he feels there'll be lots of business coming our way when the war is over.

I've run out of time, Tom. I must leave to catch my usual tram to work otherwise I'll no longer be in Mr. Dallarup's good books.

I hope to see you again very soon.

All my love

Cathy

Mum was hovering in the kitchen when Cathy dashed towards the back door.

'Your breakfast, cherub,' she offered. 'Come and sit down.'

'I haven't time, Mum. I'm going to be late. I don't want to miss the tram.'

'Wait a minute, Cathy,' Mum continued as she opened the cupboard and took out a biscuit tin. 'You can't go without anything at all. If you're in such a rush take a couple of these to have with your cup of tea.' She slipped a handful of biscuits into a brown paper bag.

'Thanks, Mum,' she replied as she took hold of the door handle ready to leave.

'And you can tell me all about that letter when you come back tonight,' Mum called after her, pointing a finger as Cathy dashed up the garden path.

She smiled to herself, knowing Mum missed nothing. She'd obviously been watching through the window when Cathy went to the mail box. But she was determined to tell Mum the truth. Whether Mum approved of her relationship with a Pom of not, there was no need to hide things any longer.

As she dashed towards the tram stop a question flooded her mind for the umpteenth time. What did the future hold and would she eventually move to England with Tom?

That thought caused a heavy fluttering in her stomach. She loved her life in Australia and if Tom was serious about marrying her it was then she would have to make a decision. The alternatives were simple. She either accepted his proposal and returned with him to England, or she rejected his proposal and remained back in Australia without him. But could she afford to do that? Could she afford to lose him?

During the next few months Cathy received several more letters from Tom none of which revealed anything about the action in the Pacific. But that was not imperative. What meant most of all to Cathy was that at least Tom was still alive.

It was early one morning. Her sleep had been spasmodic for most of the night and, rather than lying there feeling despondent, she decided to get up and have a leisurely breakfast. There was no immediate hurry to catch the tram today; she had half an hour to spare and this gave her the opportunity to chat with Mum for a change. The wireless was on in the background and Mum was telling her all about the lovely dress fabric she'd spotted in one of the local shops. It was then she was startled by what she heard on the wireless. Despite Mum's description of the material, Cathy heard the newsreader's announcement.

'British ship, the *Resolute*, has this morning anchored in Australian waters. She is currently standing off in the harbour at Circular Quay ready to move down the coast for a re-fit.'

Cathy was stunned by the news. Overwhelmed at the thought of seeing Tom again, she couldn't wait to tell Rita. Slowly she picked up her bag and casually walked to the door.

'I need to get off now, Mum. We have an early meeting. Let me know if you decide to buy the fabric, that's if you have enough clothing coupons.' She smiled. Hopefully Mum had been too busy talking about the dress material to catch on when the announcement was made. And, in any case, Cathy didn't have the time to discuss the arrival of the ship. Not that it mattered what Mum thought. But Cathy was eager to get to the office early and catch Rita before they started work.

Her excitement almost got the better of her as she sat on the tram. She wanted to tell the whole world that *her* Tom had returned to Sydney. And, once at the office building, she waited outside, impatiently searching for Rita. The minute she saw her step from the tram she ran towards her.

'Steady on, Cathy,' Rita murmured, laughing. 'What's so urgent?'

'You're not going to believe this but I heard on the news this morning that the *Resolute* has docked close to Circular Quay!'

It seemed Rita hadn't fully grasped Cathy's words and she looked across at her friend, a bewildered look on her face. 'Say again, Cathy. I don't understand.'

Cathy repeated herself. Suddenly it dawned on Rita what she was saying and she lost that vacant look. Wide-eyed, she asked, 'Are you sure it was the *Resolute?*'

'There's no doubt about it.' Tears came to her eyes but then, to stop herself from becoming too emotional, she grabbed her friend's hands. 'I can't wait to see Tom.' They jumped up and down on the pavement both thrilled at the good news.

When they stopped Rita pulled a face. 'I only hope Mike's proposal still stands.'

'Of course it still stands. What's brought that on?'

'I suppose I've lost confidence after such a long time apart.'

'Stop worrying, Rita! We'll go straight down there when we finish work,' Cathy offered, her face glowing with enthusiasm.

'I can't wait,' Rita cried out. 'I don't suppose Mr. Dallarup will give us a day off.'

'You must be joking, Rita. We've too much work to do. But there's no reason why we can't leave as soon as we finish.'

'How about if we take the tram and go down there at lunchtime?'

'Oh, I don't know. We'd be in trouble if we were late back. I don't want to lose my job.'

'I suppose you're right. Nor me, especially now that we'll need all the money we can lay our hands on for the wedding.'

'Don't you think you might be getting ahead of yourself, Rita? The boys are not exactly back for good. The war isn't over yet.'

'I realise that but we need to start saving soon.'

Cathy wiped the dampness from her eyes and they went inside, heading for the restroom to freshen their faces before starting work. But it was difficult concentrating and the morning seemed to pass so slowly for Cathy. But she was still not prepared to dash down to Circular Quay at lunchtime. That would be too risky. She would wait until they finished for the day before going down and looking for Tom.

The ship stood off in deep water and the tenders were lowered ready to take the men ashore. Tom and Mike, eager to step onto dry land, waited their turn and soon they were on their way to Circular Quay.

'What's the best plan of action?' Mike asked, looking at his watch. 'It's one o'clock now and the girls are going to be at work until later this afternoon.'

'How about if we go to the office just before five when they finish,' Tom suggested. 'I can't wait until tonight when Cathy's back home from work.'

'That's not an option for me, Tom. I don't know if Rita's told her parents yet that we're engaged and I've never met them. I've only been to the house a couple of times and both times I've left Rita at the gate. As far as I'm concerned it's for the best if we get the tram to the offices. And it'll be great to surprise them.'

'I'll say. We've two or three hours to kill and we might as well do a spot if sightseeing.' He looked across at the Harbour Bridge and smiled. 'You can see why they call it *The Coat Hanger* can't you?' he added pointing to the huge structure.

'Absolutely. I bet it's a devil to climb when it needs repairs. I wouldn't fancy my chances. I'm not too happy with heights. I think I must be acrophobic,' he advanced.

'What's with the big words?' Tom laughed.

'It runs in the family, acrophobia I mean. Dad can't even paint the upstairs window frames. He dreads going up ladders.' He grinned. 'But let's decide where we're going.'

'How about going across to The Rocks and when we come back we could sit somewhere along here,' he suggested, pointing to the buildings, 'with a pint and relax until it's time to get the tram.'

'Sound idea, pal.'

After wandering casually along the quay and visiting The Rocks, they called in one of the bars along the quayside and ordered a pint of beer. By this time it was almost four o'clock.

'We need to look out for the tram stop to get us out to the suburb. It has a foreign sounding name. I think it's called Leichardt.'

'I'm glad you have it sussed out. I haven't been there before.'

'I've been once to meet Cathy but it was a few

months ago of course. I hope I can remember the way.'

'I hope so too.' Mike paused. 'Thinking about it we could wait until Cathy and Rita arrive at Circular Quay. What do you think?'

'Let's chance it. I've a pretty good idea where the offices are. We'll take the tram. We're in good time. From what I can recall it's quite a tall building. I'm sure I'll recognise it as soon as I see it.'

There was a tram waiting when they came across the stop but it didn't leave for another ten minutes and by the time they arrived in Leichardt it was already five minutes to five. As they stepped off the tram Tom recognised the area immediately and he knew exactly where the office was situated. They reached the building and, within a few minutes, the staff started to flood out.

Tom's heart began to race the minute Cathy appeared. Just seeing her was something special. She was wearing a knee length V-neck dress in a delicate pink colour matching her shiny hair. All he could think of was kissing her lovely mouth and he stared avidly becoming so fixated with the idea he seemed to be in a trance.

'Tom! Oh Tom,' she called out to him and that brought him back from his mesmerised state.

He'd played this moment over and over in his mind so many times it almost seemed unreal. But here she was. He reminded himself he must calm down and stop thinking about what he'd like to do when they were alone. *Cut it out,* he told himself. If he didn't watch it he could easily mess up.

'Cathy,' he shouted, catching her as she ran into his arms. He couldn't believe this was happening.

'I've missed you my darling.'

'Me too,' she replied, her eyes glistening.

'Hey, don't be crying on me.' He laughed. 'You don't want to see a grown man crying do you?'

She laughed amid her tears. 'I can't help it. I thought I might never see you again.'

'Didn't I tell you I'd be back whatever happened?'

She nodded.

'I meant it. And here I am.'

They linked arms and set off towards the tram stop. When Tom looked behind him he noticed Mike and Rita were still in a heavy clinch.

'See you back on the ship,' he called out and Mike stuck a thumb in the air.

Elated, Cathy clung to Tom and when they climbed aboard the tram they huddled close together. She never wanted him to leave her again. But that was pie in the sky and she must make the most of their time together. Tom had told her his ship would be leaving for the north Pacific once the re-fit was complete and that would be in two or three weeks' time.

'Do you need to go back home?' Tom asked her as they stepped off the tram at Circular Quay. 'How about your mum and dad? Won't they wonder where you are?'

'They will, but if you're game, you're coming with me.'

'What?' Tom took a deep breath. 'I don't know about that. I thought your mum disapproved of Poms.' He laughed. It seemed strange calling himself a Pom. It had derogatory connotations to it and he knew he was as good as any man.

'I don't care what she thinks.' Cathy's voice had a rebellious tone to it. 'Although I think Mum's mellowed quite a bit since Danny's injuries and of course Dad's heart attack.'

'Your Dad has had a heart attack?' Tom frowned. 'You didn't mention it.'

'I thought you had enough to worry about and I did intend telling you when I next saw you.'

'How is he now?'

'He's fine but Mum keeps her eye on him. He doesn't get away with anything believe you me.'

'I can imagine.'

All the way back to St Peter's Cathy felt a fluttering inside. What would be Mum's reaction when she walked into the house with Tom? But why should she worry? She was a grown woman and it was time she made her own choices and her own decisions. Mum had kept hold of the reins for long enough, not that she went against all Mum's decisions but now it was different.

Cathy noticed that the door was open as they walked through the gateway and into the back garden. Mum was outside bringing in the washing from the outside line.

'Hello, cherub,' she called out and when she saw Tom she added, 'I see we have a visitor.' She smiled. 'Tom, isn't it?'

Cathy was agreeably surprised. Mum had changed her tune.

'It is, Mrs. Ellis. It's good to see you again.'

'When did your ship dock?' She shook her head. 'Cathy didn't mention you were back in Sydney.'

'We arrived this morning.'

'I see. Then it hasn't taken you long to meet up

with Cathy.'

'Tom met me from work, Mum. It was a lovely surprise.'

They went inside and it seemed to Cathy Mum had accepted the fact that she made her own choices these days. There'd certainly been no mention of Geoffrey for months.

'Now then, young man,' Frank said, standing up and shaking hands with Tom. 'It's good to see you again.' And from that point Dad took over. The two of them had an extended conversation about the war in the Pacific, Tom's reactions to it and Dad's theories as to the future whilst Cathy helped Mum finish off preparations for the meal.

It was after nine when Tom looked at his watch.

'I'd better set off back to the ship,' he said.

'I'll come to the gate with you,' Cathy offered.

'Thank you for a lovely meal, Mrs. Ellis,' he said.

'I'm glad you enjoyed it. Will we see you again?'

'I hope so. We're here for at least two weeks.'

'And where to then?' she continued.

'Back up north I expect.'

He turned to Frank. 'It's been interesting talking to you, sir,' he added.

'Another time, Tom,' Frank asserted, gripping Tom's hand and giving him a final handshake.

'I'd like that, Mr. Ellis,' he replied.

When they stepped outside Cathy closed the door behind them. Tom took her in his arms and his kiss was long and deep. 'I've been waiting all night to do that,' he told her.

'Sorry we haven't had much time together but I wanted to stand firm and take you back with me, show Mum and Dad I have a mind of my own.' She hunched her shoulders. 'And it seems to have been for the best. Dad is in his glory talking tactics and finding out what's going on. And Mum's definitely warming towards you. I notice she gave you extra slices of lamb as the special guest.'

Tom laughed. 'She did, too. I'm glad it worked out well.' He squeezed her hands. 'But tomorrow I want you all to myself.'

'You do, do you?' Cathy replied coyly. 'Then we'll see what we can arrange.'

'Outside the building again, five o'clock?' Tom suggested.

'It's a date!' Cathy smiled into his eyes and he kissed her gently on the lips before leaving her standing there. She watched him leave, his bell-bottoms fluttering in the breeze. And when he reached the brow of the incline he turned and waved. Her heart bounced in her chest and happiness flooded her body. Life couldn't be more wonderful.

She stared after him until he disappeared. She had envisaged his return to Sydney and dreamed of their togetherness over and over again but, now that he was here with her, their relationship seemed to surpass all her expectations. And she knew in her heart that whatever happened he would be her soulmate for life.

Cathy was late leaving the office. Mr. Dallarup had called her in to discuss a future trip to Broome. She tried to sound excited about it but unknown to her boss she was more excited at the thought of seeing Tom again than the proposed visit to Broome. Dallarup had no firm date as to when they were to visit the factory and Cathy only hoped it would be after Tom had left to join his ship again. The last thing she wanted was for the boss to impinge on her precious time with Tom. She certainly didn't want to miss out whilst he was on leave.

'What you do think?' Dallarup said after he'd finished explaining. He smiled and gave Cathy a look of satisfaction.

Cathy wasn't in the least bit interested in the details at this point in time. All she wanted was to get out of the office and meet up with Tom. Fixing a smile on her face she replied, 'It sounds like another interesting trip, Mr. Dallarup. It seems business is on the up. At least it'll keep our jobs safe,' she offered, her hand clutching the door handle.

'Absolutely,' he replied.

She turned to leave and, opening the door added, 'I'll see you tomorrow.' Closing it quickly behind her she dashed out of the building and down the front steps.

Tom was looking out for her and as usual he greeted her with open arms. 'You do love to make a chap wait!' he teased. 'I thought you'd changed your mind,' he added, laughing. Slipping an arm around her shoulder he gave her a fleeting kiss and led her towards the tram stop.

'How about going to the *Troc* and later having a change of scenery? I thought we might go for a bite to eat? The lads have been telling me about a little pie place in Woolloomooloo. I checked it out on my way from the ship. It reminded me of home.

I know it's nothing swish but we could eat our supper as we walked back towards your place.'

'Sounds good. I think it must be Harry's Café de Wheels. I know it closed when the war broke out but it was always very popular, especially with the forces and the celebrities. Dad was only saying a few days ago that Harry is back from war service and he's re-opened already. I went there with Mum and Dad a few times years ago as a special treat. The pies were delicious and I'm sure the quality will still be the same.'

'Then decision made.'

'You're coming home with me now, aren't you? We can travel together to the *Troc*.'

'I was hoping you'd say that.' They linked arms and headed for Cathy's.

All seemed quiet when Cathy pushed open the gate to the yard. The back door was locked and Cathy had to rummage through her handbag for the key. 'That's strange,' she said. 'They didn't say they were going out.'

There was a note on the table when she stepped into the kitchen.

Gone to cinema to see The Rats of Tobruck. *Salad in pantry. Back about 9.*

'That's a turn up for the books. Mum and Dad never go out at night.' She paused. 'Having said that, Dad did mention the film the other day and said some of the men at the market had recommended it. Apparently the two main stars are Peter Finch and Chips Rafferty.'

'Those two? They're big names at home,' he replied and then with a wicked sparkle in his eyes he added, 'Good old Dad. They should do it more often.' He clapped his hands and beamed. 'All I can say is we have time to ourselves for a change.'

'I see,' Cathy replied, smiling. 'But don't be getting any ideas.'

'I haven't a clue what you're talking about,' he ventured, making eyes at her and reflecting a devil-may-care attitude.

At first she gave a shaky laugh but then she gazed at him, fighting an impulse to press her lips to his. And it was obvious his feelings matched. He stepped forward and brought his head down, brushing his lips against hers. His kiss was gentle at first, almost playful, teasing.

The second it deepened her head began to spin. She was lost to everything around her except the feel of him close. Warmth spiralled through her body and ripples shuddered down her back. Sliding her arms around his shoulders, she ran her fingers through the curl of his hair at the nape of his neck. Physically aroused, she wanted to give in to the urges she felt but knew she shouldn't. And it was clear Tom was aroused by her closeness too but, like the gentleman he was, he took control.

Cathy came down to earth with a bang, realising he had stopped himself from taking advantage of their time alone. He gently directed her towards the kitchen.

'How about that salad your mum left for you?' He grinned. 'If we're going to Harry's place tonight you don't want a big meal. Fancy sharing it with me? I'm sure there's enough for two.'

She took the plated meal from the shelf in the pantry and sat down at the table. 'You spoke too soon. I was about to offer you some. There's more than enough. I know what Mum's like, wanting to make sure I have a proper meal, but she always makes too much. Come and sit down,' she said, patting the chair next to her.

They ate the meal in silence and once Cathy had changed into a blue and white polka dot dress they set off for the *Trocadero*.

Once on the dance floor it seemed her body was moulded with his as they swayed in time to a Latin American number. She couldn't help but comment. 'You'll end up a better dancer than I am,' she joked. 'You really have the hang of this tango.' Her eyes sparkled up at him.

'And you have the knowhow to drive me wild,' he replied, his voice low and his gaze intent on her face. Ignoring the others on the dance floor he kissed her and she felt no embarrassment.

It was nine thirty when they left the dance hall and made their way to Harry's. Cathy laughed when she saw what appeared to be a large van on wheels with a hatch at the front. 'It hasn't changed at all, but somehow it seemed bigger than this.'

'I suppose that's because you were just a kid,' Tom added, joining her in the laughter.

They savoured their pies as they set off towards the tram stop. 'I'll be fine getting back home. Go ahead and get yourself back to the ship.'

'What! And leave you to go back alone. Not a chance. I'm definitely coming with you.'

They said goodnight at Cathy's garden gate just in time for Tom to catch the last tram into the city. His last words were, 'We belong together, Cathy. Don't ever forget that.'

By the first week in July the *Resolute* was

scheduled to return to the Pacific and after Cathy's tearful farewell the ship joined the American forces off the coast of Japan. There were more dog fights and more deaths. The *Resolute* transported injured servicemen to a bigger and more modern hospital ship standing well away from the action. Towards the end of July after the allies' hard-fought battles through strategic bombing the *Resolute's* task was complete. The ship sailed south once more.

Chapter 16

1945

Frank returned from the market with the latest news. He'd heard that the presidents of the United States and China and the Prime Minister of England had issued the Potsdam Declaration outlining the terms of surrender for the Empire of Japan.

'They've brought it upon themselves,' Frank declared, 'and it's not as though anyone is calling their bluff. The big three have issued an ultimatum that the Japanese either surrender or, in their words, *face prompt and utter destruction,* whatever that might mean. It looks as though they've no alternative, although I've heard the emperor tends to stand firm.'

'Oh Good Lord, Frank. That sounds drastic. I do wish it was all over and done with. I won't be happy until my boys are safely back at home where they belong.'

'Exactly, Marj. I want them home too. And I agree the statement from the big three does sound threatening, but I think the Japs have their backs against the wall. Surely it won't be long before it's all over.'

Frank's words rang true. The three heads of state weren't bluffing. On the morning of the sixth of August Frank arrived at the market. He was early and he made a mug of tea before switching on the wireless in his little makeshift office. Whilst he tried to tune out the crackling, he caught an announcement which startled him.

'The first atomic bomb ever to be used in a military operation was dropped on the city of Hiroshima, Japan, this morning at eight sixteen Hiroshima time. The bomb, named by the allies "Little Boy," exploded one thousand nine hundred feet above the courtyard of Shima Hospital, with a force equivalent to twelve thousand five hundred tons of TNT, killing men, women, and children indiscriminately, both military personnel and civilians.'

Shocked at the news, Frank ran out of his office into the market hall.

'Bloody hell. Have you heard what's happened?' he shouted. The men stopped what they were doing and looked across at Frank. 'The allies have only dropped a bloody atom bomb on the Japs! I think they must have killed half the population.'

Aghast, the men stood around in huddles contemplating the consequences whilst Frank dashed back into his office to check if there was more news. There were comments from around the world but nothing more to report from Hiroshima apart from the devastation caused.

Still the emperor refused to surrender. And that was not the end of the bombing. Just three days later on the ninth of August a second bomb the allies named "Fat Man" exploded over Nagasaki killing forty thousand people outright. A mushroom cloud from the nuclear explosion formed and rose eighteen kilometers into the air. Although the Japanese were the enemy, the world was in shock and it was only days after the catastrophic results of the bombings that the Emperor of Japan surrendered.

'It's not surprising they've had to give in. It's a shame about what's happened but the Emperor should have taken the threats seriously,' Frank concluded.

'But what about the poor people who've been affected, the ones who've lost their families?'

'I know it's sad, Marj, but you have to remember that the Japs have carried out atrocities themselves. I'm afraid that's war, love.'

Cathy listened to what Dad had to say about the bombings and she waited expectantly to hear that Tom's ship had sailed away from the Pacific. But then she panicked after hearing a rumour floating around at the office that several ships of the Pacific Fleet were missing. Unfortunately she couldn't discover the source of the rumour but at the forefront of her mind was a major question. Could Tom's ship be one of them?

For days she couldn't stop herself from thinking about it and, not having heard from Tom for weeks, she convinced herself the *Resolute* was one of the missing ships. Her anguish when the one man she'd ever loved had left her to return to the war zone and her fears about his safety had already wreaked havoc, but now this. And the more she thought about the situation the more she worked herself up into a frenzied state. All she could think about was what might have happened to him.

It was Saturday morning, Mum was out shopping and Dad was doing an extra shift at the market. Still worried and with no news of Tom, Cathy decided to call at Rita's and ask if she'd heard from Mike. She was about to leave when she heard a knock at the front door. Perhaps it was Rita herself wondering if there was any news from the ship. But on second thoughts, it wouldn't be Rita. Her normal routine was to come to the back door not the front.

Cathy sighed, went through into the hall and her eye caught the silhouette of a tall figure through the glass panel. Her stomach churned. *Not someone from the market,* was her first thought. *Don't say Dad is ill again.* Puzzled, she opened the door.

Had she known who was standing there, she would have kept quiet and ignored the knocking. Unfortunately it was too late now. It was Geoffrey boldly confronting her and, although she'd like nothing more than to close the door in his face, she was stuck with him. This was all she needed.

'Hello gorgeous! It's lovely to see you again.' He smiled and, without invitation, stepped inside. 'I was driving past the shops when I spotted your mother. When I asked about you, she told me you were home alone.' He smiled 'I thought it was a good opportunity to call in and chat. It's quite some time since I saw you, my dear.'

Cathy felt affronted. 'I'm quite busy just now. What exactly did you want to chat about, Geoffrey?'

'I thought maybe you'd offer me a cup of tea and we could talk things through together.' He gave her a sly wink and his smile was ingratiating. 'I take it you don't have company.'

Cathy cringed. The guy obviously thought himself a charmer and well-practised in the art of seduction. But he'd chosen the wrong person with whom to try it on.

'Dad's at work this morning but it shouldn't be long before he's back.' She sighed and tried to soften her words with an apology. 'Sorry you've made the effort, Geoffrey, but I thought I'd made myself clear the last time I saw you. There's nothing to talk through as far as I'm concerned.'

'But you probably weren't thinking straight, my dear. I know how dizzy you girls can be from time to time.' He laughed. 'I thought we might start over and give ourselves a chance to develop our relationship. You know my position at the bank means I could give you a good social life with the kind of extras any girl would be envious of.' He stepped towards her, that sickly smile still dancing around his lips.

He was giving her the creeps now. Who did he think he was calling in when he knew she was alone? She had to get rid of him and quickly. But the more she backed away the more he stepped towards her, forcing her up against the wall.

'Look outside, darling,' he offered, pointing through the hall window at a shiny black car. 'That's my new car. What do you think? Wouldn't you like a spin in it?'

She gulped now wanting to puke at his nearness as well as his suggestion.

'I haven't time today, Geoffrey. I was just about to leave the house when you arrived.'

He pressed himself up against her. 'Then let me take you wherever you're going, sweetheart.' He trailed his finger down her cheek.

She closed her eyes and swallowed. The lump in her throat was desperate to escape and it clawed viciously as she swallowed once more. She was trapped, and it was no good trying to grapple with him. He was too big and too strong.

She opened her mouth and managed to answer, her voice no more than a whisper. 'Not today, thank you, Geoffrey. Maybe some other time.' She pressed her hands to his chest and tried to push him away.

His smile turned to a grimace. 'You're not taking me seriously, are you?' He knocked her hands down from his chest and placed both his hands on the wall, stopping her from moving. 'Mother tells me you've taken up with a Pom.' He smirked. 'If you're expecting anything serious you'll be lucky on that score. He's probably out for a good time, nothing more. And if he did take things more seriously he'd no doubt want to take you back with him to some squalid place over in England. Believe me, Cathy, it won't work. You'll be crying to come back in no time. And then you'll wish it was me you'd chosen.' He shook his head slowly. 'But by then it'll be too late. I'm not interested in secondhand goods!'

'How do you mean, second-hand goods? How dare you describe me as second-hand goods? And I'm not interested in egocentric prigs!' She looked him directly in the eyes and she could see he certainly didn't like what she'd said. 'And what do you know about Tom? You've never even met him.'

'Tom, is it? I don't need to meet him. They're all tarred with the same brush, out for all they can get.' He sneered. 'Get your head screwed on, sweetheart. You don't know what you're missing.' He slid both hands around her and pressed himself up against her again, his lips almost touching her mouth.

Her heart seemed to ram in her throat. She pushed her hands beneath his arms, anger coursing through her now.

'Get off me!' she shouted. 'Why don't you get it into your head I don't want you. I'm not the slightest bit interested in your job, your money or your car, or what you can do for me, you patronising idiot!' Her legs were trembling now.

His forehead took on a heavy frown. 'You don't speak to me like that. You need to be taught a lesson young lady. Where's your gratitude when I'm offering you everything?'

She was shaking now. Perhaps she'd gone too far. Maybe she should have humoured him.

It was at that moment she heard footsteps in the back yard. It was obvious Geoffrey had heard them too. Relief surged through her. Hopefully it was either Mum or Dad returning.

But before he moved away Geoffrey had to have the last word. 'Don't forget what I said. I won't give in, you know.' He pulled away and raced to the door, opening it with a flourish and putting on his false smile. 'Hello again, Mrs. Ellis. I'm just on my way. Thought I'd call in and have a word with Catherine.'

'Don't rush off, Geoffrey. Why not stay and have a cup of tea with us?' Mum asked.

Cathy could have screamed. Even Mum was on his side.

'Thank you, my dear,' he replied, patting her on the shoulder, 'but I must get on. I'm a busy man you know. But I hope to see you again soon.'

Cathy shook her head. Who did he think he was? His patronising words echoed inside her head. She hoped never to see him again.

Mum smiled after him but then she turned to face Cathy and her forehead creased into a frown. 'Are you all right Cathy love?'

'I'm fine, Mum. But I can do without Geoffrey calling in to see me. It's time he realised I'm just not interested.'

'That's fair enough, cherub. I know you're sweet on Tom. But you need to know which side your bread's buttered. I keep on telling you Geoffrey would be a good catch. But that's all I'm saying.'

Cathy hoped that was all Mum was preaching and she didn't comment further. Collecting her handbag from her bedroom, she opened the back door. 'I'm calling round at Rita's, Mum. I won't be long.'

It was a relief when she left the house and

headed to her friend's just a couple of streets away. But still she had that churning feeling inside. Geoffrey had said it wasn't the end. What did he mean by that, she wondered? She'd definitely watch her step in the future and make sure she didn't open the door to him again.

Rita was standing at the door when Cathy arrived. 'I was just about to come round to yours,' she said. 'Have you heard anything?' she whispered, closing the door behind her and stepping out into the yard.

'Not a bean. I'm worried, Rita. What if something's happened to them?'

'I know what you mean.' She linked her arm through Cathy's. 'Let's go down to the soda bar.' She turned to see if anyone was looking through the window. 'I don't want Mum listening in.'

'Haven't you mentioned anything yet?'

'No. I'm waiting until the boys are back. There's no point telling Mum and Dad too soon. They'll only get on at me.'

'I think Mum still has ideas about Geoffrey. I've had him round to see me,' Cathy told Rita.

'Geoffrey Grant?' Rita laughed. 'What did he want?'

'It's no laughing matter, Rita. He's nothing but a creep. He was quite threatening and I'm worried he might come back.' She told Rita exactly what had happened. 'When I think about him touching me it gives me the shudders.'

'I'm not surprised. I didn't realise you were in such a state. Sorry I laughed.' She slipped her arm around Cathy's shoulder. 'You're shaking, Cathy. You need to mention it to your dad and you need to be careful. The last thing you want is that dingo pestering you!'

'I know but it's tricky. I'm in a dilemma. I don't want to spoil Mum's relationship with her friend, Irene. I didn't tell her what happened, just that I'm not interested. And I don't want Dad involved either. If he knew he'd probably go round there and beat the living daylights out of Geoffrey.'

'I know what you mean. It's a difficult one. But be careful in the future.'

It was several days later when the letter arrived. As usual it was in a brown envelope. Cathy looked at the postmark. If it was a recent letter at least the ship had left the Pacific and he was still alive. She stuck her thumb inside the flap and ripped it open eager to read its contents. But her stomach flipped when she read the first line of Tom's letter.

My darling Cathy
We're back from the Pacific and are now in Darwin where it seems we're going to remain until our next orders. I know it's disappointing that we've not returned to Sydney but I suppose if we're scheduled to go back to England that's not going to happen because we'd be going off course.

Cathy swallowed hard and tears pricked the backs of her eyes. At least he was safe but what if she never saw him again? Her world would be shattered. An immense feeling of dread enveloped her like a shroud, and she tried desperately to control her emotions. She struggled and squeezed her eyes tight shut. But was she being premature in her reactions? She brushed the tears from her eyes and continued to read.

I'm not sure how long we'll remain here but I'm not going to let anything come between us even if I have to return to England and save every penny I can to pay for your passage so that you can be with me. I only hope you're still of the same mind and want us to be together.

Sailing to England? It couldn't be true. Her worry returned. He was going back without seeing her and that was something she had always dreaded hearing. The breath rushed from her lungs and her heart began to race. He'd mentioned her following him although he hadn't touched on the possibility of their marrying. But it seemed that was the only course of action now that she knew she couldn't forsake him.

But stay calm, my love. I'll keep in touch. Please write back to me and tell me your feelings. I'm hoping you'll still want us to be together and I can't wait to hear from you.
All my love forever, darling.
Tom

Cathy dried her eyes. She didn't want Mum to see her like that and she had to be sensible. Most importantly Tom was alive, and he seemed adamant they would be together at some point in time. All she could do now was hope it would not be in the too distant future. At least now he was back from the war zone he would keep her informed as

300

to what was happening.

She took out her notepad and wrote back telling him she would miss him if he went directly to England. But she stressed she couldn't live without him and she wanted to be with him forever.

Tom did keep in touch and he wrote to her almost every day. But after several weeks there was no mail for four or five days and Cathy began to wonder what was happening. Had his ship set sail for England?

Throughout the day at the office she couldn't lift the dark mood she seemed to have developed and when it was time to leave she couldn't get away from the office quickly enough. She dashed out of the building the minute five o'clock chimed, intending to meet up with Rita at the tram stop as usual and they'd travel home together. At least Rita had the engagement ring and a promise. Cathy relied on her friend to cheer her up. Despite the boys being away, Rita was always optimistic and not a worrier like Cathy.

She stepped out into the bright sunlight but what she hadn't bargained for was a completely different scenario.

Tom was outside waiting for her. He wasn't wearing his uniform and she couldn't believe her eyes when she saw him, arms wide open, dashing towards her.

'Oh, Tom. How have you managed to get here?' She fell into his embrace and he kissed her gently, not wanting to make a scene.

But before he had the chance to answer Rita was beside them.

'Tom, it's great to see you,' she offered, her

voice filled with excitement, her eyes alight with expectation. 'I take it the ship is back in Sydney.' She looked around and when she turned back to face Tom she had a heavy frown on her face. 'But where's Mike?'

Tom looked embarrassed. 'I'm afraid he's not back, Rita. He's still on the ship in Darwin. But Mike is expecting to hear from you. Have you received his latest letter?'

'No but hopefully it'll be waiting for me when I arrive home.' Puzzled now, she shook her head. 'But how is it you're here and he's back in Darwin?'

'I've made my own way down but it's all quite complicated so I'd prefer for you to wait for Mike's letter. It's better to hear from him.'

'I hope he hasn't changed his mind. I hope he hasn't called off our engagement.'

Tom placed a hand on her shoulder and looked her in the eyes. 'I'm sure it's nothing like that. In fact I think you'll be surprised and pleased when you read it. But I don't want to spoil it for you.'

Rita seemed a little more mollified when they took the tram together and travelled back to St Peter's. But she was quiet all the way back, obviously wondering what was happening and, when the tram drew up at their stop, she turned to leave.

'I can't wait to hear from Mike,' she said. 'I need to get back and see if the letter's arrived.' She hurried down her street eager to check out the mail.

Tom took hold of Cathy's hand and pulled her towards him. 'It's so good to see you again.'

'Please, please tell me what's happening, Tom.

I'm on tenterhooks. I can't believe you're back but why are you here and not Mike?' She frowned. 'I know it's something you didn't want to say in front of Rita and I felt sorry for her. Has Mike left her in the lurch? And as for you, you haven't deserted have you?'

Tom laughed out loud. 'So many questions! Deserted? What at this late stage? You've got to be joking, Cathy. But steady on. Mike hasn't left Rita in the lurch. He's on the ship and as far as I know the arrangements are still the same. Rita has promised to leave for England as soon as they can organise a passage for her.' He pondered and took a deep breath. Cathy knew he had something on his mind.

'What is it then?' she asked him. 'I can tell something wrong.'

'Nothing's wrong. I have something to ask you, nothing more.'

'Oh, yes and what's that?' Cathy challenged, curious and hoping it was something good.

'Come with me right now,' he stressed, taking her hand and pulling her towards the nearby park. They sat down on one of the benches.

'Don't keep me in suspense, Tom,' she urged. 'What's it all about?'

Tom stood up from the bench, bent down and knelt on one knee. He stared into her eyes and took her hand in his.

'I've been waiting to ask you this for ages but the time had to be right.' He swallowed hard. 'Now that I've been demobbed there's nothing holding me back.' He took a deep breath. 'Will you marry me, Cathy?'

At first the words didn't seem to register. And then, shocked but delighted Cathy leant forward and threw her arms around his neck.

'I will, I will.' Her eyes glistened as she pulled herself back before kissing him soundly on the lips. 'But when, where?'

'Hang on. Give me a chance to explain.' He laughed. 'You're not going to believe this but the reason I'm here is that I've volunteered to stay in Australia.'

Cathy interrupted. 'But...'

'Hear me out, sweetheart.' He smiled and his eyes lit up. 'We were given the option by the Australian government of staying back here in Australia with the proviso that if we couldn't settle they'd pay our passage back home.'

'But what about your family?'

'The reason you haven't heard from me is that when we arrived in Darwin and the offer came through I contacted Dorothy to run it past her before I made a final decision. I wanted to hear her reaction before I told you. I hope you understand that we've always stuck together as a family and I thought maybe Dorothy would expect me to go back to England.' He sat down on the bench and squeezed her hands. 'She wrote back giving me her blessing to stay, telling me there was nothing to rush back for now that they had no contact with Mum, and Dad had passed away. She said since she married George they'd settled well in the house and made it their own.' He stared ahead seemingly deep in thought. 'She's so caring. All she wanted was for me to be happy.'

'And Billy?'

'Naturally Billy is disappointed but if all goes well I've offered for him to come over and stay with us once he leaves school. I'll save as much as I can to pay his fare.' He gripped Cathy's hands. 'Dorothy says she's expecting me to take you over there to meet her once things are settled and we can afford to visit. What do you think?'

'It's wonderful news, Tom. I can't believe you're not going back to England without me. I know Rita has agreed to go but, to be honest, Tom, I was worried about leaving Mum and Dad, especially after Dad's heart attack. Even so I would have gone to England had that been the only option.' She turned to him and brushed her lips against his. 'I think the first thing we have to do is go back to mine. You realise you need to have Dad's permission at some point in time, unless of course you want to wait until I'm twenty-one.'

'I don't want to wait,' Tom told her and then he coughed. 'Mm, I know I need his permission and I'm dreading it.'

'Don't worry. I'm sure he'll agree. I know for a fact he's liked you since the first time you met. And there'll be no problem now that you're staying in Australia and not whisking me back to England. I think he'll be glad about that. Mum certainly will.' She paused. 'But it might be an idea to give them time to get used to seeing you around again before you approach Dad,' she suggested.

'I don't want to wait too long,' Tom told her.

Cathy laughed. 'Such impatience!'

'I'm not impatient; I'm desperate to make you my wife.' He pulled her up from the bench, took her in his arms and kissed her sending her into a spin.

When he released her she smiled, knowing his words had come from the heart. 'We'll give them a week. How about that?'

'You're on!'

During that week Tom began looking to move from his temporary accommodation in the Sydney hostel. Unfortunately he didn't come across anything suitable.

When he did take the plunge and asked Frank for his daughter's hand in marriage, Frank stood up and offered his hand.

'I'm glad it's you, Tom. And you've made a sound decision to stay over here in Australia. I don't think for a minute you'll regret it, especially now that you have a life to look forward to with my little treasure.'

Tom took his hand and Frank shook it vigorously. 'You're right there, Mr. Ellis. She is a little treasure and, don't worry, I will look after her.'

'I'm sure you will, Tom and now that we're going to be related, I think it's time you called me Frank,' he suggested. 'I can't do with all this formality.' He pondered. 'Now if you're going to keep my little girl in the luxury she deserves, you'll need a job,' Frank said, laughing at his own comment, 'unless you're already sorted.'

'I've been looking since I returned but jobs seem to be a bit thin on the ground. I'll take anything to get myself started, even labouring work. I could tackle that.'

'Why don't I ask around at the market? At least it would be a start. You're big and strong enough to do some portering work.'

'That would suit me fine if there's anything going. I'd be eternally grateful, Frank.' Tom paused. 'I don't suppose you know where I can get reasonably priced accommodation? The hostel I'm in just now is quite basic. And I'm right in the centre of town.'

Frank turned to Marjorie. 'Didn't Mrs. Jakes say she was willing to take in a lodger, Marj?'

'I believe she did.' Marjorie turned to Tom. 'Her house is in the next street.' She turned to Cathy. 'It might be an idea if you took Tom round to see her, cherub.' She paused. 'She can be strict but she's a very fair woman. If she'll take you in I can guarantee you'll be comfortable.'

'Thanks for mentioning it, Mum,' Cathy replied. 'I hope the room is still available. What do you think, Tom? Shall we go round now and see her?'

'The sooner the better as far as I'm concerned. It sounds just the ticket for me and if she'll take me in I'll be more or less on the spot.'

Mrs Jakes, an elderly woman possibly in her late sixties made a firm offer to Tom listing her rules and regulations such as mealtimes and lock-up time at night.

'I'm so grateful. Don't worry, Mrs. Jakes, I'll do whatever you say if you'll only give me a chance.'

'Then it's a deal,' she said, holding out her hand for Tom to shake. 'Move your things in whenever you're ready.'

Tom was certainly ready and the following day he gave notice at the hostel and moved into Mrs Jakes's house. 'If there's anything you need me to do, say the word. I can more or less turn my hand to anything if you have any problems in the house.'

It seemed they had a reciprocal arrangement and Tom felt sure Mrs. Jakes was as pleased to have him stay as he was to be there.

But Marjorie didn't take the news of Tom's proposal as willingly as her husband and she took Cathy on one side.

'I suppose I'll have to let Irene know.' She shook her head. 'She'll be disappointed Geoffrey's missed out. You've let a good one go there.'

'You're joking, Mum. I didn't tell you when you last saw him here but he was quite threatening. He's certainly not my type. But Tom is. He's so gentle and thoughtful and loving.'

'Threatening? I don't know what you mean. You didn't say anything before.'

'I didn't want to cause any trouble between you and Mrs. Grant, Mum. You've been friends for so many years. So please keep what I'm telling you to yourself.'

But the problem of Geoffrey didn't stop there. Rita was concerned for her friend and she didn't forget it. When she read Mike's letter telling her the ship would be sailing for England within the next week he said he was so sorry he hadn't been able to take up the offer to stay in Australia because he needed to see his family back in England. He had very close ties with his parents and his brother and sisters and he couldn't make such a decision on the spot. Unfortunately he hadn't been able to get permission to travel down to Sydney to see her before he left but he hoped she still wanted to join him in England once her passage could be arranged.

She wrote back immediately, telling him she was definitely up to following him to England. And, during the course of the letter, she also mentioned the problem Cathy had faced when Geoffrey had visited her. She stressed to Mike how worried she was for her friend. 'I know Cathy won't have said anything to Tom about Geoffrey, but I wondered if you'd pass the message on to Tom discreetly when you write to him again.' Rita disliked Geoffrey intensely especially after what Cathy had told her and she worried that he might make another approach.

Chapter 17

1945

Frank and Marjorie were out visiting Irene and Walter Grant when Tom called in with the engagement ring. It wasn't a deliberate ploy to visit when Cathy was alone in the house. He hadn't known her parents would be out. His plan was to take Cathy to the park and present her with the ring at the exact spot he'd proposed to her. But now that he'd discovered they would be alone together he made a slight amendment to his plan. Why not take advantage of their time together alone in the house? His idea was still to visit the park and slip the ring on her finger there, but later. The problem was that he couldn't stop thinking about what they could do together whilst her parents were out. But he told himself he must slow down and stop that train of thought.

'I didn't expect you so early, Tom. I'm not quite ready,' Cathy told him.

'No problem, sweetheart. I'll sit right here and wait,' he offered before taking her hand and pulling her down next to him. 'Just a little kiss and a cuddle first, seeing we're alone.'

Cathy laughed and he gathered her in his arms, kissing her tenderly. Just being there with her made everything about their relationship so worthwhile. He'd told her he couldn't wait to marry her; he couldn't wait for her to be his wife. And he meant every word of it. He smiled to himself feeling so smug that he was marrying the most beautiful girl in the world. And, when he looked into those rich brown eyes riveted to his, it was as though she was reading his thoughts.

He pulled her to her feet and slipped his hands on her hips, drawing her in. She looked so relaxed and happy. His pulse quickened and he pressed his face to her neck.

'You smell delicious,' he whispered and he slid his mouth to hers. The kiss was long and passionate but when her arms linked around his neck he realised it was rather too long. But he couldn't help himself and he backed her towards her bedroom door, his lips gliding over her neck. 'I have something for you,' he told her and she laughed but he caught the hitch in her breath and felt the quiver when he pressed his lips to hers once more.

Cathy had never felt like this before and her heart was racing. It's so wonderful, she thought, and she closed her eyes wanting to bask in the feel of his body close to hers and his lips searching for hers.

The sound of the doorbell startled her and she pulled her thoughts together before drawing away. 'I must see who it is.'

'Don't be long,' Tom stressed still drinking in her loveliness. They would soon belong to each other.

Cathy went into the hall and opened the front door. There he was yet again, Geoffrey Grant.

'I told you I'd be back, darling,' he offered, stepping into the hall, taking her by the elbows and pushing her up against the wall.

'And I told you I wasn't interested,' she replied, struggling to release herself from his clutches.

'I am not to be rebuffed,' he stressed, an official tone to his comment. 'I'm the one who gives the orders.' He drew his face close to hers. 'Now here's a bit of sound advice for you, Catherine my dear, and this is my final offer. Pack in your relationship with the Pom and I'll overlook the scathing comments you came out with the last time we met.'

Cathy was so stunned at his egotistical attitude she almost burst out laughing. But she held back. Whilst she felt safe in the knowledge that Tom was in the house with her, the last thing she wanted was for him to learn of Geoffrey's threats. But that didn't stop her from saying exactly what was on her mind.

'I meant every word I said, Geoffrey, scathing comments, the lot,' she replied, staring him in the face and trying to keep her voice down so that

Tom wouldn't hear.

'Now, come, Catherine. That's no way to treat someone in my position. You must learn to obey. And as I told you before, you need to be taught a lesson.' He pressed her up against the wall, held her there with one hand and started to claw at the buttons on her blouse with the other. 'The Pom is more certainly the one who'll get the soiled goods when I've finished with you,' he sneered.

The blow seemed to come out of the blue. Cathy felt the impact as Geoffrey's hands slid from her and he crashed to the floor.

'We'll see about that, old pal!' Tom shouted, staring down at Geoffrey who now appeared to be shaking.

Geoffrey tried to pull himself up from the floor but struggled. Scowling now, he rubbed his head. A trickle of blood dripped from his lips and he wiped it away with the back of his hand.

'You'll be hearing from my lawyer,' he mumbled, his voice shaky as he finally pushed himself up and tried to straighten his suit. 'Grievous bodily harm, that's what it is, you Pommy bastard!' he shouted.

'I doubt it'll stand up in court, old boy, not against attempted rape.' Tom slipped an arm around Cathy. 'Run along and tell your parents you tried it on with Cathy, that's if you dare!'

Geoffrey's eyes were bulging now. He was furious that someone had got the better of him. He turned, threw open the front door and left it wide open behind him.

Tom dashed his hands together. 'I'm glad I've seen that pompous idiot off the premises. You won't be hearing from him again.'

Cathy's eyes were wet with tears. 'You came in at the right time, Tom. How did you know about Geoffrey?'

'The grapevine, Cathy! Mike gave me the tip off. Rita apparently mentioned in one of her letters that the moron was threatening you.' He squeezed her and pulled her close. 'I've been biding my time, waiting until I came up against him.' He smiled and shook his head. 'He's one of those idiots who thinks he's God and is allowed to treat a woman as though she was his possession. He's got away lightly. When I saw him manhandling you it made my blood boil. I had to control myself not to go any further.' He kissed her on the cheek. 'But there's nothing to get upset about, my darling. He's out of your life forever now.'

'But I'd hate Mum and Dad to find out. They're round at Irene's at this very minute, either that or they're on their way back.' She shivered.

'Stop worrying, my love. Do you think any of them will find out from Geoffrey exactly what's happened? He's too much of a coward. He'd be mortified if they knew. He threatened me with his lawyer to cover his embarrassment. It's over and done with now. End of story.'

'I do hope so, Tom.'

'Now, where were we?' He took her hand and smiled down at her. 'I told you I had something for you, didn't I?'

Cathy nodded.

That could have been something else, but he disciplined himself. The important thing now was for him to present her with the ring.

'I'd like us to go to the park if that's OK with you.'

'Yes, that's fine.' She gave a weak smile. 'But I'm curious to know what it is.' Her face lit up.

'You'll find out once we get there. Do you want to finish getting ready and then we'll go?' He studied her intently. She was a vision of loveliness in his eyes and he had to make himself stop thinking of leading her back into the bedroom to pick up where they'd left off.

Cathy cried with joy when Tom slipped the ring on her finger. 'There it's official now!' he told her.

'I didn't need a ring from you to make it official, Tom. Your promise was enough for me. But I love the ring.' She stared at the diamond cluster. 'It's beautiful and it's exactly what I would have chosen. And I can't believe that it fits so perfectly. You have a good eye for sizing things up.'

'I agree. I sized you up quickly enough didn't I?' He laughed.

'Cheeky. That's not what I meant.'

'I know but there you go. I have my ways of finding out these things.' Unknown to Cathy he'd brought back a size card and measured one of her dress rings against it to check on the size. 'All we need now is to set a date.' He rubbed his hands together. 'Once I start the job at the market we can begin to save.'

'We don't need anything too expensive or elaborate, Tom, but I think Mum and Dad will expect us to marry at the church.'

'I agree wholeheartedly, my angel. I want everything to go perfectly for you. I love you so much.'

Some sort of weakness attacked her body. 'Oh,

Tom!' She shivered and he pulled her close. 'It's so exciting. I thought the time would never come when we'd be together.'

'But it was my plan from the minute I set eyes on you, Cathy my love. I need you, desperately.' His voice shook with emotion as he soothed her face with his fingertips. 'You're beautiful and I love you so very much.'

Encapsulated in his arms, she reflected on their closeness and smiled up at him. He kissed her once more. She felt alive, vibrant and she whispered, 'Cathy Crossley. It has a lovely ring to it.'

Tom laughed and pulled her close. Her bright eyes sparkled with pleasure as she drew herself up on tiptoe and kissed him gently on the mouth. He heard her moan in a quiet sound of surrender. She pulled gently away and cupped his face with her hands, smiling up at him in a way that told him they would be soulmates for life.

This Large Print Book for the partially sighted, who cannot read normal print, is published under the auspices of

THE ULVERSCROFT FOUNDATION

THE ULVERSCROFT FOUNDATION

... we hope that you have enjoyed this Large Print Book. Please think for a moment about those people who have worse eyesight problems than you ... and are unable to even read or enjoy Large Print, without great difficulty.

You can help them by sending a donation, large or small to:

**The Ulverscroft Foundation,
1, The Green, Bradgate Road,
Anstey, Leicestershire, LE7 7FU,
England.**
or request a copy of our brochure for more details.

The Foundation will use all your help to assist those people who are handicapped by various sight problems and need special attention.

Thank you very much for your help.